Praise for DEBORAH WOODWORTH's SHAKER MYSTERIES

"A complete and very charming portrait of a world, its ways, and the beliefs of its people, and an excellent mystery to draw you along."
Anne Perry

"A first-rate series; warm-hearted, richly detailed, and completely enthralling. Mystery fans should be sure to give them a try."
Publishers Weekly

"Bits of Shaker lore add a fresh slant...But it is Rose herself—intelligent, compassionate, and very strong— whom readers will especially want to see again."
Star Tribune (Minneapolis/St. Paul)

"Woodworth writes with grace and intelligence."
Carolyn Hart

"A fascinating framework of period detail."
Alfred Hitchcock's Mystery Magazine

"Woodworth does an admirable job of opening up the world of these peaceful and industrious people to the reader...But she doesn't idealize her characters, who exhibit the same small and large sins as the rest of us, even in their cloistered, orderly world."
Denver Post

To Debbie,

DEBORAH WOODWORTH

Happy reading!

DANCING
DEAD

A SHAKER MYSTERY

Deborah Woodworth

8/28/02

AVON BOOKS
An Imprint of HarperCollinsPublishers

AVON BOOKS
An Imprint of HarperCollins*Publishers*
10 East 53rd Street
New York, New York 10022-5299

Copyright © 2002 by Deborah Woodworth
ISBN: 0-380-80427-1
www.avonmystery.com

First Avon Books paperback printing: March 2002

Avon Trademark Reg. U.S. Pat. Off. and in Other Countries,
Marca Registrada, Hecho en U.S.A.
HarperCollins® is a registered trademark of HarperCollins Publishers Inc.

Printed in the U.S.A.

10 9 8 7 6 5 4 3 2 1

For Marilyn Throne, with gratitude and affection

AUTHOR'S NOTE

The 1869 Shaker Tavern, in southern Kentucky, served the traveling public for about thirty years. The South Union Shakers owned the building but did not run the tavern, which was located at a railroad stop a few miles from their village. The Shakers also owned and leased out the Shaker Store across the street from the tavern. South Union Shakertown closed its doors forever in 1922, but the Shaker Tavern still operates today as a bed-and-breakfast hotel. The building retains its unique combination of Shaker simplicity and Victorian elegance. In addition to the tavern, several other original South Union Shakertown buildings have been restored and are open to the public. However, North Homage Shaker Village, located somewhere in northern Kentucky, and its own Shaker Hostel are entirely fictional, as are all the characters who live there.

Deborah Woodworth
April 9, 2001

DANCING
DEAD

Languor County Courier

Languor County, Kentucky,
April 22, 1938

The Haunting of Shaker Village

If you are out for a midnight stroll in quiet North Homage Shaker Village, take care. You might find yourself sharing the path with a ghost. Recently folks visiting the village have reported spotting the form of a young girl, dressed in a loose gown and long cloak, floating inches above the ground. They say she passes right through the thick walls of Shaker buildings. She appears at windows and spins like a slender cyclone, then reappears seconds later on the grass. No one has seen the face of this restless shade or heard her utter a word.

Why has she come? What does she seek? We think we have found the answer. The following story is drawn from Memories from the Life of a Shaker Brother Dur-

ing the Era of Manifestations, *penned during the period between 1834 and 1840, by a Shaker known only
as Brother Joshua. Presumably, the brother left the
North Homage Shakers in 1840, taking his journal
with him. Brother Joshua's writings were only recently
discovered and published by a descendant, who
chooses to remain anonymous for fear of retaliation.*

As the story goes, it was on April 16, 1838, one hundred years ago, that a lovely and desperate young
woman ended her own life. We believe that the Shakers
of North Homage, right here in Languor County, have
conspired for a century to keep this tragedy a secret.
But now the story can—indeed, must—be told, for the
shade of this sad girl has chosen to return to her place
of death.

Her name was Sarina Hastings. She had lived with
the Shakers from the age of six, and she had just become a Shaker sister. At the time of her death, she was
a mere eighteen years of age, slender and fragile, with
bright gold hair and clear blue eyes. She set many a
man's heart to racing, whether they were Shaker brothers or men of the world. But Sarina was of a pious nature—or so it was thought.

One day in the autumn of 1837, Sarina met someone
who stirred her own heart. The man's name is lost to
history. Perhaps he was a brother, perhaps not. Whoever he was, he urged Sarina to leave the Shakers and
follow him. Brother Joshua wrote that this temptation
sealed her fate.

A century ago was a time of great activity among the
Shakers. They believed that Mother Ann, their dead
foundress, was working among them, through "instru-
ments" who received "gifts of the spirit." Sarina was

one such instrument. She could twirl for hours without rest, speak in tongues, and pull beautiful songs from the air. She heard the voices of dead Shakers whispering in her ear as she whirled in a trance.

These voices, wrote Brother Joshua, turned against Sarina. They told her that her worldly love was evil and must be killed. The poor girl whirled and twirled until her mind was incapable of reason, hoping to cure herself of her worldly passion. But to no avail. Sometimes the whispering urged her to kill the man she loved; other times, to kill herself. The more she danced, the greater her confusion, until she heard a voice that said she must purge her body with fresh herbs. The muddled child wandered through the Shaker garden early one morning, eating whatever was beginning to poke above ground. Brother Joshua wrote that she ate the new leaves of the rhubarb plant. Indeed, the poison killed her worldly love, for weak as she was from fasting and dancing, it also killed her body.

Recent reports from an anonymous source in North Homage indicate that the ill-starred Sarina has reappeared to roam the village where she died. She has been seen spinning through the gardens at early dawn, and her form floats about at night, carrying a lantern through abandoned buildings. Perhaps she seeks her lover and will never rest until she has found him. Or perhaps her shade has been trapped forever in a dance of death.

ONE

MINA DUNMORE WONDERED IF IT MIGHT BE TIME TO give up her widow's black. She had long ago ceased to mourn, if indeed she ever had, and her outfit made her look too much like a Shaker sister. Someone might notice the resemblance before it was time. The hat was especially troubling. It was an old, black, bonnet-shaped thing her mother had worn after her husband, Mina's father, had packed his bags and abandoned them. Her mother had worn widow's weeds until her death.

Mina, who was only seven at the time, had been forbidden to tell anyone that her father had left. She was to say he had died in a train wreck. Being a quick and imaginative child, Mina embellished the story each time she told it, filling in details she picked up from peeking in the lending library's more lurid novels, until she nearly believed it herself. The accident, she would tell her entranced schoolmates, had happened on an icy winter night in the mountains of Pennsylvania. Snow clogged the tracks and ferocious winds buffeted the cars. Her father was on his way to a very important meeting with the governor, that's why he had to travel during such dreadful weather. Sometimes she'd say he was racing to an emergency meeting with the President of the United States, or perhaps His Holiness the Pope, depending on the gullibility of her audience. Just at the stroke of midnight, the train derailed and tumbled down the mountainside, killing everyone on board. If you found the right mountain and were foolhardy enough to be there at midnight, you could still hear the screams and the crack of metal against rock.

By the age of eight, Mina had become an accomplished liar.

She sighed with exasperation as she tried to get a view of herself in the small, cloudy mirror hanging from some pegs in her room. These Shakers might have given more thought to appropriate furnishings before they'd opened up their hostel. Maybe the sisters didn't want to see themselves, but Mina did. And she couldn't afford to just go out and buy a mirror. Not yet, anyway. The reminder of her lifelong poverty fired the smoldering resentment in Mina's heart. She took several moments to compose herself. It was essential, for now, that she not draw attention to herself, and losing her temper would set her apart.

The hat must go, she decided. Though she had just turned forty, her hair was still a thick, rich brown, and she had cut it herself to just below her ears. If she waved it, she'd look more like a modern woman of the world. She was still fairly slim—just a shade thick around the waist, but the black dress helped hide that, so perhaps she could pretend to be younger. She glanced at the small clock the Shakers had placed on her bedside table. There was just enough time to dampen her hair and crimp it with some pins before dinner.

Mina smiled into the mirror. She now felt almost peaceful. Soon it would be her turn. Very soon.

What a stroke of luck! Saul Halvardson straightened his bow tie so that it was perfectly centered between the lapels of his dinner jacket. He leaned toward his shaving mirror and straightened the part in his dark hair, noting with approval the silver streaks. He'd always been successful at his job, even throughout this pesky Depression, but business had improved markedly since he started going gray. He believed it made him look boyish and distinguished at the same time. Ladies were far more inclined to buy silk stockings and toiletries from a handsome man than from a plain one.

He'd had especially good luck with the ladies recently. There were two staying at the hostel now; he might just give them a try. They were old enough to be flattered. They didn't look particularly wealthy, but in Saul's experience, a woman could usually be induced to retrieve a dollar or two from the flour canister for a pair of stockings or a small vial of eau de toilette. Besides, it was a diversion. Then there was that young thing with the red-brown curls, Gennie something or other. She'd been quiet at meals. Saul had noticed her engagement ring, and he had the impression she was a friend of the Shakers. He'd keep his distance from her, pretty though she was.

The real luck had been finding out about the Shakers opening this hostel in one of their old buildings. He'd been staying here since it opened, just a couple days earlier. He saw an opportunity, and he jumped on it. Just in time, too; the place had filled up fast. He considered this his smartest move in a lifetime of smart moves—starting at age twelve, when he had run off to live with his colorful grandfather, rather than stay with his Bible-thumping, belt-wielding father. It was his grandfather who'd taught Saul to use flattering words and a smile to sell anything to anybody. Granddad was something—he could sell snake oil to a quack, and he'd taught Saul all his tricks. Granddad had warned him he was too cocksure, and, yeah, he'd had a few troubles lately. Nothing that couldn't be cured with a bit of clever effort. No better place to do it than here, either.

He'd even managed to get the room that most perfectly suited his needs. That quiet woman, Miss Prescott, had wanted a more secluded view and asked to trade her room at the top of the stairs for his at the west end of the building. Just another example of his incredible luck.

It was still a while till dinner, so he relaxed in his rocking chair and gazed with appreciation around his room. The North Homage Shakers might be just scraping by, but they had a wealth of finely made furniture. The desk was pine, of simple design but sanded to a satiny smoothness. They'd left a maple box, oval with swallowtail joints and a snug-fitting lid, lying on the desk. He supposed it was to hold his loose change, his pocket watch, and so forth. He'd take it along when he left. It would impress future customers. *Yep*, he thought, *call something Shaker and folks will figure it's got to be quality.*

Saul loved possibilities, and North Homage was teeming with them. Meanwhile, the weekly rent was cheap, the food was good, and with attentiveness and his usual luck, he could turn near disaster into a windfall.

* * *

Daisy Prescott twisted her honey-blond hair into a bun and secured it with pins at the nape of her neck. She studied her image in the large mirror she had propped up on the plain desk in her room. It didn't provide the elegance she preferred, but it would have to serve as a dressing table. She leaned forward and tilted her head this way and that as she examined every inch of her face and hair. Nothing seemed out of place, yet somehow . . . By her right hand was a large rosewood box with leaves carved into its sides. Daisy smoothed the tips of her fingers over the lid, lightly tracing the ivory inlays that pieced together into the shape of a rose. She opened the lid and selected a pair of wire spectacles. Spinster secretary was the look she was aiming for, and she was certain that squinting all day at the tiny words emerging from a typewriter would have her wearing spectacles in no time. Such a foolish pursuit, reading. Not only did it ruin one's eyes, it distracted one's mind from more lucrative activities.

She examined her makeup critically, then wiped off a layer of rouge. Pale was better. Easier to overlook. Granted she had an exquisite figure, tall yet small-boned and willowy, but she must take more care to disguise it. Her face and her body were valuable assets in her work; she knew how to use them, and when. Now was not the time.

Daisy thickened her painted eyebrows by a fraction of an inch, then smiled shyly at her reflection. She tried gazing up through her pale lashes. Yes, much better. She gathered up her toiletries and her rosewood box and put them, with a number of other objects, inside the cupboard built into the wall of her room. There was no lock on the cupboard door, which was unfortunate, but adding one herself would draw too much attention. At least there was a solid, new lock on the door to her room. She pushed the items far to the back of the cupboard and stacked some folded lingerie in front until nothing showed. It would have to do. The room and its furnishings were so carefully constructed, she had yet to find so much as a loose floorboard under which she could hide anything.

Gennie Malone rocked slowly and stared out the window of her second-floor room in the new North Homage Shaker Hostel. Supper would be soon, but for once she had no appetite. All she wanted was to rock and stare and think what to do about her engagement to Grady O'Neal. She had grown up in North Homage, under the loving care of the sisters, and it was here that she was drawn when she was troubled. Grady had given her a blue roadster as an engagement gift, and she'd used it to travel the eight miles from her boardinghouse in Languor to North Homage. She felt a little guilty using the car, under the circumstances, but she'd have felt worse about asking Grady for a ride. At least she had some savings from her job in the Languor Flower Shop, enough so she could pay for about three weeks in the Shaker Hostel. That was important. She needed to feel she wasn't depending on Grady.

Gennie had been seventeen, sheltered and unworldly, when Grady came into her life. Seven years older and from a well-to-do family, he now served as Languor County sheriff. She had fallen madly, deeply in love. She was still in love, if it came to that. But now she was a woman of twenty. She had lived in the world, held a job, even traveled all the way to Massachusetts with Sister Rose. She had found in herself a love of adventure and an independent mind. Sister Rose, her friend and North Homage's eldress, and the other sisters had taught her about devotion, compassion, and the equality of all people. Gennie had been shocked to find that as a wife she would be expected to grant her husband the final say in nearly all matters. Growing up in North Homage, she had been taught to obey the sisters and brothers, naturally. Rose and Sister Charlotte, who taught and cared for the orphans being raised by the Shakers, had been strict with her. And she had always followed their instructions—well, nearly always. She was a child, and they were her parents. Marriage, though, that was supposed to be different, wasn't it?

In so many ways, Grady's childhood had been the opposite of hers. He'd been a privileged child, the only son in a wealthy, tobacco-growing family. Though surrounded by poverty, he had never known hunger, never lost a parent. On the other hand, he had learned compassion, and he served as a low-paid county sheriff because he felt a duty to protect those less fortunate. Gennie loved him for that. Yet that sense of duty . . . well, it just didn't seem the same as the deep compassion she had witnessed in Rose and the other Shakers. Grady's people, their friends, even Grady himself, they were good folks, but they all put themselves a bit higher than the hardscrabble farmers around them. It rankled when Grady treated her the same way, as if she couldn't survive without his guidance and protection.

Gennie squirmed and inched her rocker closer to the window so she could get a view of parts of the kitchen and medic gardens and, beyond them to the north, the herb fields, where oregano, thyme, and other perennials were unfolding their first tender spring leaves. By leaning, Gennie could just see the corner of the white clapboard Herb House. After she'd finished Shaker school at fourteen, she had spent much of her time working with Rose on the herb industry. Her mood perked up a bit at her memories of busy, happy days spent harvesting, drying, and packaging herbs for sale to the world. She closed her eyes and could still smell the burst of flowery sweetness as she stripped dried lavender buds from their stalks and pressed them into round tins. Her mouth watered at the remembered scent of pickles when she brushed against long bunches of dill weed hanging from the rafters in the second-floor drying room.

Shaker brothers and sisters began to emerge from buildings and walk toward the Center Family Dwelling House, and Gennie realized the bell must have rung for the evening meal. It was unusually cool for April, and she'd had her window closed. Next time she'd open it, even if it meant wrapping up in a blanket. She loved to hear the bell again. The hostel had no bell. Everyone was expected to gather at five-thirty or they missed supper. According to her clock, she had just enough time to clean up. Suddenly she was very hungry. It happened every time she remembered the smell of herbs.

TWO

SISTER ROSE CALLAHAN, ELDRESS OF THE NORTH Homage Shaker Village, straightened her aching back, wiped her dust-covered hands on her apron, and pushed some wisps of curly red hair back under her white indoor cap. So much dust, as if fog had settled inside the Ministry House library. It shouldn't be this way, Rose thought, not without some guilt. Their foundress, Mother Ann, had warned her early followers that good spirits would not live where there was dirt. In days past, when the North Homage Shaker community was filled to bursting with converts, there would have been many hands available to keep each corner clean enough for an angel to visit. But now the Believers were so few. Their hearts still reached to God, and their hands to work, but much less got accomplished these days.

Rose gazed around the small room with a sadness she hadn't expected. She would miss it. Some of the pegs lining the walls were worn and needed replacing, the mustard paint on the trim could use refreshing, and the pine floor was scuffed, but in the short time she had lived in the Ministry House, this room had become her favorite. As eldress, she had met friends and visitors from the world here, kept her daily journal and written letters at the desk, and studied the devotional and historic works that had lined the bookshelves.

However, it was she who had wanted to move. Brother Wilhelm Lundel, the village's elder, was not above reneging on his reluctant promise to close the Ministry House and move into the Center Family Dwelling House, where the rest of the village lived. When Rose had first become eldress, only a couple of years earlier, she'd had difficulty standing up to Wilhelm. He was a powerful personality, in his early sixties, while she was still in her late thirties and far less experienced. Wilhelm had pressured her into moving to the Ministry House and remaining separate from the community. She had moved against her better judgment and her deepest desire, which was to be with her Family.

She and Wilhelm must provide spiritual guidance for the Believers of North Homage, with that they both agreed. Beyond that, they held opposing views on nearly everything. Wilhelm believed they should live apart from other Believers to preserve distance and authority. Rose believed they could light the way best if they lived among their Children. Somehow, she had prevailed upon Wilhelm to move with her back to the dwelling house. With their dwindling membership, she had argued, it was wasteful to keep an entire extra building open just for two people. Besides, they'd had more than their share of tragedies in the last few years, and the brothers and sisters needed the presence of their elder and eldress. Wilhelm had relented when she reminded him that their own Parents, the Ministry at

Mount Lebanon, New York, had grown increasingly concerned about North Homage's stability. It was a major concession on Wilhelm's part, but he'd been sure to place a price on it. Rose must accomplish the move herself. Everyone else, Wilhelm had asserted, was needed for spring planting.

Wilhelm had made her life difficult for so long, she almost wondered what she would do without him. Almost. His ferocious will cleaved to the notion that the Society must go back a hundred years to a time of strength and growth, and he spent every minute of every day thinking of ways to do that. He had adopted an archaic form of speech, which made a simple request to pass the peas sound like a homily. Before she had become eldress, he'd forced the North Homage Believers to exchange their simple but modern clothing for the old-fashioned loose dresses and brethren's work clothes worn at least a century earlier. The sisters had spent weeks sewing, working far into the night to cut, fit, and stitch, using the old patterns. So unnecessary, when they had so few hands.

There I go again, wallowing in uncharitable thoughts. Rose dusted another pile of books and packed them in a cart, to be transported to the dwelling house. She had gotten what she'd prayed for, so she would be wise not to complain—at least not in Wilhelm's hearing. Though perhaps, since she had convinced Wilhelm to move, she might try her hand at returning the North Homage wardrobe to a more modern condition. *Now I've added hubris to my lack of charity.* Best to choose her struggles carefully, out of spirit, not pride.

The front door of the Ministry House opened and closed, so Rose busied herself with another stack of books. It would not do for Wilhelm to find her wasting time. She felt eyes watching her from the doorway and concentrated all the harder on her dusting.

"You shouldn't be doing this all alone, Sister."

The voice was not Wilhelm's, and Rose lifted her face with a welcoming smile. Brother Andrew Clark, North Homage's trustee, grinned back at her. "I suppose this is your penance for convincing Wilhelm to move?" He grabbed a nearby rag and a pile of books. "I'll cart these over to the dwelling house when you're ready. Yea, I know what you are about to say, you are strong enough to do it yourself, and I am busy closing up the retiring rooms in the Trustees' Office, but nevertheless, let me help. The task will be done all the more quickly, and you can return to more important work."

"You've convinced me," Rose said. Andrew had been sent to them only about a year earlier, from another village, but she felt they had been brother and sister forever. At times, other feelings stirred, but she struggled to release them and asked for assistance from Holy Mother Wisdom. It was her profound belief—and Andrew's, she knew, as well—that by doing so, she strengthened her love for God and for all others. But it wasn't always easy.

They worked in companionable silence for a time, interrupted by the occasional sneeze. Rose began to notice something odd—each time she crossed from the cart back to the shelves, she passed the library window, and she saw a surprising number of strangers pass by. At first she simply felt irritated because they were walking in the grass, rather than using the paths. Then she caught a man and woman staring through the window right at her. They gazed around the room, shook their heads, and turned away.

"Andrew, what on earth is going on out there? Are we having a public auction and no one told me?"

"Nay, they are just curious," Andrew answered, without glancing up.

"Curious about what?"

"Oh, the ghost, of course. They will become bored and leave when they realize it's just nonsense."

"Andrew, I have no idea what you're talking about. *What* ghost?" Another man peeked in the window and looked Rose up and down as if assessing her qualifications as a specter. He squinted as if trying to see through her.

Andrew frowned at the man, and he retreated. "I'm so sorry, Rose, I thought you knew, but of course you've been too busy with this move. The *Courier* printed an article this morning about a ghost supposedly roaming about North Homage at night. It's idiotic, the sort of thing I usually expect closer to Halloween." He related the contents of the article to Rose.

Rose picked up a book, dusted it, then put it back on the shelf. Then she did the same with a second book.

"Rose?"

"Yea?"

"What are you doing?"

Rose looked at the clean row of books she'd begun to replace on the shelf. "Apparently, I am moving back in," she said, with a laugh that died quickly. "I don't like this, Andrew. Why would someone write such an elaborate lie just now as we are opening a new business?"

"Well, if it is meant to destroy the Shaker Hostel, it seems to be having the opposite effect. We'd filled all the rooms before we opened, and in the past couple of days I've had numerous calls and letters from folks who want to stay here. So the story has boosted business." Andrew looked sharply at Rose. "You can't suspect that one of us planted the story—to lure people here?"

"I don't know what to think," Rose said. "I'll wait and see."

The cart was filled with books, and Andrew said, "The supper bell will ring soon, so I might as well take this over to the dwelling house. Where shall I leave it?"

"In the smaller meeting room. We'll save the larger one for worship when the weather is bad."

"We won't be closing up the Meetinghouse, will we?"

"Not if I can help it, and I know Wilhelm is equally determined. I was so saddened to see the Meetinghouse in Hancock Village empty and deteriorating." Abandoned buildings were not the only sadnesses Rose had witnessed during her recent stay in Hancock Shaker Village, in Massachusetts, but she had no wish to speak of them again. Andrew merely nodded. He began to push the cart toward the library door, then stopped and turned to face Rose.

"I was wondering," he began. Dark brown waves grazed his forehead as he frowned at the floor.

"Is something worrying you?"

"Yea, but it is my problem, and you have your hands full."

"Tell me," Rose said. "If I can help, I will. Is it to do with the new hostel?" She hadn't spent much energy on the hostel's development, apart from throwing her support toward Andrew and away from Wilhelm, who had opposed the project.

"Yea, the hostel worries me. Or perhaps it is Wilhelm who worries me." Wilhelm had made clear his conviction that the hostel provided an opening through which the world could invade the Shakers. He watched it carefully for any hint of evil, while Andrew guarded it like an infant. "Nothing I can put my finger on, just . . . Something doesn't feel right. I ate supper with the guests yesterday evening, and it was a bit uncomfortable. I found myself longing for a quick, silent Shaker meal. Perhaps I've forgotten what it's like to be in the world, among the world's people, but everyone seemed, well . . . cross." Andrew met Rose's eyes, and the furrow down his forehead deepened. "There were harsh words, and even my presence did not stop them from being spoken." He shook his head and shrugged. "I'm just an herbalist," he said. His thin face relaxed. "I can search out the hidden possibilities in plant life, but I'm stymied by human motivations, especially worldly ones. You are much better at that sort of thing."

Rose laughed. "And yet, as our trustee, you do business daily with the world, and you do it well."

"That's different."

"Yea, I suppose it is. Is one particular guest causing discord, perhaps making critical or unkind remarks that set tempers on edge?"

Andrew ran his hand through hair that was just a shade longer than Wilhelm preferred. "I would have to say that none of the guests has mastered the art of pleasant conversation—none except Gennie, of course. Even Gennie doesn't seem her normal sunny self."

"Nay, she is not. I believe she is in need of rest, so she might be unusually quiet while she is here. She is always observant, though. Shall I speak with her? She may be able to put into words what you perceived." Gennie had moved to the hostel from her boarding-house in town to, as she'd put it, "give the place a boost." She had confided her real reason to Rose alone.

Rose had been pleased with Gennie's decision, mostly because it meant having her back in North Homage. Rose never gave up hope that someday Gennie's heart would bring her back to live in the village, to sign the Covenant and become a Shaker sister. In the meantime, their friendship endured.

"Yea, perhaps consulting with Gennie would help," Andrew said, "but I would appreciate it greatly if you would have supper in the hostel this evening. Then you could judge for yourself. I'm probably worried for nothing, but . . ."

"It's nearly time for supper now," Rose said. "I doubt the food will stretch to include another person."

"I know. That's why I took the liberty of telling Mrs. Berg to expect you."

Rose couldn't help laughing. "Truly, Andrew, you should be an elder."

"Supper'll be on the table in a minute, if nothin' gets in my way." Beatrice Berg stared hard at the invader to her kitchen. The man just smirked in that silly way he had and kept his fat behind on the stool. She wanted to be ruder, usually couldn't stop herself, but she really was in a hurry. Horace von Oswald was a guest at the Shaker Hostel, and so was she, but only by grace of her willingness to work for it. The housekeeping was tedious, though she enjoyed seeing what all folks had in their rooms—especially the things they tried to hide away. And she did love the cooking. If Sister Rose or Brother Andrew got wind of her being lax in her duties, she'd be thrown out, no doubt about it.

"Anything else I can help with?" Brother Linus Eckhoff put the last thin piece of aged wood in a box by the kitchen door and brushed off his hands on his work pants. Brother Linus was a slight man with a kind face. Beatrice liked him, even though he had a strike against him for being a man. At least he was respectful.

"Come back in an hour," Beatrice said, as she squinted at a handwritten recipe. "Does that say 'dill' or 'fill'?" She held out the paper to Brother Linus. "Gotta be dill. Don't make no sense otherwise."

Brother Linus took the paper, being careful not to touch Beatrice's hand. He held it at arm's length. "I don't have my spectacles, but I'd say it's dill."

"Shall I read it?" Horace asked, extending his hand.

Beatrice ignored him. "Come back after supper, like always," she said to Brother Linus. "I'll have a passel of victuals for you to cart back." She wished she could ask him to stay and keep Horace out of her hair. At least Linus was willing to work. He didn't sit around on his behind asking fool questions.

"So tell me, how do you like working for these Shakers?" Horace asked, when Linus had left. Horace had a pasty, round face and one of those little button noses, so when he smiled he reminded Beatrice of an unbaked gingerbread man. No one should be that well-fed; it wasn't right. What was he getting at with these questions? Was he testing her?

"They're fair to me," she said.

"Yes, they certainly have that reputation, but . . ." Horace cocked his head at her. He had messy, uneven hair, as if he hacked at it himself and then never combed it. His clothes looked secondhand and stretched tight across his round body, as if they'd been made for someone thinner. And, mercy, those eyes— they could scare the bejabbers out of a person. Small, round, and black, like clumps of dirt.

Beatrice plunked a serving platter on the table a little too hard. She wasn't going to say another word, and that was that. Horace could hint till he shriveled up and died; she wasn't going to fall for it. If he wanted to know about the Shakers, he could go and ask them.

"You'd best get to the dining room," she said. She figured he wouldn't budge, and he didn't. She leaned over to read the next item on the recipe that the Kitchen Deaconess, Sister Gertrude, had given her to try out—another potato soup, the third since the hostel had opened. Each time it was different. Gertrude was trying out various combinations of herbs and vegetables. Beatrice had been instructed to follow each recipe exactly and to save a portion for Gertrude, Rose, and Andrew to taste. Beatrice didn't like being told how to cook. Sometimes she would add a little something extra and have a good laugh to herself. She probably shouldn't tonight, though, what with the eldress coming to supper.

Beatrice heard Horace take a breath like he was going to open his fool mouth again, so she turned her back on him and pretended to be searching the kitchen for an ingredient. The kitchen was small; she couldn't go very far.

"What do you think of this story we've been hearing about a ghost in North Homage?"

"What ghost?" Beatrice asked, turning around in spite of herself.

"Oh, you haven't heard," Horace said, with that irritating grin. "There was an article in the paper about it, just this morning. Someone is supposed to be roaming around the empty buildings at night, someone who died unjustly."

Beatrice felt a sudden chill as if ectoplasm had passed right through her. Some people were afraid of snakes or mice or of catching influenza, but not Beatrice. Nothing scared her—nothing except ghosts. Ghosts terrified her. If there was a ghost around here, she'd have to skedaddle. She'd wait and see, though. This was the best place for her to be, all things considered. Safe and out of the way. She'd have to find out more about this ghost, but not now. If she didn't get this food on the table lickety-split, she wouldn't be worrying about no ghost. She'd be out on her ear.

Ignoring Horace, Beatrice lifted the heavy pot of potato soup from the old wood-burning stove. One of the reasons she'd gotten this job was that she'd grown up cooking on one of these old things, and the Shakers couldn't afford to buy new kitchen equipment. They'd raided the old stuff from kitchens they no longer used.

"You'd best find yourself a place," Beatrice said to Horace. "Get the victuals while they're hot." She sloshed some soup into a tureen and put the pot back on the stove to keep warm. When she turned around, Horace was gone. The kitchen felt safe and cozy again, as if Horace himself had been the unquiet shade seeking vengeance. Maybe he was. Maybe he'd been sent right to her, which meant there was no place for her to hide, not on this earth. Beatrice clucked impatiently at herself as she lifted the heavy tureen and headed for the dining room. No ghost could do anything to her, she told herself, except maybe scare the bejabbers out of her, and that was only if she let it. From now on, she'd keep an eye out.

THREE

ROSE ARRIVED A FEW MINUTES BEFORE THE OTHERS AND took a seat at one end of the old trestle table Andrew had moved into the Shaker Hostel dining room. She wanted a clear view of everyone present, while keeping her distance from the men. She suspected the hostel guests would skip saying grace before eating, so she bowed her head and gave silent thanks for the coming meal. If the smells wafting from the kitchen in the next room were any indication, supper would be well worth her gratitude.

Andrew had done a good job with the room. He had struck a subtle balance between traditional Shaker simplicity and the more elaborate decoration of the world. Blue cords with silky tassels gathered sheer white curtains into graceful curves. Instead of wooden pegs, hooks encircled the pale blue walls, and framed photos and small bookshelves hung from some of them. Another hook held an old Shaker candleholder on which Andrew had placed a red glass vase, which a grateful visitor had once given the community. Since Wilhelm wanted them to follow the old rules, the village grew no tulips or daffodils for spring bouquets. Flowers, he reminded them, should be useful, not decorative. Andrew had bent the rules, as he often did, and a basket of dried calendula and sage served as a centerpiece.

The table itself had been used decades earlier in this very building, previously named the West Dwelling House. The building had once housed the outside family—folks who weren't quite ready to make the commitment to sign the Covenant and live the Shaker life. Hence, the former dwelling house had only one entrance and one stairway, instead of the two normally provided so brothers and sisters would not accidentally brush against one another. Rose thought the building a perfect choice for worldly visitors, and she was glad to see it in use again.

A large man with an unhealthy pallor entered the dining room from the kitchen. He stared at Rose a moment longer than was polite, then dragged a ladder-back chair from the side of the table over to the end opposite Rose, so that he faced her. The action felt like a challenge, perhaps to her authority, yet his perpetual smile seemed friendly enough. Andrew had briefly described the guests to her, and she was certain this man must be Horace von Oswald. Horace had been vague about his profession, but he had paid for his room two weeks in advance, so he clearly had funds.

"So," said the man, "you must be Sister Rose. You are eldress, are you not?"

"Yea, I am."

"How long?"

"I beg your pardon?"

"How long have you been eldress?"

The bluntness of his question startled her, and she hesitated. Never before had a stranger from the world expressed any curiosity about her tenure as eldress.

Horace's black eyes never left her face. She was saved from answering when a middle-aged woman dressed in black entered from the hallway.

"Well, aren't we honored. The eldress has come to have supper with us." The words might be construed as welcoming; the tone could not. Rose felt her stomach clench.

Horace's attention diverted to the woman. "Mina, you're here," was all he said. So this was Mina Dunmore, Rose thought. A widow living on a small inheritance, Andrew had told her. Not the cheeriest of women, but she was, after all, a widow.

"Can't think where else I'd be," Mina said. She took a seat to Rose's left and as far from Horace as she could get.

"I haven't seen you all day," Horace said. "What have you been doing?"

"Don't see it's any of your business," Mina said. She spread her white linen napkin on her lap and smoothed out wrinkles that weren't there. "I went shopping in Languor," she said finally. North Homage used a roomy 1936 Plymouth for its own needs, but they still owned its predecessor, an old black Buick. Brother Linus had gotten it cleaned up and running smoothly, so the hostel residents could borrow it for trips into Languor. "It's certainly a poor excuse for a town," Mina said, "but I did find a place to have my hair done." She patted her crimped curls. "Not that there's any reason to dress up around here. There's no place to go. When my husband was alive, we were always off somewhere—dinner parties, dances, the theater."

"Ah," said Horace. He turned again to Rose with the smile she felt sure she would come to dread.

A boisterous male voice, coming from the hallway, provided a welcome distraction. A man and woman walked together through the wide doorway into the dining room. Since Beatrice must be in the kitchen, Rose assumed these two were Saul Halvardson and Daisy Prescott. Saul wore a dark blue, double-breasted jacket and matching pants with a crisp, straight crease down the front of each leg—the latest of worldly styles, as far as Rose could remember. Andrew had said he was a traveling salesman who sold ladies' lingerie. If it had been Wilhelm telling her, rather than Andrew, Rose never would have known about the ladies' lingerie. Andrew and Wilhelm had both lived to adulthood in the world, but Wilhelm was repulsed by it. Andrew, though he preferred life as a Shaker, accepted the world as it was, sometimes with pity.

With a flourish, Saul pulled out Daisy's chair for her and eased it forward as she sat down. Daisy settled at the table without acknowledging Saul's gesture. She spread her napkin on her lap, then entwined her fingers in a prayerful position on the edge of the table. She fixed her gaze on the dried flowers in front of her, and her eyes did not waver when Saul appropriated the seat next to her, placing him at Rose's right. Rose was fairly certain Daisy was not actually praying; her silence had a calculated air to it. Rose was intrigued. Daisy was slender and fine-boned, a bit taller than average. Her dress was a dowdy brown, with a waist down around her narrow hips. Rose was woefully behind on women's fashions, but the style seemed out-of-date; she'd never seen Gennie wear anything like it.

As if on cue, Gennie entered the dining room. Saul leaped up and helped her with her chair. She rewarded him with a wan smile. Rose noticed that Gennie, despite her withdrawn mood, had taken the time to dress for dinner. Grady's family had been training her, and she had become very much a woman of the world. Still, Rose told herself, miracles do occur. Maybe Gennie would come back someday, and if she did, she would bring so much to the Society.

A clattering from the kitchen attracted everyone's attention. The door swung open, and the fragrance of dill and onion wafted into the room, along with the solid figure of Beatrice Berg. She thumped a tureen on the table and gave Horace a hard stare. He had taken the cook's place at the end of the table, nearest the kitchen. He appeared not to notice her irritation.

"Eat it while it's hot," Beatrice said, and she disappeared back into the kitchen. Horace began serving himself at once, without offering to serve the women first. He filled his bowl to the top and picked up his soupspoon, as Beatrice reentered with two plates of bread. She took one look at Horace and carried the bread down to Rose.

"Somethin' wrong with your eyes?" she asked Horace. He stared at her, his spoon hovering just beyond his lips. "There's other folks at this table. Maybe they want to eat, too." She reached over for Daisy's soup bowl, which she filled with soup and returned. "See?" she said, again to Horace. "Don't take no strength at all."

Gennie was struggling mightily to suppress a giggle. It emerged as a little chirp.

"Why don't we pass our plates down?" Rose suggested. "We can eat when we've all been served." She felt a bit like a sister in charge of the Children's Dwelling House, teaching manners to orphans who'd had no chance to learn them before. Horace didn't change expression, but his eyes seemed to grow smaller and darker.

Beatrice returned bearing plates of butter. Saul half rose from his chair, but Beatrice didn't wait for him. She scraped her chair away from the table, plunked down, and scooted it close again. Though she was seated just in front of the soup tureen, she held her bowl out to Horace. He hesitated a moment, then deposited one ladleful in her bowl. Beatrice didn't move. With clear reluctance, Horace added another ladleful.

The diners ate their soup and bread in silence. Beatrice cleared away the empty bowls and brought in a baked ham and tender buttered asparagus. Rose's jittery stomach began to relax. The Believers in the Center Family dining room would be eating plainer food, but these were people of the world, and Andrew knew they expected more. She felt only the slightest guilt since, after all, Andrew had engineered her attendance here. She was working.

Horace finished his portion well before the others and made the mistake of reaching across Beatrice's plate for the platter of ham. Beatrice whacked him with the flat of her fork.

"We ain't eatin' slop in a pigsty," she said. "Did your mama teach you to reach like that? I swear, you do this every meal. Next meal comes around, and danged if you don't do the same thing all over again."

Horace lowered his head, but Rose was certain she saw him smiling. Daisy and Mina continued their meals, looking straight ahead as if nothing had happened. Gennie poked at her food.

Before the drama could reach its next scene, Rose turned to Mina and asked, "Are you enjoying your stay here? Is your room comfortable?"

Mina hesitated as if she had to translate the questions into another language, or perhaps she was looking for some hidden meaning behind the words. "It's okay, I guess," she said finally. "Room's a little barren, not quite what I'm used to, but it'll do for now."

"What are you used to, Mina?" Horace asked her.

Mina slowly sliced her ham into square bites and didn't so much as glance at Horace. Rose was beginning to understand the discomfort Andrew had struggled to describe. It seemed that both Mina and Horace were suffering from simmering resentment, and Beatrice was none too cheery, either. Rose turned her attention to Saul Halvardson, seated on her right. He chewed with apparent pleasure as his quick eyes settled on one person, then another. He seemed unaware of the tension at the table—or else intrigued by it.

"Tell me, Mr. Halvardson," Rose said, "how did you hear about our new hostel?"

Saul turned to her with a surprised expression. "Saul," he said. "Please call me Saul, Sister."

"And do call me Rose."

"With pleasure." He inclined his head in a slight nod, as if bowing. He took a bite of ham and gazed across the table at Mina. Rose realized he had not answered her question, and she felt certain his omission had been intentional. If he hoped to hide from Rose, however, he had taken the wrong course. His behavior piqued her interest. She sat still and watched him ex-

pectantly, waiting for his answer. He gave in and
turned back to her. As if no time had elapsed since her
question, Saul said, "I saw an advertisement for it. I'm
sorry, I don't remember where. I travel so much."

"Of course," Rose said. "Tell me, what is your sales
territory?" She wasn't ready to let him off the hook.
Anyway, she'd grown impatient with the secretive un-
dercurrents at the table.

"Are you interested in sales?" Saul asked.

"Yea, of course," Rose said. "I used to be North
Homage's trustee, before I became eldress. As trustee,
I oversaw the community's businesses and had the
pleasure of working with businessmen from the world.
I used to send our own brothers on sales trips, so natu-
rally I'm curious about your route."

Saul nodded and smiled, but his eyes flitted around
the room. Again he delayed answering, busying himself with passing platters in case someone wanted seconds. Rose studied his profile. She was not so
unworldly that she didn't notice his striking looks. His
wavy dark hair was streaked with silver, and his face,
though thin, had a bit of softness that made him seem
ingenuous at first glance. He offered the platter of ham
to Daisy, who thanked him with a shy glance up
through her lashes. Out of the corner of her eye, Rose
saw Mina's body tense as she watched the interchange.

With a suddenness that startled Rose, Saul turned
back to her and said, "My sales route is usually north
of here. Up as far as Cleveland, that area. I suspect
your salesmen normally go south—southern Kentucky,
Tennessee, and so forth?"

Rose nodded. "So you must have seen our advertisement in the Cleveland paper?"

"Of course, now I remember," Saul said, smiling brightly and revealing well-tended teeth. "That was where I saw it."

Rose chewed on a bite of bread, allowing Saul to return his attention to the worldly women, who clearly interested him. She intended to keep an eye on Saul Halvardson. Thinking it was too far north, Andrew had not placed an advertisement in any Cleveland paper. He had focused his attention on southern Ohio and farther south, since their inhabitants might be more accepting of the summer heat in Kentucky.

Rose turned to Daisy Prescott. "Tell me, Miss Prescott, what brings you to our hostel?"

Daisy placed her utensils neatly across the upper edge of her plate and looked directly at Rose. Behind her spectacles, her eyes were a luminous blue-green. "I was in need of a vacation," she said. She spoke barely above a whisper, giving the impression of terrible shyness.

"From what?" Horace asked.

"Oh." Daisy's hands fluttered, landing on her knife and fork. "Well, work has been quite demanding lately, and I'm so tired." She took a bite of ham and chewed slowly.

The other guests had lost interest in Daisy, except for Mina Dunmore, who studied the younger woman's face as if critiquing her makeup. "Nothing like a quiet vacation," Mina said. "That's what Mr. Dunmore used to say."

Daisy did not look up from her plate.

The platters emptied rapidly, and Beatrice cleared them off, along with the soiled dinner plates. She returned from the kitchen carrying a pie with a golden crust and sugary bubbles sneaking out the edges. Pecan pie. Gertrude's recipe used orange rind to cut the sweetness, and Rose's mouth watered in anticipation. Even Gennie perked up. Beatrice nestled the pie plate beside the basket of herb flowers, close to Rose and as far as possible from Horace.

"Mrs. Berg, this looks absolutely delicious," Rose said, as she accepted the pie cutter. She divided the pie into eight slices, intending to save one for Andrew and Gertrude to taste. The mood in the room had mellowed considerably. Rose handed the warm pie plate to Saul, who served Daisy and Beatrice, then himself. He handed the plate toward Horace. Quick as a garter snake, Beatrice snatched the pie plate, scooped out one slice for herself, plopped another onto Horace's plate, and handed the pan across the table to Gennie. Horace's obsidian eyes locked on the pie. Clearly he coveted that extra slice. Rose would not have been surprised if he'd grabbed the plate away from Gennie, but he applied himself to his own portion. Beatrice had outsmarted him, and her smirk said she knew it.

The telephone in the hallway rang, and Beatrice jumped up to answer it. As Rose watched, Horace's eyes fixed on Beatrice's untouched portion of pie. His hand twitched. With disconcerting suddenness, he shifted his gaze and caught Rose watching him.

Beatrice reappeared and gestured to Rose, who reluctantly put down her fork. It crossed her mind to be glad that Horace wasn't sitting next to her, ready to seize her unprotected plate.

"One of the sisters," Beatrice said. "I think she

called herself Charlotte or something." She made haste back to her chair, probably sensing the danger to her portion of pecan pie.

"Rose, I'm so sorry to pull you away from your meal. I hoped I could sort this out on my own, but . . ."

"Charlotte? Are the children all right?" Rose spoke softly to avoid being overheard in the dining room.

"Yea, except . . . well, it's Mairin again. She was with us in the Children's Dwelling House, but somehow she slipped away while we were walking to the dining room for the evening meal. Nora is beside herself."

"Have you questioned the other children?"

"Yea, all of them. No one saw her leave, including Nora, who always watches her so carefully."

Rose heard a child's sob in the background, and Charlotte turned away from the receiver. Rose pulled over a small wooden chair and sat, anxious for Charlotte to return. Rose felt a deep fondness for the small eleven-year-old girl known only as Mairin. Mairin was a mixed-race child who had suffered terrible neglect before the Shakers had taken her in. She had attached herself to Rose and to Rose's own friend and spiritual guide, the former eldress Agatha Vandenberg. Mairin had seemed to be progressing so well, emerging from the cloak of aloofness in which she'd wrapped herself, safe and tight. Then Rose had rushed off to Massachusetts to help the Hancock Shakers solve a murder within their quiet village. It had never occurred to Rose that she should take Mairin aside and explain why she must leave—and that she would certainly come back.

"Rose? Are you still there?" Charlotte sounded both frightened and irritated. Rose gave thanks, not for the first time, that she herself did not bear daily responsibility for the children being raised by the North Homage Shakers.

"Yea, Charlotte, I am here, and I'll begin the search at once. You stay with the other children. Keep a careful eye on Nora. You know how she is—she's likely to set out on her own to find Mairin, and then we'll have two lost girls. I'll go now and ask the brothers to begin searching the grounds, and the sisters can look for her indoors."

"Shall I search the Children's Dwelling House again?" Charlotte asked.

"Nay, I'll send Gertrude over to do that. You just keep Nora under your eye."

"All right, I'll be sure to—"

"Charlotte? What's wrong?"

"Oh, Rose . . ." Charlotte was clearly in panic. "It's Nora, she's gone. I only turned away for a moment."

"Run and find her. Now!"

Rose didn't bother to explain her departure, she just hurried toward the front entrance. As she passed the dining room door, she glanced in to see Gennie staring out at her. Rose made a split-second decision. Gennie knew Mairin, and they got along well. She also knew Nora—and how to handle her. It would take Gennie's mind off her own problems to be of help with the children. With a quick wiggle of her index finger, she gestured for Gennie to follow her, then she moved past the doorway. Within seconds, Gennie appeared in the hallway.

"Come," Rose said. "I need your help. I'll explain along the way."

"Rose, dear, do come in and tell me what all the commotion is about." Sister Agatha Vandenberg's small, frail body looked doll-like, tucked into her rocking chair with a fluffy powder-blue blanket woven for her by a friend from the world. Her thin white hair was pulled back from her face and covered by a light indoor cap. Her eyes, cloudy with growing blindness, nevertheless saw more than many whose eyesight was clear. Right now they saw through Rose's deliberate calm to the distress she truly felt.

"Sit down," Agatha said, in her gentle yet commanding way.

"I wish I could," Rose said. "Mairin has run away, and Nora has gone off to find her. I'm afraid Mairin will leave the village and Nora will follow her."

"Nora is a good friend."

"Yea, but a foolish one. She is only nine years old, but she has always been quite sure she is an adult. She doesn't know how dangerous the world can be. And Mairin is only eleven."

"I believe Mairin knows better than anyone the cruelty of the world," Agatha said quietly.

"Of course you are right," Rose said. She wasn't thinking clearly, and it was no use trying to hide her muddled state from Agatha. "Perhaps I will sit, just for a moment." She pulled a ladder-back chair over from the desk and placed it near Agatha. "I was hoping Mairin would come to you. She has such a special connection with you."

Agatha reached a thin hand toward Rose and squeezed her arm. "Yea, Mairin touches my heart. But her strongest connection is with you, you must know that."

Rose shook her head. "I thought so. I truly thought I could help her, but perhaps that was hubris. She seems as unreachable now as when I first found her, hiding in a tree in our orchard."

"Nay, she is not that same child, and yet she always will be," Agatha said. "Her soul has ventured into the light. We have both watched it happen, and it will surely happen again. You must have patience and let her come to trust us in her own time. And eventually she will understand that when even we, being mortal, leave her behind, she can always trust her Holy Father and Mother. This will take time. The world has betrayed her far too often for her short years."

Agatha sank back in her chair and began to rock gently. Rose endured more than a twinge of guilt at the fear she was exhausting Agatha. Several strokes over the past few years, plus a severe chill last winter, had left the former eldress physically weak and fragile, though her will seemed untouched.

"You're tired," Rose said. "Rest and let us handle this. It isn't fair to burden you with such problems."

"Hush, now, Rose," said Agatha, with a touch of irritation. "Such problems are the reason I'm still here. When I can no longer help in any way, I pray I'll be called home. I have no desire to put off that moment by resting any more than I must, so I don't welcome coddling."

"Yea, I understand," Rose said, with unaccustomed meekness.

"Good. Now, everyone is off looking for Mairin, so you can stay a few moments and discuss what to do with her when she is found—and she will be found. We cannot force her to trust us before she is able, but we must discourage her from running away."

Rose stood and paced to the window. She tried to let herself enjoy the freshness of the spring leaves, their yellow-green tinted with pink by the setting sun. But the sunset reminded her that, if they could not find the girls, Mairin and Nora would be alone in the coming night. Rose turned back to Agatha and sat down. "I don't know what to do," she said. "When any of the other children misbehave, we keep them home from outings or assign them extra chores. None of that seems to have any effect on Mairin. She simply runs off again. I want so to help her, yet I am angry with her. I try to hide my anger, she ignores me, and I become even angrier. I pray for guidance and none comes. I'm at my wit's end."

Agatha chuckled. "At your wit's end is a perfect place to start. I remember being there myself once, oh, about thirty-five years ago, when a little four-year-old with a quick temper and a will of iron refused to do anything the sisters told her to do."

Rose squirmed. "It's uncomfortable to remember how impossible I was my first few years here, but surely my situation is different from Mairin's. I'd been neither starved nor beaten; I was simply willful and spoiled."

"Nay, Rose, you were not spoiled. Willful, yea, but not spoiled. You'd been passed about from relative to relative after your mother and father died, and young as you were, you'd learned that nothing lasts. You fully expected we'd pass you along, too."

"I don't remember any of this," Rose said, "but I do remember that you were quite stern with me on more than one well-deserved occasion."

"Indeed, I was. You missed numerous special outings, as I recall." Agatha's smile softened her taut, thin features. "It took several years for you to understand that we were going to keep you. You might have to miss a hayride, but we weren't going to deposit you on a stranger's doorstep just because your temper got the best of you now and then."

"I began to trust you. And then to love you, all of you." Rose felt her shoulders relax and her hope return. "Though I'm afraid you didn't cure my temper."

"Nay, that we did not." Agatha sighed with unusual force. "Some things are up to our Holy Mother and Father—and I wish them luck."

Rose threw her head back and laughed. Agatha had not teased her in a long time, and it felt delicious. "All right," Rose said, "I'm beginning to understand. I'm still frightened by Mairin's running away, though."

"Of course you are. I am, too. When you find her, perhaps you should tell her just how frightened we have been. Her heart will hear you. In time." Agatha leaned her head back against her rocker and closed her eyes. Rose lightly touched her hand in farewell and slipped out of her retiring room, easing the door shut behind her.

FOUR

GENNIE MALONE HAD BEEN MORE THAN HAPPY TO abandon dinner in the hostel to join the search for the missing Mairin. She didn't think she could have endured many more minutes with her fellow guests, even for pecan pie. She'd never before met so many unpleasant people gathered in one place. After three weeks with them, Grady and his world might seem far more tolerable. Or perhaps she'd just up and leave it all—take a train to somewhere way far away, maybe a big city like Louisville, find a job, and live on her own for a while. Away even from Rose.

Gennie stopped suddenly and looked around. The sun had nearly set, and she hadn't been thinking at all about poor Mairin. From long-ago habit, she was heading for the Herb House in the northeast corner of North Homage. She turned around and scanned the rest of the village. Windows glowed with bright lights as Believers searched for the missing girl. Gennie looked toward the Herb House. Perhaps it was because of the memories that still haunted her—memories of a violent death she could never seem to forget—but the Herb House looked dark and foreboding, even to Gennie, who loved it.

Gennie was never one to let a little foreboding hold
her back. She was still dressed for dinner, so to save
her new tan kid high heels, she stayed on the path instead of taking the shortcut through the grass. She
eased open the Herb House door, hoping not to send
any errant children inside deeper into hiding. She
needn't have worried; the hinges were well-oiled. She
closed the door behind her.

Leaving the lights turned off, she stood very still,
listening. She shut her eyes and listened harder. She
heard something; she was sure of it—a murmuring
sound, just above her, as near as she could tell. She
opened her eyes. Massive shapes seemed to jump out
at her, but she knew they were just machines the brothers used to press herbs into tight packs. The presses
wouldn't be used until later in the season, when large
amounts of medicinal and culinary herbs would be dry
and crumbly, ready for processing. Then the air would
be heavy with sweet and sharp scents, but now it
smelled like dusty, dry grass. She saw no movement in
the shadows.

With a guilty lilt of pleasure, Gennie picked her way
through the dark room toward the staircase. The drying
room was upstairs. It was early in the season, but there
would already be some bunches of herbs hanging upside down to dry. Pungent young oregano, surely, and
perhaps some sage, newly picked and not yet as musty
as when it had fully dried. It all came back to her and
reminded her of Rose. If she were running away, this
was where she'd come.

Gennie's feet still remembered each stair, and which
planks squeaked. By the time she was halfway up, she

knew her instinct had led her to the right place. She could hear the urgent voice of a child behind the closed drying room door. Unless she missed her guess, the voice belonged to Nora. Gennie ran up the last few steps and flung open the drying room door.

Two small, startled faces—one pale and blond, the other honey-brown and framed by fluffy hair—snapped toward her. They sat cross-legged on the floor in the middle of the room, leaning toward each other. Gennie put her hands on her small hips and raised stern eyebrows at them. In a flash, Mairin was on her feet, darting toward the drying room door. But Gennie was young and quick. As Mairin rushed past, Gennie scooped her up and held her by the waist. Mairin wriggled and kicked, but she was tiny, her growth stunted by malnutrition, and Gennie was determined.

"Oh no you don't," Gennie said, holding the girl tightly against her. "You've caused us all a heap of worry, and it's time you faced the music."

Mairin made a sound between a grunt and a scream, then she kicked Gennie in the shin.

"Ow! You little . . ." Gennie grabbed the girl's knees with one arm to avoid another attack, but Mairin squirmed all the harder. Though she was still small for her age, good Shaker food had added pounds and strength to her frame. Gennie was afraid she was about to lose her grip on the child when Nora came over and clutched Mairin's ankle with both hands.

"Mairin, please stop that," Nora said, in a surprisingly adult voice. Gennie suspected Nora had heard those words herself, spoken to her by a desperate sister. "Gennie is a nice person, she only wants to help you. *Everybody* wants to help you, really and truly. Cross my heart and hope to die and *everything*."

Mairin stopped wriggling. However, Gennie did not loosen her stranglehold. This was one unpredictable child. Mairin twisted her head around and stared at Nora for several moments, then let her body go limp.

For the first time, she spoke. "Let me down."

"Can I trust you not to run away?"

"Yea."

Gennie was startled by Mairin's use of the Shaker form of "yes." It seemed to give her promise added weight. Gennie lowered Mairin to the floor, then let her go. Mairin didn't move. She stood with her body rigid and her face puckered in a defiant frown. It struck Gennie that Mairin expected a beating. Gennie dropped to her knees with no thought for the safety of her light tan dinner dress. The copper flecks in Mairin's eyes glittered with fear.

"No one is going to hurt you, Mairin. I promise. It's just that all of us, and Rose especially, have been terribly, terribly worried about you. When you disappear, we get scared that something awful might have happened to you. Can you understand that?"

Mairin's small face relaxed. She nodded. "I don't mean to make everyone worry about me," she said, in her low, melodious voice. "Sometimes I just need to be outside."

Suddenly Mairin seemed far older than the wiggling child Gennie had so recently restrained. Gennie swung a small, short-backed chair from its wall pegs and moved it next to a larger ladder-back that was standing by a well-worn desk. She gestured for Mairin to sit in the smaller chair.

"Nora, you run along to the dwelling house and let the village know that Mairin is safe. I'll bring her back in a few minutes."

Nora hesitated and fixed Mairin with a parental look, protective and stern.

"Run along now," Gennie said. "Rose is beside herself with worry."

"Okay." Nora spun around and ran out of the room. Gennie closed the door behind her and turned to face Mairin.

"We need to have a little talk." As Gennie walked toward her, Mairin flinched. Gennie noticed but said nothing. Words would not convince Mairin she was safe in North Homage—time might do so, and gentle care, but never words.

"Mairin, would you tell me something?" The child's small chin jutted out defiantly, but Gennie continued. "Why do you sneak off? It's more than just wanting to be outside, isn't it?"

Mairin shrugged her shoulders.

"Mairin, I want you to listen very carefully." Gennie's voice had dipped to a deeper, less gentle level. Mairin's eyes flicked toward her, then focused on the floor. "No one here will harm you," Gennie said, "but that doesn't mean we aren't angry. Angry and disappointed. The Shakers have treated you well. Rose and Agatha love you and want only the best for you. Every time you disappear, you hurt them."

Mairin was still.

"So why do you run away, Mairin?"

"I don't know."

Gennie watched the girl's face for several silent moments. Her simple response had revealed nothing. Gennie had the nagging sense she was keeping something back. Yet maybe she really didn't know why she ran off. "All right then," Gennie said, "where do you go?"

"Nowhere special. Just all around. It's more fun outside."

"What makes it more fun?"

Mairin grinned, a rare occurrence that transformed her face. "It's the people," she said. "They do strange things. I sit in the trees and look down on them." She giggled softly.

Gennie had a bad feeling. A very bad feeling. "Um, Mairin, what people are you talking about? Shakers?"

Mairin wrinkled her nose. "Nay, not the ones who live here," she said. "All they do is work. But there's been lots of other folks around. I don't know them. Sometimes they act funny." She giggled again.

Gennie was wishing herself just about anywhere else. She feared that young courting couples might be using secluded parts of the village, thinking they were alone. She was glad Grady hadn't visited her since she'd moved into the hostel. In the past two and a half years, Gennie had grown from an innocent child to a mature and knowledgeable woman, but she was unprepared to explain courting to an eleven-year-old. She cleared her throat nervously. "Can you describe to me what you saw?" she asked.

"I saw lots of different things. I see folks dance around in a really funny way," Mairin said. She slid off her chair and began twirling around the drying room.

Her malformed bones, the result of untreated rickets, caused her to stumble and bounce off the edge of the worktable, but she just kept going.

Gennie sank back in her chair with relief. Mairin had seen Shaker dancing, that's all it was. Dancing was so much easier to explain than a cuddling couple.

"Come sit down again, Mairin, you're making me dizzy. I know you've seen some dancing worship before. Did Rose or Agatha ever explain it to you?"

"Sort of."

"Well, you see, a long time ago, Shakers used to dance in the Meetinghouse when they had a worship service. Sometimes the sisters and brothers would twirl and twirl until they went into a trance—that's like a magic place where they talked to Shakers who were already in Heaven. Or they heard angels singing beautiful songs and were shown lovely drawings, which were given to them as gifts."

Mairin stopped whirling about and tilted her head like a curious puppy. *She really is an endearing child*, Gennie thought.

"I know all about *that*," Mairin said. "This was different." She began spinning again, this time throwing her head back so that she faced the ceiling.

Make that endearing and irritating. Gennie was about to scold Mairin when the child lost her balance and fell backward, crashing into a table holding several large screen trays used to dry small, delicate herbs, such as chamomile flowers. Mairin tumbled to the floor, the screens cascading on top of her.

With a cry, Gennie rushed to her. She tossed the screens aside and took Mairin by the shoulders. "Are you all right? Does anything hurt?"

Mairin sat rigid under Gennie's grasp. She opened her mouth as if to speak, but instead her lower lip quivered.

"Oh dear, you're hurt, aren't you? Don't move. I'll get Sister Josie right away. She'll know what to do." Now in her early eighties, North Homage's Infirmary nurse had handled many a crisis.

"Nay! Don't tell anyone, please." Ignoring the warning to stay still, Mairin clutched at Gennie's arm. "I'm okay, so nobody needs to know, do they?"

Gennie laughed. "You didn't knock down the whole Herb House, Mairin, just a few trays. They were empty, too. See?" She gathered up the screens and revealed the floor underneath, which needed a sweeping but wasn't littered with ruined herb flowers or crumbled leaves. Mairin stared forlornly at the floor, then lifted her face to Gennie.

"What are you afraid of?" Gennie asked.

"Sister Rose is going to leave me again."

"What?"

"She left because I'm bad. I'm bad a lot."

Gennie clicked her tongue. "If you're bad," she said, "then I'm badder. I used to do more than knock down empty screens, believe me. I always loved the smell of herbs. In the late summer and early fall, when this room was full of herbs hanging upside down in bunches, I used to spin around and fling out my arms and hit them on purpose. That would release their fragrances. Of course, sometimes I'd knock them clean off their hooks."

"Then what happened? Did you get punished?"

Gennie hesitated. She'd dug herself into a deepening hole, wanting to reassure Mairin. She hadn't been punished because she'd always managed to rehang the herb bunches before anyone found out. She'd told herself that the floor was kept clean, it didn't matter that the herbs had fallen on it. But she stopped short of encouraging the same sneaky behavior by Mairin, who was already sneaky enough. So far Mairin hadn't paid the full price for her transgressions because Rose was being careful with her, trying to keep her from running away from the village.

"Well," Gennie said, "whenever I or one of the other children was punished, no one ever spanked us or anything like that. The sisters would just make us stay home when the other children went on an outing, like swimming or sliding in the snow."

"I'd just sneak out again," Mairin said. She was matter-of-fact, merely stating the obvious.

"Mairin, I think they're on to you—the sisters, I mean. They'd probably have one of the older girls watch you. There'd be no way out. Believe me, you'd have to stay put and be bored."

Mairin stuck out her lower lip in a pout. Gennie reached out her hand to help her off the floor. "Come on, up you go. Time to go see Sister Rose."

Reluctantly, Mairin took Gennie's hand and let herself be pulled to her feet. They headed out the drying room door and down the stairs. Gennie paused in the middle. "Mairin," she said, "you said you saw a woman dancing. Where was this?"

"Last time it was in that place where those things are that the sisters sit at—you know, like they're playing music but they're really making blankets or something?"

"Looms? Do you mean the Sisters' Shop?"

"I guess so."

"The sisters didn't see the woman, too?"

"They weren't there." Mairin hung her head. "It was night," she said. "I sneaked out after Nora fell asleep, and I saw a light on at the top of the building. So I watched. That's when I saw her dancing around."

"Who was she? A Shaker sister? Was it this ghost everyone has been talking about?"

Mairin shrugged. "I'm ready to go now," she said.

"Oh, Mairin . . . You've got to promise me never again to sneak out at night. Will you do that?"

"Yea."

Gennie didn't believe her for a moment, but it was the best she could do for now. She would have a talk with Rose as soon as possible. Right now, she just wanted to go back to her room and rethink the whole idea of marriage and children. In the past half hour, Gennie had become convinced that, should she ever have children, God would ensure that they were every bit as difficult as she had been as a child.

Gennie sat alone in the parlor of the Shaker Hostel, curled in a wing chair, a light blanket covering her knees. She sipped at a cup of spearmint tea she'd fixed herself in the kitchen. It was well past midnight. Everyone else had gone to bed, but she knew that sleep would elude her. She had a lot to think about. For once, it wasn't Grady who occupied her mind—well, not all of it, anyway. Little Mairin and her nighttime adventures kept interrupting Gennie's attempts to sort out her own future. That dear and exasperating child had crept into Gennie's heart, just as she had already done with Rose and Agatha. Yet Mairin trusted none of them, not completely.

Gennie held the steaming tea to her chest and inhaled the sweet fragrance. The days were warming up, as they did quickly in April, but it could still be chilly at night. She knew her room would be colder still. At least here she had two dying fires—one in the fireplace and another in the black cast-iron stove against the wall. The old stove was the only distinctly Shaker object in the room. Otherwise, Brother Andrew had used worldly furniture and décor, as in the dining room. Gennie had come to feel at home in such surroundings, yet a part of her always yearned for the simple Shaker life she'd known as a child. *I've probably grown soft, too*, she thought. *It wouldn't hurt me to do a little physical labor*. Then she remembered standing in a kitchen all day, cooking for forty people, and going soft didn't sound so bad.

A creak above her head startled her. She listened for a few moments, but all was quiet. The house itself was settling down to sleep. Gennie irritably kicked off the blanket. This wouldn't do. She'd been ruminating for nearly a week, and she wasn't getting anywhere except frustrated and—yes, bored. She needed to *do* something. Mairin's haunting hazel eyes popped into her mind again, and Gennie knew exactly what to do. Right away.

Her heart fluttering in a familiar and pleasant way, Gennie folded the blanket over the chair back, returned the empty cup to the kitchen, and climbed the stairs to her room. Without bothering to flip on her light, she reached around to a wall peg just inside her door and grabbed her light spring coat. She'd changed out of her dinner clothes into a comfortable cotton dress and low-heeled shoes, so she was all set for adventure. She threw on her coat and hurried down the hall, giving no thought, in her excitement, to the noise she made. She slowed down only when she passed a door under which she could see a faint glow of light. Someone else couldn't sleep. As she remembered, it was Mina Dunmore's room. She didn't hear any movement as she tiptoed past. Maybe Mina had fallen asleep reading. To be safe, though, Gennie made a mental note to avoid the view from Mina's window.

She closed the front door behind her, grimacing as the latch caught with a click. North Homage still didn't lock its buildings, even the hostel, so she didn't have to fuss with a key. She turned and looked around her. She could see the north side of the village, all of which was dark except for one light in the Infirmary. She'd heard that Sister Viola, now in her nineties, was down with a spring chill, so Josie was probably sitting up with her. It was unlikely that a dancing ghost had materialized anywhere near Josie—if it dared disturb a patient, she'd give it a tongue lashing it would remember for eternity.

Mairin had seen the ghostly dancer in the Sisters' Shop, which was at the south end of the village, southeast of the Shaker Hostel. Was the ghost drawn to one place, or was it roaming the village, building by building? What did ghosts normally do? While she was growing up, Gennie had heard lots of stories about Shakers receiving communications from the dead, but she'd never heard of an actual shade haunting a Shaker village.

Gennie walked around to the east side of the hostel so she could see the Sisters' Shop. The building was dark, as it should be so late at night. Gennie would have to pass three buildings to reach the shop. The South Family Dwelling House was no problem; it had been abandoned for some time. The Schoolhouse would also be empty. But then she'd have to slip by the Children's Dwelling House unseen. Sister Charlotte and the children still lived and slept there. Rose had wanted everyone to move to the big dwelling house, but Wilhelm drew the line at children. He didn't like them much to begin with, and their numbers had grown in the past year because so many had been left with the Shakers by desperate parents crushed by this relentless Depression.

All children slept in the north end of the building, to be closer to the village. But that didn't mean they'd stay in their rooms. Gennie had only to remember herself as a child to realize that. It would be just like Mairin to have slipped out of her bed and into one of the empty east-facing rooms. That's probably how she first saw the ghost.

In the distance, the Sisters' Shop showed no sign of life, either corporeal or ethereal. The spring air still carried a damp chill, and Gennie's enthusiasm was waning. Before just giving up, however, she walked toward the back of the hostel to get a closer look at the shop. As she rounded the corner, she saw what she'd been waiting for—a brightly lit window that should have been dark. Not in the Sisters' Shop, though. Instead it was to her right, in a second-floor window of the Carpenters' Shop.

At times in the past, a brother might work into the night and then sleep in the Carpenters' Shop, but Gennie knew no one did that now. Anyway, if someone were working late, the light would be shining on the first floor. Gennie approached the building slowly, keeping her eyes on the window even if it meant wandering off the path and into the dew-soaked grass. She didn't care about her shoes or stockings.

Gennie had ventured within about a hundred feet of the Carpenters' Shop when she saw movement through the window. It looked as if an arm had reached across and yanked shut the thin white curtains. Gennie stood still and waited, half expecting the light to go out. Nothing happened for several moments. Gennie chided herself for her overheated imagination and was more than ready to leave when a silhouette appeared in the window. The translucent curtain turned the image into a dark, faceless apparition with an unusually large head.

The figure bowed directly toward Gennie—or so it felt. Could it possibly see her? The creature turned sideways and bowed again, twice this time, as if someone else were in the room. Now Gennie could see that the large head was really the hood of a Shaker cloak pulled forward, hiding the face. Did ghosts have faces? Gennie was caught between the world and her Shaker upbringing. In fact, it was her worldly experience that made her believe this creature might be a real ghost. Grady would laugh at her, but his sister, Emily, loved séances and regularly used a Ouija board to guide her life. This was just the sort of ghost Emily believed in— dark and mysterious and probably very evil. It was nothing like the Shakers who had passed on, the ones Agatha used to tell her about.

The apparition faced the window again and bowed, then repeated its sideways double bow. Gennie caught her breath. *It's dancing.* That stylized bowing was so like part of a choreographed Shaker dance of worship. The figure stretched its arms straight up, which expanded its width as the cloak unfolded like the wings of a bird. Circling slowly, it turned its face toward the ceiling. Miraculously, the hood did not fall backward.

Gennie ignored her damp feet and ruined shoes as she watched the ghost twirl faster and faster till the cloak billowed out like a tent. The specter whirled out of sight, then reappeared and twirled across the window. Gennie stood breathlessly still, waiting for it to return. Seconds passed. She began to count them. A minute went by, then another. Gennie's heart was battering at her chest in anticipation of the next surprise. Three minutes passed.

"Well, I guess the show's over." The voice came from behind her. Gennie yelped and spun around. At first she saw nothing; her eyes had been glued too long on the bright window. As she adjusted to the darkness, a figure emerged, then another. Three people had been standing behind her, watching the window. She glanced around and located two more observers peeking around the corner of the Schoolhouse. As they approached, she realized they were all strangers.

"Look, she's leaving," said a woman in a hoarse whisper. She pointed toward the window. Gennie turned just in time to see the light fade out. The group waited several more minutes, but no other window lit up, at least in the part of the building visible to them.

A man took off in a sprint, circled the Carpenters'

Shop, and returned, out of breath. "All dark," he reported.

"Haven't seen you before," a woman said to Gennie.

"This is my first time."

"We been here every night this week," the woman said. "At least most of us have. It's better'n the circus. Why, I like to fainted dead away first time I seen that ghost prancing around."

"How did you hear about this?" Gennie asked.

"Oh lordy, *everyone* knows about her by now. It's been in the papers and so forth. My cousin down in Bowling Green heard about it even. I'm surprised there ain't more folks here, but there's probably lots watching the wrong buildings. Anyway, nothin' much happened till a few days ago. We guessed she'd be at this building because she's already done all the other buildings in this area, 'cepting that boardinghouse or whatever it is." The woman seemed to have appointed herself the group's storyteller, because the others had pulled back and were whispering among themselves. One of the women broke away and began spinning gracelessly. She collapsed, laughing, into the arms of a man.

"I'm Betty, by the way."

"It's nice to meet you, Betty," Gennie said, without giving her own name. "Do you really think she's a ghost?"

"I reckon so. There's different stories going around, don't know which is right. There's them that says she's a Shaker girl done in by her lover, and others think she done herself in, out of love for some man that jilted her. Me, I figure she got herself murdered and she's come back looking to punish the man that did it."

"But wouldn't he be dead by now, too?"

"Well, more'n likely," Betty said, "but if she's been gone for a hundred years, maybe she got confused."

Gennie gave up on any attempt to wring logic out of Betty.

"Have you seen her face—that ghost's, I mean?" Gennie asked.

"Nope," Betty said, with regret. "She's always got that hood pulled forward or something. Maybe ghosts ain't got faces."

Gennie didn't venture an opinion on the subject. As her excitement dwindled, her discomfort grew. She'd begun to notice that her shoes were soaked through. She wanted to go to her room, dry off, and snuggle under her covers. She forced herself to ask another question. "How many times have you seen her?"

"Oh, me and Arlin—that's my husband—we been out here five nights in a row, ever since we seen that story in the Lexington paper, while we was visiting my sister. The first night we just wandered around, didn't see nothin', but we figured we'd come back and try again. That's when we met those folks." She pointed toward the others, who chattered as if they were at a church social.

"When we finally seen her, it was in that building over there." Betty's arm swung toward the abandoned South Family Dwelling House. "Next night she was over there, and then last night over there." She'd indicated the Schoolhouse and the Sisters' Shop. So the specter had jumped around a bit but stayed in the same area, avoiding the buildings occupied at night. Would it stick to the abandoned or empty buildings or become bolder and begin to haunt the Shakers' living quarters? If the ghost ventured into the Children's Dwelling House, it would surely have an audience of one very determined little girl. Gennie smiled into the darkness at the thought of Mairin following the phantom from room to room. If someone was perpetrating a hoax, Mairin would soon figure it out.

Betty stared at the South Family Dwelling House, her face scrunched up as if it hurt to concentrate. "Now I think of it," she said, "I did notice something the other night. Arlin seen it, too. That ghost looked like she was fat. We didn't notice it at first, not while she was dancing—maybe 'cause her dress was puffed out by all that spinning around. But when we was back in our wagon heading home, we caught sight of her running between a couple of buildings, and it sure seemed like her cloak was still pushed out, you know, like it would be over a fat person. Arlin, he didn't think a ghost could have fat, not solid fat anyways. She was supposed to be a pretty young thing, too. So I reckon she was, you know, in the family way. Maybe that's why she killed herself—or got killed. Makes sense, don't it?"

"What buildings was she running toward, do you remember?"

"Oh honey, these buildings are so plain they all look alike to me." A tall man who must be Arlin called to Betty. "Time for bed," Betty said. "You take care now, hear? Get yourself dried off. Ain't worth a chill."

Gennie no longer cared about her cold, wet feet. A pregnant ghost—this was something she should take to Rose. And Agatha, too. If anyone would remember a story about a Shaker girl who got into trouble and died as a result, it was Sister Agatha. Gennie's morose mood had melted away. She could put aside this endless fussing about Grady and Marriage. Adventure was in the air.

FIVE

LIKE ALL OTHER DAYS, SATURDAY WAS A BUSY ONE FOR the Shakers of North Homage. Normally they would give themselves an extra half hour of sleep on Saturday morning, but planting season had begun. The ground was warm enough to till, the air was sweet with apple blossoms, and the brethren were hard at work outdoors. Rose, however, was unlucky enough to be shut indoors with Elder Wilhelm Lundel. Gennie had reported all she'd seen and heard the previous night on her ghost-hunting adventure, and Rose had felt compelled to relate the information to Wilhelm. She and Wilhelm shared responsibility for the spiritual guidance and care of the North Homage Believers, but often Wilhelm had difficulty remembering he was not sole leader of the community. This was one of those mornings.

"Wilhelm," Rose said, "it is not Andrew's fault that this odd specter has seen fit to inhabit our buildings." She arranged another set of books on the shelves that their carpenter, Brother Archibald, had refinished for the library's new location in the Center Family Dwelling House's smallest meeting room.

"Then it is *thy* fault, for encouraging Andrew to

open that . . . that place." Wilhelm, for once, was helping Rose with the move. She suspected it was only because he wanted the room arranged his way, not hers. Why he should care, she didn't know. Wilhelm had established his beliefs long ago and saw no reason to deepen them with spiritual study. He preferred working outdoors.

"It's only a hostel, Wilhelm, not a den of evil."

"It is something of the world, right within our village. It brings an evil influence, which has called up this creature from Hell."

"You don't think it possible that this manifestation might be a long-dead Believer who has returned to tell us something?"

"Nay, I most certainly do not. She would have spoken by now. She would be watching over us, not performing for the world."

Rose had to admit he was probably right. "Wilhelm, do you remember hearing any stories about a young Shaker sister who died here under strange circumstances a hundred years ago? Did Obadiah ever mention anything like that happening?"

Wilhelm snorted derisively. "Obadiah was far too busy as elder to worry about such foolishness." He flicked a bit of dust from a copy of *Mother Ann's Testimonies* and placed it gently on a shelf. "As am I." He scooped his broad-brimmed work hat from a wall peg and faced Rose. "Sister, I leave it in thy hands to rid us of this intruder. If she is not gone soon, we will be forced to close that hostel."

"Wilhelm, that's—"

"I haven't time to argue, and we haven't time to waste. We have people of the world wandering around the village day and night, and who knows what fresh evil they will bring with them. All this nonsense only creates spiritual confusion for our Children, for whom we are responsible, are we not?"

Rose could think of nothing to say. Wilhelm had turned her own argument against her, the very words she had used to convince him to move with her to the dwelling house.

"Good," Wilhelm said, as he strode toward the door, "then we understand one another." He paused with his hand on the doorknob. "One other issue. That child, Mairin—I hear she has been roaming the village at night, disobeying her elders."

"Mairin is my responsibility," Rose said.

"Precisely," Wilhelm said, turning to face her. "And she is a bad example to the other children. If she cannot be controlled, we will have to send her away. We will send her to an orphanage—one of those orphanages that operate farms. She obviously does not appreciate all that we provide for her, asking only light work and study in return. Working on a farm might teach her gratitude."

"Nay, we will not send Mairin anywhere." Rose drew in her breath and prayed for calm. Her prayer was answered in the form of a sudden inspiration. "You yourself know that Mairin has shown spiritual promise. Don't forget her gift drawings."

Wilhelm's face tightened, and Rose knew she'd won a point. Though Mairin had drawn nothing lately, she had in the past used crayons to translate elaborate images from her dreams. They had impressed Wilhelm, at least for a while.

"It seems the spirits have abandoned her, however,"

he said. "Perhaps they don't find her a worthy instrument."

"Perhaps she is again serving as an instrument, and we just aren't listening. The child is drawn to this apparition. Maybe it will speak only through her."

Wilhelm thrust out a stubborn chin but said nothing, which told Rose that she had earned some time. The period in Shaker history to which Wilhelm most wished to return was the Era of Manifestations, or the years of Mother Ann's Work, beginning in the 1830s. Then, the gifts of the spirit—the dances and songs and drawings, the trances, the speaking in tongues—had first been sent through young girls. Rose was torn. She believed in the presence of spirits, but she couldn't help feeling that they were inclined to communicate more quietly nowadays.

But who knows, perhaps Mairin truly is an instrument.

Maybe Holy Mother Wisdom, in her compassion, had chosen to speak through a troubled child. Anything was possible.

"Mairin may indeed show herself to be an instrument," Wilhelm said, turning back to the door, "and perhaps she will not. We cannot afford to wait much longer to find out. See that she reveals herself soon."

After Wilhelm's warning, Rose gathered up Mairin and the two of them made straight for Agatha's retiring room. When they heard the quiet command to enter, it was Mairin who pushed first through the door. Without waiting to be prompted, she dragged a small chair from the desk over to the rocker where Agatha sat. Mairin settled her small body against the wooden back slats and gazed at Agatha with intensity.

"Are you sick?" she asked.

"Nay, child, I am recovered from my chill. How kind of you to ask."

Mairin said nothing, just continued to stare as if assessing Agatha's strength for herself. Rose quietly lifted a ladder-back chair from its pegs and sat some distance from the two.

"Are you mad at me, like everybody else?" Mairin asked. Her voice was matter-of-fact, without hint of a childlike whine.

Agatha leaned forward and touched Mairin's arm. Her thin hand was pallid against the girl's warm, fawn-brown skin.

"I was frightened," Agatha said, "like everyone else."

Mairin's gaze darted over to Rose, then dropped to her lap. "Gennie said I was scaring people." She raised her impassive face to Agatha. "I'm sorry," she said. She did not promise never again to put everyone in such a state, and neither Rose nor Agatha demanded she do so.

"My poor memory has grown old," Agatha said. "Tell me again, Mairin, when is your birthday?"

For once, Mairin looked startled. "I don't know," she said. "Nobody told me for sure, just that it was in the spring sometime."

"Rose? Have you any information?" Agatha asked.

"Nay, I haven't. We tried to hunt down Mairin's birth certificate in Indianapolis, but we could find nothing."

"Well, then," Agatha said, "what is to stop us from creating a birthday? Today is April 23, isn't it? And it is Saturday. Tomorrow is the Sabbath. How about April 25 for your birthday, Mairin? We always celebrate each child's birthday, you know. The Kitchen sisters can bake you a cake—I'm sure Sister Gertrude would be delighted to do it herself—and right after school Sister Charlotte will gather all the children together for a party. Would you like that, Mairin?"

Mairin nodded with more vigor than usual. "Would you and Rose come, too?"

Rose opened her mouth to remind Mairin of Agatha's frailty, but the former eldress held up a shaky yet authoritative hand. "Rose will be there, of course, and I will come if I am able," she said. "Now, you run along back to the Children's Dwelling House. I know Sister Charlotte has special Saturday lessons planned, and you don't want to fall behind. Besides, Rose and I have some things to discuss."

Mairin slid off her chair and stood awkwardly before Agatha's rocker. "Thank you, Sister." She reached out her hand and touched Agatha's with the tips of her fingers, then pulled back quickly. Another child would have jumped up and down with glee, but Mairin's body tightened, as if she wanted to keep her excitement from escaping. She closed her eyes and hugged herself. She stood that way for so long that Rose became alarmed.

"Mairin, are you all right?" she asked.

Mairin opened her eyes. "Yea. I was just telling Mother Ann that my birthday will be perfect if she'll let my angel come, too." In the time it took Rose and Agatha to digest her words, Mairin had scampered from the room.

"Her angel?" Rose scooted her chair close to Agatha's. "Could she mean this apparition she's been following about?"

Agatha frowned, her cloudy eyes focused inward. "We must watch the child carefully," she said.

"Do you believe she is in danger?"

"I believe she has gifts," Agatha said. "Extraordinary gifts. But she is too young and inexperienced to know how to follow them properly, to listen to them. I'm afraid she might misunderstand and put herself in danger."

"But if they are gifts of the spirit, how can they lead her astray?"

"I'm not worried about the gifts that are part of her," Agatha said. "I'm worried about the part of her that is human." She closed her eyes and leaned her head against a thin blanket folded over the back of her rocker.

"You're exhausted," Rose said. She worried constantly about Agatha's health and felt guilty each time she asked her elderly friend to help her solve a dilemma. Agatha, Rose knew, would be content to move on to the next stop on her spiritual journey, but Rose had no desire to hasten the process. "I'll keep a close watch over Mairin," she said. "You needn't worry."

Agatha's blue-veined eyelids shot open. "Mairin came to us starving and unloved," she said with renewed force. "We fed her and we've loved her, yet in some way she hungers still. *That* is why I fear for her." Agatha released a long sigh and seemed to shrink in her chair. Rose leaned over her and lightly kissed the smooth skin of her forehead.

"I think I understand," Rose said. "Now you rest. I'll keep you informed." She closed the retiring room door behind her. She wasn't certain she really did understand what Agatha had tried to tell her, but she knew enough to listen to the message. If she didn't keep a close eye on Mairin, something even worse than an orphanage might be in the child's future.

Rose made a quick telephone call to Sister Charlotte, who assured her that Mairin had returned to the Children's Dwelling House and that she and Nora would watch her carefully. She then visited Sister Gertrude in the kitchen to request a birthday cake for Monday and perhaps some homemade ice cream.

"I know just what I'll bake," Gertrude said. "We have just enough of last fall's crop to make a lovely dried apple cake. The young'uns love that one." Gertrude's large, bony hands splashed in a deep sink full of hot, soapy water as she washed up the dishes from the noon meal. Rose found a clean linen towel and began to dry. She'd been lax lately about helping the sisters with their work. Physical labor was important for her humility, and to be honest, she loved working alongside the sisters.

"Oh, no need to do that, Rose," Gertrude said, waving a dripping hand toward the clean dishes. "Unless you want to, of course. I mean, you've got your hands full with that hostel, don't you?" Gertrude clearly hoped for a serving of gossip.

"Andrew handles most of that," Rose said. She gave a final wipe to a shiny copper-bottomed pan and hung it on a peg next to its comrades.

"Oh, of course it's Brother Andrew's project, I know, but what with this latest excitement and all, I reckon you're up to your ears keeping everyone calm over there."

"Calm?"

"Well, a ghost, after all. Even if those folks are from the world, they can't be used to sharing a house with a ghost."

Rose reached for another pan. "I wasn't aware that this apparition had been seen in the hostel, let alone that it lived there," she said.

"Yea, it most certainly has been seen there." In her excitement, Gertrude scrubbed a little too vigorously, and the pan she was holding slipped out of her hands, sloshing foamy water on her apron as it hit the sink. Gertrude scooped up the pan and renewed her scrubbing. "Why, I had it straight from the housekeeper, Mrs. Berg. She's a bit of a gossip, you know."

"Nay, I didn't know." Rose tried mightily not to smile. Amusement would surely hurt Gertrude's feelings—and it might stem the flow of information.

"Oh goodness, she does go on. But this time she saw it herself—the ghost, I mean—wandering the halls of the hostel."

"When was this?"

"Well, it was just this morning I spoke with her—she came to talk over my new recipes. I reckon she felt like having a chat. I thought that dill potato soup was right tasty, didn't you? Anyway, she said she'd been up and about the night before. Couldn't sleep, she said. Thought she'd warm up a cup of milk. Goodness, I better remember to drop her by some extra milk tomorrow.

●

"Anyway, she went down the back stairs to the kitchen, and she swore she saw a shade in a Dorothy cloak—she didn't know it was a Dorothy cloak, of course, just thought it was an old-fashioned cloak, but I knew what she was describing when she said it was real long and had a short cape over the shoulders. Where was I?" Gertrude stopped scrubbing and stared at the dirty bubbles in front of her.

"Mrs. Berg saw the ghost."

"Yea," Gertrude said, nodding vigorously. "It was in the kitchen, she said, or at least it was just leaving. She said it glided through the door without opening it and disappeared."

Rose was beginning to suspect that Beatrice Berg had been imbibing something far stronger than warm milk. "Had she any idea what the apparition was doing in the kitchen?"

"Nay, but she did say it was a mighty plump ghost, so maybe it was eating." Gertrude cackled, then stopped suddenly. "Do ghosts eat real food?" she asked.

"To be honest," Rose said, "this is my first experience with ghosts, so I don't know."

"My, there's certainly been some odd doings in the village since that ghost appeared. Mrs. Berg complained that a new wooden spatula just up and disappeared from the hostel kitchen, and Sister Isabel said some of the best wool went missing from the Sisters' Shop. Then Sister Gretchen said a big old basket disappeared from the Laundry—you know, the kind they use to take out the wash when they hang it on the lines? Why, it's almost like that ghost is setting up housekeeping." Two young girls arrived to help her prepare for the evening meal, and Gertrude quieted down. She obviously wanted more gossip fodder, but she knew better than to dig for rumors in the hearing of impressionable young ears.

Rose hung the last clean pan and made her escape. She had an idea, and she wanted to follow up on it right away. Ignoring the path, she cut east through the medic garden behind the Infirmary and went straight for the Laundry. The story of a plump Shaker sister who danced alone at odd times, and for unknown reasons, was beginning to sound far too familiar.

Despite unseasonable coolness, the Laundry had already reached midsummer temperature. When Rose opened the door, a cloud of heavy, hot air enveloped her. No one was on the ground floor, where the huge washing tubs, with their community-sized agitators, had finished their work for the day. Since no one had been hanging clothes outside to dry, Rose guessed the sisters would be upstairs ironing as much as they could before the outdoor heat made it impossible until autumn.

Rose paused a moment to pray for guidance—and for patience. As eldress, Rose held primary responsibility for the sisters. They confessed to her regularly, and she endeavored to help them open themselves to deeper spiritual understanding. She guided them through the sometimes turbulent waters of community life. At times she doubted herself, yet she always did her best for the sisters, and they seemed to know that and to appreciate her assistance.

All but one, that is. Since the day she'd arrived, Sister Elsa Pike had been a source of frustration and the cause of many of Rose's pleas for patience. Elsa was a firm supporter of Wilhelm's plans to thrust North Homage far into the past, and she felt protected by him. She openly defied Rose, resisted confession as long as possible, and made little effort to live in harmony with the rest of the Family. More than once, Rose had been prepared to tell her she must leave the village and go back to the world, where she'd lived most of her life. Yet each time the moment arrived, Elsa changed her tune. She would suddenly confess with great vigor and meekly do as she was told for as long as it took to show the community she was contrite. Rose suspected that Wilhelm coached her. Rose always let her stay, then soon enough came to regret her decision. The timing was just about right for Elsa to shed her contrition and return to her normal self. Fevered dancing worship, ecstatic enough to please Wilhelm, was one of Elsa's specialties.

It was no use waiting to calm down. This ghostly activity smacked of Elsa; Rose could see no other possibility—or at least no other possibility that felt convincing. She marched toward the stairway leading up to the ironing room. Before she reached it, a quiet pair of feet in soft cloth shoes slipped down the steps, and Sister Gretchen, Laundry Deaconess, appeared. Gretchen was normally a reserved, even-tempered young woman. Today she looked harried. Dark brown hair had escaped in clumps from her white indoor cap, and her eyes darted furtively back up the staircase.

"Don't tell me," Rose said, "you've spent the day alone with Elsa." She shouldn't have said such a thing, of course, but experience had taught her that the other sisters tolerated Elsa far better when they knew their eldress sympathized.

Gretchen flashed a quick smile and maintained a diplomatic silence. "Are you here to speak with me?"

"Nay, with Elsa. Alone, if you don't mind."

"I don't mind in the least. I have some clothes to collect off the lines. Elsa is upstairs." She didn't add *and you're welcome to her*, but Rose was fairly certain she'd thought it. She was out the door with a speed born of relief. Rose, on the other hand, was dangerously ready for a confrontation.

Elsa heard her footsteps and began talking before Rose reached the landing. "Don't see no rhyme or reason to pressing these old work shirts," she said. "The brothers just mess 'em up five minutes into wearin' 'em. Those men don't pay no never mind to how much work we womenfolk put into keeping them in nice, clean clothes." She didn't glance up from the brown shirt she was going through the motions of ironing.

"The brothers work very hard, Elsa," Rose said. "They have little time to worry about the wrinkles in their clothing."

Elsa's head popped up in surprise. She was a sturdily built hill-country woman with a broad, flat-featured face that did not hide her emotions. At that moment, irritation pulled her thin lips straight and hardened her eyes.

"Waren't expecting thee," she said. Elsa made a sporadic but determined attempt to use Wilhelm's archaic form of speech, but when combined with her hill-country vernacular, the result often triggered fits of giggles among the unprepared. Rose allowed her to speak as she wished. Language was the least of her problems with Elsa.

"You may leave the ironing for now, Sister. I have an important matter to discuss with you."

Elsa hesitated with her hand on the upended iron and her eyes on Rose. Apparently she decided that obedience would be a good idea, because she let go of the iron. She stayed behind the board, however, perhaps to keep an obstacle between herself and her eldress.

"Come and sit with me," Rose said. She indicated two ladder-back chairs with well-worn taped seats. "This shouldn't keep you from your work for long. I know you want to get back to it."

Elsa sat without protest.

"It has been some time since you cleansed your mind and your heart in confession, Elsa."

"Is that what this here's about?" Elsa threw out her rough hands in a gesture of impatience. "I got a passel of work to do, and lessen you want to do it for me, I got no time for confessing." Her "thees" and "thous" tended to slip away in the face of almost any emotion.

"We all have very full days, Elsa. The other sisters put their hands to work every bit as hard as you do, but they make time to put their hearts to God."

"My heart's with God all the time. I wake up prayin' and go to sleep prayin'. I ain't got a minute free of prayin', so when would I do somethin' needs confessing?"

Rose took an especially deep breath and fixed Elsa with her sternest stare. "Perhaps you would feel more appreciated in the world," she said, "where your spiritual fervor might serve as a beacon. Surely you are wasted here among us poor Shakers."

Elsa's face tightened in a stubborn scowl. Rose had played this game with her many times, and both knew the rules. Elsa knew it would be difficult for Rose to send her away over Wilhelm's objections. Difficult, but not impossible.

"Ain't got nothin' to confess," Elsa said, chastened but ever stubborn.

"Well then, it won't bother you to tell me how you've been spending your time these past few days."

A shadow passed across Elsa's face. It was either doubt or confusion; Rose couldn't tell which. "Ain't done nothin' worth the tellin' of it," Elsa said. "I work, eat, sleep—and worship, of course."

Noting Elsa's ever-expanding waistline, Rose thought that eating probably came first. It was another in a long string of uncharitable thoughts about Elsa that Rose continually confessed to Agatha. At least she was able to hold her tongue this time. However, she dropped all attempts at delicate indirection and asked, "Have you been indulging in dancing worship alone at night?"

"What? Why are . . ." Elsa's mouth dropped open. Her astonishment quickly dissolved into red-faced fury. She stood up and planted herself in front of Rose, fists on her rotund hips. Rose stood as well, to avoid letting Elsa look down on her.

"I ain't that spook that's been dancing around at night, if that's what you bin thinkin', and you got no call to go around accusin' me. That there's a real ghost. I seen it myself."

"Oh? When and where did you see it?"

"I wasn't out when I shouldn't a-bin, if that's what you're thinkin'. I couldn't sleep, that's all. Couple nights ago, it was. My retiring room's at the end of the hall, looks out south over the village. I was just sittin' in

my rocker by the window, and there she was, prancin'
around in front of a window on the second floor of the
South Family Dwelling House. Gave me a turn, she
did." Elsa looked offended, as if the specter had appeared with the primary intention of upsetting her.

Still, Rose was dubious. "You were able to see her
from such a distance?"

"I got good eyes."

"Are you certain you weren't closer?"

"I said what I saw, and it's the God's honest truth.
God can just go ahead and strike me down dead if I'm
lyin'." She stuck out her chin and glared at the window,
daring the heavens to send a lightning bolt through the
glass.

There was no point in pressing further, and Rose
knew it. She swung her chair up on some wall pegs.
"All right, you may return to your work now," she said.
Elsa was not a particularly bright woman, but she had
often proven herself to be a natural actress, so Rose
had no idea if her protestations of innocence were true.
The answer required investigation. Rose had nearly
reached the doorway when she heard Elsa clear her
throat in a calculated way. Rose paused, knowing more
was coming.

"If I was thee," Elsa said, a sneer in her voice, "I'd
look closer than Heaven for that ghost."

Rose glanced back over her shoulder.

"By which I mean, I'd keep an eye on those folks
y'all invited here—thee and thy friend, Brother Andrew, that is. I'm bettin' one of them's the ghost. Gennie's on the outs with that man of hers, that's what I
hear, and I reckon that could drive a girl like her right
over the edge."

Rose reached for the doorknob.

"That little girl you like so much, that Mairin, you'd best keep an eye on her, too," Elsa said. "I seen her stealing from the kitchen more'n once these last few days. Wouldn't surprise me none if Mairin's in cahoots with the ghost. Maybe the ghost's really a devil, and that girl's in its power."

Rose didn't bother to answer, but she closed the door behind her more forcefully than was strictly necessary.

SIX

ROSE WAS NOT IN THE MOST TRANQUIL OF MOODS AS SHE left the Laundry after her irritating and unenlightening talk with Sister Elsa. She still couldn't say for certain it was Elsa playing ghost at night, nor could she eliminate her. Some outdoor work sounded good. Maybe it would clear her head. Right now she was ready to toss Elsa out of the community on her irksome ear, Wilhelm or no Wilhelm.

She borrowed an old, empty basket from the Infirmary, then made her way toward the Meetinghouse, across the unpaved path that cut through the center of the village. She'd been noticing that the grounds were littered with debris left behind by the thoughtless people of the world who came nightly to watch for the ghost. So many hands were needed for spring planting that no one had time to tidy up the lawn.

The minutes passed quickly and Rose's basket was half full, when she glanced up and saw the brothers' door to the Meetinghouse swing open. Perhaps one of the brethren had been making repairs to the large meeting room, she thought, in preparation for worship on Sunday afternoon. She knelt to snag a fragment of paper ground into the grass. As she stood again, she saw a woman sail through the open door as if leaving her own home. Rose recognized her easily from dinner at the Shaker Hostel. It was Mina Dunmore.

Mrs. Dunmore had discarded her widow's black for a belted dress in a garish shade of pink, which accentuated her thick waist. She favored Rose with a brief smile, the sort a lady might bestow on an admirer, and turned in the direction of the Ministry House. She left the door to the Meetinghouse wide open.

Appalled, Rose left her basket on the grass, hurried to the Meetinghouse, and closed the door. Then she picked up her skirts and jogged toward the interloper.

"Mrs. Dunmore," she called out as she caught up to the slower woman, "might I have a word with you?"

"Yes?" There was an imperious edge to Mina Dunmore's voice.

Daily physical labor kept Rose's limbs strong, so she had no need to catch her breath. She did, however, need a moment to control her flash of temper. For Andrew's sake, she wanted to avoid antagonizing hostel guests, no matter how improper their behavior.

"What did you think of our Meetinghouse?" she asked.

"I beg your pardon?" Mina Dunmore looked genuinely puzzled.

"Our Meetinghouse—the building you just left. I assume you wanted to have a look around, see where we hold our worship services? We will worship tomorrow after the noon meal, if you'd like to see what a service is like."

"Ah yes, the worship service. I hadn't realized . . . I mean, I'm sure it's quite intriguing." Mrs. Dunmore backed away.

"You are certainly under no obligation," Rose said. "I only thought, because you took the trouble to explore the building, you might be interested. I wondered if you'd heard something about the service?" She knew she was goading the woman, but she wanted to create discomfort. She wanted Mina Dunmore to stay out of the village's private buildings unless she'd been invited.

Mrs. Dunmore snickered. "Oh yeah, I heard a thing or two about those services of yours. I was raised strict Methodist myself, so I don't hold much with all that dancing. I've heard it gets mighty wild sometimes."

"Nay, it's normally quite tame," Rose said.

"I'll take your word for that." Mina stepped farther away. "Well, I know y'all work real hard, so I won't keep you from it." She turned and walked straight to the Ministry House. Without hesitation, she entered.

So much for the subtle approach. Next time I'll have to block the way.

Rose considered marching into the Ministry House and dragging the woman out by the sleeve, but she saw Wilhelm cross the path and head directly toward the building. He was probably planning to work on his last bit of personal packing for the move. For once, she was delighted to see him. When he caught the worldly Mina Dunmore wandering through the Ministry House, the woman would wish she had stayed in her room all day. Rose was tempted to follow and watch, but there was work to be done.

Children burst through the Schoolhouse as if sprung from a trap. Sister Charlotte had assigned them a few hours of Saturday work, to allow them to end the school year more quickly. Most of the children followed Charlotte to their dwelling house, where they'd be given time to expend their energy before enduring a silent evening meal with the adults. A small group ran toward a cluster of parents, who waited with cars or wagons to tote their offspring back to town or to their farms. The Shaker school was known as the best in the county, so it never lacked for students, and the local farmers were glad for the chance to have their children finish the year in time to help with planting. Rose stood with the people from the world, watching for Mairin.

Nine-year-old Nora, Mairin's best friend and self-appointed protector, emerged from the Schoolhouse, followed closely by the older but smaller girl. They stopped and leaned their heads together, sharing a secret, giggling. Rose waited, not wishing to intrude. In time, the two girls saw her, waved, and raced each other to reach her. Nora, whose limbs were normal, was winning until she pulled back to let Mairin catch up. They arrived at the same time.

"Hello, you two. How was school today?" Rose asked.

"Mairin read part of a story," Nora said. "She did it perfectly, too. Sister Charlotte said so."

Mairin kicked at the ground.

"Mairin, I'm so pleased with your progress," Rose said. She touched the girl's shoulder lightly. Because of a lifetime of beatings, before the Shakers took her in, Mairin was leery of being touched. However, she raised her face to Rose and beamed. She had come far, and she knew it. A few short months earlier, she had been unable to read or write more than her name and a few words.

"Nora, would you run along with Sister Charlotte? I'll take good care of Mairin. I want to talk with her about something."

"Okay. See you later, Mairin." Nora turned a cartwheel, knowing that Rose wouldn't mind, and ran off toward the group Charlotte was leading to the Children's Dwelling House.

Mairin watched Nora race off, then gazed up at Rose with a mixture of pleasure and uncertainty in her eyes. As always, Rose felt her heart constrict. She had grown deeply fond of this odd, vulnerable little girl. She held out her hand, and, to her delight, Mairin placed her own within it.

"Let's walk a while, shall we?"

Mairin said nothing, but followed Rose docilely. The afternoon had grown steamy, a harbinger of summer. Rose led the way past the burned-out foundation of the old Water House and into a thick grove of sugar maples. The trees had leafed out but were still a light spring green, and the budding undergrowth was studded with wildflowers. A faint, not unpleasant whiff of moist soil and decomposing foliage wafted up as their feet kneaded the earth. Mairin yanked on Rose's hand and pointed to a delicate, pale purple cress flower poking up through the previous autumn's coverlet of leaves. They arrived at a small clearing and sat on a fallen log shaded from the afternoon sun.

"Are you still mad at me?" Mairin asked. Her voice, like her face, was expressionless, as if she didn't care about the answer. Rose knew better.

"Nay, I am not." Rose gazed intently into Mairin's

eyes. "Are you still angry with me for going away for a while?"

Mairin's small chin lifted. "You promised you'd help me with my reading," she said.

"I know I did, and I should have told you I was going. I forgot my promise; that was wrong." The apology felt somewhat like a confession, and it crossed Rose's mind that Mairin might someday be called to become a Believer, perhaps even an eldress.

"Mairin, have you been going out at night just because you are angry with me?"

Mairin shook her head, and the sunlight burnished her fluffy brown hair. "Well, maybe at first," she admitted, with a shrug, "but then I forgot to be mad anymore because I met the angel."

"You mean the sister who dances at night?"

Mairin nodded.

"And you think she is an angel, not a ghost?"

"I'm sure she's an angel."

"Why?"

"Because—" Mairin stopped herself and avoided Rose's gaze. She slid off the log and knelt in the grass to pick a tiny wood violet. "These smell sweet if you have a whole bunch of them," she said, "and they taste good, too." She chomped the flower off its stem and chewed.

Rose refused to be distracted. "What is an angel, Mairin? Can you tell me?"

"It's someone God sends to help you and protect you," Mairin said, with confidence.

"I see. This woman you've seen dancing, how does she help and protect you?"

Mairin was silent so long that Rose wondered if

she'd even listened to the question. Finally, she said,
"If I tell you, will you promise not to tell anyone else?
Not even Nora?"

"Did the angel ask you to keep this secret?"

"Nay, but I'm afraid they'll take it away and—"

"Take what away, Mairin? Your angel?"

Mairin shook her head. "Come with me," she said,
"and you'll see." She scampered back toward the village, leaving Rose to follow as fast as she could. When
they reached the edge of the maple grove, Mairin ran
through the grass to the back of the abandoned South
Family Dwelling House. She stopped at the cellar
door, where once the South Family brethren had
brought root vegetables into the earthen basement for
winter storage. Mairin pulled open one side of the
heavy door, grunting with exertion, and disappeared
down the steps. Rose hurriedly followed.

Small, low-ceilinged storage rooms opened onto a
narrow hallway with a dirt floor, which ran the length
of the root cellar. The cool air smelled of dampness
and neglect. It was a place the Shakers rarely had occasion to go anymore, and, probably for that reason, it
had become one of Mairin's favorite hiding places.

Mairin led Rose to an inner room near the few stairs
leading up to the basement kitchen. As she approached
the opening, Mairin began to tiptoe. She stood at the
entrance and peered inside for a moment. Rose was
ready to explode with curiosity. She looked over
Mairin's head into the cavelike room. All evidence of
stored vegetables and jars of preserves had long since
been removed, but in one corner, perched on a low
shelf, Rose saw a deep, round utility basket. One of its
wooden grip handles had broken off and stuck straight

up. Rough spots indicated places where the wood had cracked and popped out of the weaving. An old, well-used basket—yet Mairin approached it as if it were a holy relic.

A small, piteous cry came from inside the basket. "Good heavens, Mairin, do you have a baby in there?" Rose rushed toward the basket.

"Shh, you'll scare it," Mairin said. Rose had never heard so much emotion in the child's voice. Mairin reached into the basket and scooped up a tiny bundle of fur—calico fur. With intense gentleness, she held the tiny creature to her chest and stroked its head with two fingers.

"It *is* a baby," she whispered. "And it doesn't have a mother, just like me. That's why the angel sent it to me, because I know what it's like not to have a mother."

"May I hold it?" Rose asked.

"Well, all right, but be very careful. It's so little."

"I promise." The kitten had almost no weight. It couldn't be more than a few weeks old. It was a miracle the creature had survived.

"She's beautiful," Rose said.

"How do you know it's a girl?"

"Well, see her coat? All those colors? That's called calico, like the fabric, and a calico cat is nearly always a girl. Where is her mother, do you know?"

"She died." Mairin's tone had gone flat. "I buried her in the orchard and said a prayer and everything. There was another kitten, too—a black one with one white paw—but it died, too. I buried them together. I think they'll be happier together. Can I have her back?"

Rose handed the kitten into Mairin's eager hands. "Where did you find them?"

"Out back, under those big bushes. They were all alive when I found them, but the mama and the black kitty were real sick. I tried to feed them. I took some milk from kitchen, and I found some soft rags in the Sisters' Shop."

So that's what Elsa was talking about when she accused Mairin of stealing food. Rose glanced into the basket and saw it was lined with the fine blue wool used to make cloaks. Maybe she wouldn't mention to Sister Isabel that she'd found the missing wool. Not yet, anyway.

"Mairin, is this where you've been coming the past few nights when you've run away?"

"Mostly. I wait a little while, and if I think folks are looking for me, I hide somewhere else. I wanted the kitten to be my secret." Mairin stroked the kitten's fur and leaned close to hear her purr. "I didn't even tell Nora. She's going to be real mad at me."

"She will forgive you if you explain."

"I tried hard to save the other kitties," Mairin said. "I put them all in the basket and carried them in here and watched them as much as I could. But first the baby died and then the mama died, and I was really worried about this baby, but she's okay, isn't she?"

"She seems to be," Rose said, "but she's terribly young to be without her mama. We need to take her to Sister Josie. She will know how best to care for her."

"Nay!" Mairin turned away, hugging the kitten tightly. "The angel gave her to *me*." The kitten mewed sharply. Mairin loosened her grip, and the kitten burrowed into the crook of her arm.

"No one will take her away from you, Mairin. You saved her life, and she needs you. But she's still a tiny

baby who may be sick. We must bring her to the Infirmary. Josie will know if she needs medicine to get
stronger."

"But I can keep her?"

"Yea, you may keep her. If Josie says she's well
enough, we'll move her to an empty room on the top
floor of the Children's Dwelling House until she is big
enough to go outside. Come now, put her in her basket,
and we'll carry her together."

Mairin nestled the kitten in her bed of wool. *An angel might or might not be responsible for bringing
these two together, but this kitten might prove to be a
godsend.* Mairin now had something to care for—a
creature, weaker than herself, who needed her. If the
kitten did not survive, though . . . Rose sped a silent
prayer to Mother Ann, who had lost all four of her children and knew how it felt.

Rose offered Mairin the utility basket's one good
handle and grabbed the other side, so they could transport the kitten together. Awkwardness was less important than encouraging Mairin's protective feelings.
Rather than negotiate the heavy cellar door, Rose
guided them through the abandoned dwelling house
kitchen. Gray light from a grimy window, forgotten
during the building's final cleaning, barely lit the
empty room. A few worn items still hung from pegs—
a broom with a cracked handle, a tattered cloak, a pan
with a charred bottom. The old stove and sink were
missing, pressed into service in the Shaker Hostel
kitchen.

They moved through the bare dining room and into
the hallway. One cracked bench; empty pegs lining
the wall; dust motes swirling in sunbeams, like bits of

colored glass in a kaleidoscope . . . Had the shade of a long-dead Shaker sister twirled her way though these sad corridors? *Why?* And if not a shade, then what? Who?

Dread stabbed Rose like a hunger pang. She stopped and put down her end of the basket. "Mairin, why did you say the angel *gave* you the kitten?"

"Because I found her the night the angel danced here. She was dancing to get my attention. I could see her from the window of my room. She kept bowing to me, and I knew she wanted me to come closer, so I sneaked out to watch. The angel was in the window, looking right at the mama kitty and her babies. She wanted me to see them. She wanted me to find them and take care of them." Mairin knelt beside the basket. Her hand hovered over the sleeping kitten. "I couldn't save them all," she whispered. "I tried really hard."

She's talking to the angel, Rose thought. *Seeking forgiveness? Is she frightened?*

Rose knelt across from Mairin, with the basket between them. "Have you seen the angel close up?"

Mairin's eyes flitted sideways.

"It's okay, you can tell me. I won't be angry."

"I just wanted to thank her." Mairin twirled a soft brown curl around her finger. "For sending me the kitten. So I sneaked out again, even though I knew I wasn't supposed to."

"You went out the next night?"

Mairin shook her head. "The same night. I got some milk from the kitchen and fed the kitties, and then I moved them one at a time into the root cellar. I didn't think about making them a bed until the next night." Regret lowered her voice. "After I moved them the first night, I went to find the angel, to thank her. I went all through this building looking for her. I was getting really tired."

"But you kept going till you found her?"

Mairin nodded. "I went all the way up to the attic, and that's where I found her. It was really dark up there, I could hardly see. She was moving a little bit, bending over—bowing, I think. She bows a lot. I didn't know what to say right off, so I made a sound to tell her I was there."

Rose held her breath, her excitement growing. "Did she turn around? Did you see her face?"

"She didn't have a face."

Mairin had whispered so faintly that Rose wasn't sure she'd heard correctly. "The angel had no face?"

Mairin's lips parted, giving her the look of a much younger child. "I don't think so," she said. "She stood up when I made a noise. She was facing away from me, and her hood was down on her shoulders, but . . . I think she had a head maybe. I'm not sure, it was so dark. But she had a black lump like . . . like maybe she'd been dead for a really long time, and . . ."

The unemotional Mairin had returned, which indicated to Rose that the experience had been terrifying. She hated to press, but she had to. "Did you see the angel's face at all? Did she turn around?"

"Nay." There was a hint of relief in Mairin's voice. "She pulled up her hood. So she must have had a head, right? Because the hood stayed up."

"Did you speak to her?"

"Yea. I just said, 'Thank you, Angel, for the kitty family. I'll take care of them.' She just stood there for a really long time, so I said I was leaving to check on them again. Then she bowed again, but not toward me, toward the wall. I was a little bit scared, so I left."

"She sounds scary."

"But she's really good. She wouldn't have given me the kitties if she wasn't good."

"Okay," Rose said, as she lifted the basket and walked toward the sisters' entrance, "but we might want to leave her off the guest list for your birthday party. I suspect she might frighten the other children."

"I guess so. Anyway, she's *my* angel. I don't want to share her."

They walked out of the gloomy building into a late afternoon that was nearly as gray. Bright spring sunshine was rapidly giving way to charcoal thunderclouds. It would surely be an inhospitable night for ghost watching, and Rose had never been so grateful for a coming storm.

SEVEN

"You seem to have an inordinate disdain for the Shakers, Mrs. Dunmore. One wonders why you wish to remain in their hostel." With his black eyes fixed in a wide-open stare, Horace von Oswald looked like an owl about to swoop down on its prey.

Lightning slashed across the thinly curtained window, followed by a blast of thunder that rattled the panes. All the Shaker Hostel guests, trapped by the violent storm, had gathered in the parlor after dinner. Mina and Horace had appropriated the wing chairs nearest the fireplace, leaving the others to make do with rockers or the small settee.

Gennie had positioned a rocker so she could watch both the fire and the other guests. Learning from Rose about how Mairin had found her kitten had whetted her curiosity about the folks who had chosen to stay in the Shaker's new hostel. Could one of them be this ghost-angel that so fascinated Mairin?

"Now, now, let's not bicker," said Saul Halvardson, flashing a dazzling smile at Mina Dunmore. He managed to include the other women, as well. He was dressed in a black wool evening suit with fashionably wide lapels. His black silk bow tie accentuated the blinding white of his crisp cotton shirt. Gennie had been sampling her future father-in-law's library, and Saul looked exactly like Jay Gatsby, as she had imagined him.

Mighty fancy for a salesman, she thought.

Saul had provided two bottles of port; one was now nearly empty. On such an evening, port had sounded good to everyone, including Gennie. With a flourish, Saul refilled Mina's glass, then Horace's. He opened the second bottle and made the rounds, topping off each glass with boyish eagerness.

Horace von Oswald was not to be distracted. He leaned toward Mina as if about to divulge a secret. His paunch bulged out, causing one button of his brown cardigan to pop its buttonhole. Mina drew back and held her glass in front of her chest, like a talisman. "Tell me, Mrs. Dunmore," he said, "why *are* you staying here?"

"I don't see why that's any concern of yours."

Horace leaned back, and his fleshy lips curved into a faint smile. "Call it curiosity," he said. "I've always been interested in people—why they do what they do."

"You're just naturally nosy, you mean."

Horace's shoulders mounded in a shrug. "I prefer to think of myself as interested in others. When I observe that what someone says differs from what she does, I can't help but wonder why." He drained his glass. "For instance," he said, "I notice that, while you claim to have no interest whatsoever in the Shakers, you spend quite a lot of time exploring their private buildings."

Mina's cheeks reddened, but she did not respond. Gennie studied her haughty profile. Something about the grim set of her jaw and her heavy features reminded Gennie of someone, but she couldn't think who it might be.

"I've also noticed—"

"Why don't you bother someone else for a while," Mina snapped. She gulped her drink, and Saul appeared to give her a refill so fast he must have been hovering nearby, listening to the conversation. When he refilled Horace's glass, the two men locked eyes. Saul's hand shook, and he spilled several drops on Horace's sweater. Horace's gaze never left the younger man's face.

"This Depression has been so hard on so many," Horace said.

"Well, yes," Saul said, "I suppose it has." He edged away.

"I'd assume that most women can't afford fancy underwear."

"Oh, you'd be surprised," Saul said. "Lifts the spirits and all that." He glanced around the room, seeking another glass to fill. "Drink up, everyone," he said. "I can always bring down more from my room." He veered toward Daisy Prescott, who sat alone, leafing through a copy of *American Home*.

Gennie heard an odd choking sound and realized that Horace was chuckling. "That boy sells more than underwear," he said, so softly that Gennie couldn't be sure she'd heard him right.

Hail sputtered against the windows like machine-gun fire, and Gennie shivered. Small quilts hung over the backs of each rocker. She pulled hers around her shoulders like a shawl. She wished she were closer to the fire. Horace was unlikely to relinquish his chair, and Mrs. Dunmore seemed to take perverse pleasure in sparring with him. Now, though, the storm had silenced even those two.

Gennie closed her eyes, feeling cozy and sleepy. Drifting into a nap sounded pleasant, but another burst of lightning and thunder startled her. She opened her eyes to find Beatrice Berg standing near her, fists on hips, scowling at Horace. She must have finished up in the kitchen and decided to join them, though she seemed the last person who'd want more of their company. She still wore her work clothes, a shapeless dress of faded brown cotton with irregular dark patches where food stains hadn't washed out. A narrow black belt barely indented the middle of her square figure. Gray pincurls had turned to frizz from bending over steaming dishwater, and she hadn't bothered to smooth them back into place.

"Took the best seat for yourself, I see," Beatrice said to Horace. "I reckon you'd've took both of them, if you could've figured out how."

"Mrs. Berg, how charming to see you again," Horace murmured.

"Ah, Mrs. Berg, you've joined us," said Saul Halvardson, with every appearance of delight. "Come sit on the settee. I'll be right back, just going to fetch another bottle." He relinquished his seat with a bow, and left the room. Through the open parlor door, Gennie saw him bound up the stairs two at a time.

Daisy Prescott hugged one end of the settee, bent over her magazine. As Beatrice sat, Daisy stood and mumbled something involving the word "sweater." Only Gennie and Beatrice paid any attention to her.

She seemed to fade from the room, but her back was straight as she glided up the stairs.

"That's an odd one," Beatrice said to no one in particular.

"What do you mean?" Horace asked. He twisted in his seat to look at her.

"Didn't mean anything by it, so you can keep your nose to yourself, mister."

"You don't have much use for us poor menfolk, do you, Mrs. Berg?" Horace's voice—smooth and faintly menacing—never seemed to vary, no matter what the provocation.

Beatrice's hands fluttered as if seeking something to hold on to, then folded across her stomach.

"Why should she?" Mina Dunmore's question came out with such venom that all heads turned toward her. Mina didn't seem to notice. She didn't sound drunk, but red splotches had spread across her cheeks and down her neck. She stared into the fire, her shoulders hunched. A crack of thunder and a ferocious blast of wind failed to startle her.

"We're supposed to be the weaker sex," Mina said. "What a laugh. Men are nothing but children playing grown-up. When the rest of the world doesn't want to play, men just up and leave, and it's womenfolk who have to carry on."

"It is my understanding, Mrs. Dunmore, that your husband passed on," Horace said. "Surely you can't believe that doing so was a childish abdication of responsibility?"

Mina didn't answer, didn't even glance at him.

"Or perhaps you are speaking of someone else?" Horace asked.

The rattling of glass on glass announced the return of Saul Halvardson, holding two bottles of port in one hand and a box of cigars in the other. "Here we are," he said. "All set for a long, rainy evening."

Daisy Prescott slipped into the room soon after Saul. She had changed into a thin wool suit with a jacket, and she carried several magazines. After a glance at Beatrice Berg's uninviting presence on the settee, she chose a chair across the room, near the windows.

"You ain't smoking them things in here," Beatrice said.

"Nonsense," Horace said. "A gentleman needs his smoke in the evening. I'll take one, Mr. Halvardson, if you please."

"Rules of the house," Beatrice said. "Shakers don't like smoking, and that's that."

"I understand they don't care for drinking, either," Horace said, "yet there you are, sipping port."

Saul hesitated, his exuberance wilting. "I'll just leave the box over here on the table," he said.

"We are not here to join the Shaker order," Horace said. "We are paying guests, and I for one intend to smoke." He gave himself a push out of his chair. By the time he'd lumbered over to the table near the windows, Beatrice had claimed his chair.

Horace didn't so much as glance at Beatrice. He bit off the end of his cigar and lit it. Thick, acrid smoke puffed out his mouth. "I don't suppose our ghost will make an appearance on a night like this," he said.

"Would a ghost care about the weather?" Saul hovered near the box of cigars. "I mean, maybe she's out there right now, floating through some building, looking for her lover, but no one is there to watch her."

"How romantic," Daisy said, glancing up from her magazine.

"How do you know it's a lover she's looking for?" Horace asked.

"Well, isn't that what the newspaper account said—that she'd been killed by her lover?"

"That's one story, anyways." Beatrice scooted her wing chair sideways, so she could have a better view of the room and still enjoy the fire. "I heard others." She leaned her head back and half closed her eyes. Only Gennie and Mina were in a position to see her smirk.

"Well?" Mina asked. "What else have you heard? You might as well blab, we've got nothing else to do in this hole."

Beatrice opened her eyelids just enough to glare at Mina.

"We would like to hear, you know," Saul said. While attention had been on Beatrice, he had lit a cigar. Smoke clustered above the men's heads as if the storm had invaded the room.

Beatrice shifted her chair so she could see everyone. She hesitated, scanning her audience. Only Daisy seemed to have lost interest, her head bent over a magazine so only the smooth top of her hair showed. Beatrice waited. In time, Daisy must have felt the silence. Her head jerked up, lips parted.

"What *I* heard," Beatrice said, holding Daisy's gaze as if afraid it would drift downward again, "is that it ain't no lover that ghost's looking for. No sirree, she's looking for something a lot more valuable. What I heard is there was this pretty young thing the Shakers had raised from a babe, and when she'd growed up, she turned Shaker 'cause she didn't know nothin' else. She never knowed who her people was, couldn't remember her ma or pa. Then one day this lawyer come to the village and said she was a long-lost rich girl that'd been stole away as a babe. Her folks was dead, and before they died, they hired this lawyer to find her and make sure she got her money."

"That hardly seems like a reason to kill oneself," Horace said.

"Just keep your britches on," Beatrice said. "I never said she killed herself."

"Ah," said Horace. "This is getting interesting." He squeezed his bulk into a rocker and flicked his cigar ashes on the floor. Beatrice pursed her lips but didn't object.

"Like I said, this girl was rich, real rich, but she was a Shaker, too. Them Shakers, they don't hold with private property, you know. So they figured the money belonged to them. They told the fancy lawyer to give them everything because this girl—this Sarina, her name was—she warn't allowed to have nothin' of her own. Sarina put up a fuss, said she wanted out. Wanted all that money for herself, and wouldn't you if you was in her shoes? Specially . . ." Beatrice took a slow sip of her port. "Specially when the lawyer brought out her ma's jewels. There was diamonds and sapphires and rubies, not a one of 'em paste, and all in these fancy necklaces and rings and such like. There was one crown sort of thing—"

"A tiara," Horace said.

"Yeah. I heard it had fifty perfect diamonds in it. What normal young girl wouldn't want to dance all night wearin' somethin' like that?"

"Very few, I'd imagine," Horace said.

"You wanna tell this story?"

"No, no, do go on. You're embellishing nicely."

"You bet I am. And it gets better, too—but not for poor little Sarina. Them Shakers had other ideas. They told Sarina she could leave anytime she wanted, but the money and jewels stayed here 'cause she was a Shaker when everything come to her, so she had to give it all up."

Gennie squirmed and fidgeted, wanting to interrupt and object to such a crass view of the Shakers, yet longing to hear the end of the story—even if it was pure fiction, as she suspected.

"So Sarina, she begs the lawyer to help her keep the money. He knows he'll get paid a bundle, so he says, sure, he'll help out. He does some lawyer thing or other to keep the Shakers from getting their hands on the money and jewels right away. He tells Sarina to leave, so she can say she ain't a Shaker, and then the judge will give everything to her.

"It was a night like tonight, with thunder and lightning and rain coming down in buckets. Sarina was packing her bags. The Shakers had locked her in her room, and a brother was standing guard so she couldn't get out. But the lawyer, he said he'd come on horseback, just after dark, and sneak her out the window. She waited and waited and waited. That lawyer never showed. The road had turned to mud, and his horse slipped off into the gully, and the lawyer broke his neck."

Nature railed at the unfairness of such a death by loosing a double crack of thunder.

"Good heavens," Saul said. "How awful."

"It isn't awful at all," Mina said. "You're making it all up. None of this happened."

Beatrice shrugged. "Have it your way," she said.

"Oh, do go on, Mrs. Berg," Horace said. "I'm sure we all want to know what happened to poor Sarina."

Beatrice nodded. "I figured you would. Well, Sarina cried her eyes out. But she was a spunky girl, and after waitin' a spell, locked in her room, she decided to run away by herself. She didn't know the lawyer was dead, she just thought he changed his mind on account of the storm. She couldn't stand to stay with the Shakers for even one more night, so she made herself a long rope with her sheets and blankets, and then she tied her little bundle of clothes around her waist and pried open her window.

"She was up on the third floor, and the rain and wind was blowing in on her, but she tied one end of the sheet-rope to the door of a cabinet built into the wall of her room—you know, you've all got 'em in your rooms." Beatrice chuckled as if enjoying a secret joke. "She tied it to the knob, I reckon. Then she climbed out the window.

"But that Shaker brother outside her room, he got suspicious what with all the ruckus she made opening the window. He unlocked her door and come right in, never mind him being a Shaker man and all. He saw the rope, and he saw the open window. And he didn't see any Sarina. So he ran to the window and looked out." Beatrice leaned forward in her chair and lowered her voice. "Sarina was just out the window, hanging three big floors above the ground, wet and scared and helpless as a newborn babe. And you know what that brother did?" With a smug grin, Beatrice studied her listeners, face by rapt face.

"He took out a penknife and he sawed right through that sheet."

Daisy gave a tiny squeak, but no one else made a sound. Beatrice held up her half-full glass of port and looked through it, staining one cheek blood-red.

"Three stories, that's how far she fell. Broke her neck. Two broken necks in one night." Beatrice lowered her glass and drained it in one gulp. "The Shakers inherited her entire fortune, jewels and all. That's why the ghost is here, goin' through every building. She's lookin' for her mother's jewels. And she won't rest till she finds them."

"Or perhaps," Horace said, "until she avenges her own death."

EIGHT

THE STORM RAGED UNTIL JUST PAST MIDNIGHT, TAPERING off in the early morning hours. What little sleep Gennie got was tainted by lurid dreams about falling bodies and necks snapped in two. At one point, she'd bolted upright in the dark, sure that skeletal fingers were clawing at her window, but it was just another burst of hail. Toward morning, she'd finally dropped off. By the time she woke up, sounds in the hallway told her she'd miss breakfast if she didn't hurry. It was Sunday, and Beatrice had hinted at a more substantial meal than usual.

It was a dreary group that gathered around the table that morning. Puffy eyes and feeble conversation said that no one had slept well the night before. Breakfast still hadn't been served when Gennie arrived, even though she was late. She had several seats to choose from, so she sat next to Saul. He was likely to be the most cheerful. Moreover, he was lifting a pot that, unless she was mistaken, held coffee.

"Have a cup, Gennie," Saul said. "I bought this in Languor yesterday, thought we'd gone long enough without coffee for breakfast. I mean, it's fine for the Shakers not to drink coffee, but they shouldn't expect everyone to go without."

Port, cigars, and coffee—quite an expensive shopping trip. "Heavenly," Gennie said. That ended conversation for another minute or two. The coffee brought Gennie to semi-alertness, and for the first time she realized that someone was missing.

"Is Mrs. Dunmore ill?" she asked.

"We're not sure," Daisy said. "No one wanted to disturb her."

"She imbibed a fair amount of port last evening," Horace said. "I suspect she is nursing a painful head. It's likely her appetite is not at its best, either." He gulped his coffee as if it were water and held his cup out for more.

"I'll check on her after breakfast," Gennie said. She didn't relish the idea of awakening a hung-over Mina Dunmore, but, for Rose's sake, she felt responsible for the well-being of the hostel residents.

"Such a sweet mother you will make, my dear," Horace said.

No one responded. Gennie stared into her coffee cup and found herself missing Beatrice and Mina, who would have put Horace in his place.

The harsh smell of burning grease drifted in from the kitchen, where Beatrice was clattering what sounded like a full orchestra of pots and pans. "Dammit!" she screamed, followed by a crash. Beatrice appeared in the doorway with grease dripping down her front and mud stains on her shoes and ankles. "Don't expect breakfast anytime soon. That darn Brother Linus never did bother to show up with the food and wood for the stove, so I had to go out and get it all myself. After that gully-washer last night, it's a swamp out there. If I catch a chill, it'll be on his head."

"May I help?" Saul asked. "I can fetch whatever you need, and I've been known to cook an egg or two in my time."

"I don't need no clumsy menfolk in my kitchen." With that, she withdrew, and the cacophony began again.

"Maybe I'll go check on Mrs. Dunmore now," Gennie said. "All this noise must have woken her. I'll bring her some coffee."

She half filled a clean cup and held it steady as she climbed the narrow, winding staircase to the second floor. Mina's room was about halfway down the hallway. Gennie knocked lightly, in case Mina really did have a headache, then with more power when no one responded. The Shakers had installed locks on the hostel's bedroom doors, but Gennie tried the knob anyway. It turned, and the door opened. The curtains were closed, keeping the room in darkness. Gennie had to step inside to see anything.

"Mrs. Dunmore? It's me, Gennie. I've brought you a cup of coffee." No sound came from the rumpled bed, so Gennie tiptoed closer. The bed was empty. The sheets looked like they'd been dumped on the bed in a pile. The bottom sheet had been pulled off the mattress, and the pillow was missing. Gennie walked around to the other side of the bed and found the pillow on the floor. The blanket lay half off the mattress, as if Mina had fallen out of bed and pulled it along with her.

On the floor, poking out from under the blanket, an empty bottle of port lay on its side. Gennie didn't need to see any more. Mina must have continued drinking after retiring to her room. Most likely she was suffering the consequences in one of the two bathrooms shared by hostel guests.

Taking the coffee with her, Gennie closed Mina's door and checked the bathrooms. Both were empty. Neither showed any evidence that someone had been sick in it. In fact, Gennie realized that she'd smelled nothing noxious since leaving the dining room. More than anything, Mina's room had smelled . . . empty. As if no one had been there for some time. The guests had all received their clean sheets on Saturday, so there hadn't even been the odor of dirty bed linens. If Mina had slept in the bed, it couldn't have been for very long.

Gennie could think of only one explanation—Mina must have felt unwell and gone out for a walk in the fresh morning air. It sounded unpleasant, given the volume of rain that had fallen the night before, but perhaps Mina had found mud preferable to staying trapped indoors. Gennie had no intention of mentioning her discovery to the other guests; she was inclined to let Mina learn her lesson in private. On the other hand, Mina might be seriously ill, so she'd better alert Rose.

At the other end of the hall was a small parlor. Gennie had seen a phone on the parlor wall. She hoped it worked. To get to the parlor, she had to walk past the stairway landing. She tiptoed close to the inner wall to avoid being seen or heard downstairs. She didn't want to trigger curiosity in the dining room. At the end of the parlor was a door that led outside to a second-story porch. Just to be sure, she opened the door and poked her head outside. The porch was empty.

The phone worked. To her great relief, Rose had just finished breakfast and was at work reconstructing the Ministry library in the Center Family Dwelling House.

"I can barely hear you, Gennie. Are you ill? Shall I get Josie?"

"No, Rose, I have to speak softly. Just listen hard, okay? It's about Mrs. Dunmore, you remember her? Well, she's . . . I guess she is sort of missing."

"*What?* Do you have any idea what's happened? Has Brother Linus gone looking for her?"

"Now that you mention it, maybe he did. Mrs. Berg complained that he didn't come to help her this morning, so maybe he saw Mrs. Dunmore out somewhere and became concerned. Anyway, it looks like Mrs. Dunmore might have had a bit too much to drink and gotten sick during the night. Her bedroom is empty, and she isn't in either of the bathrooms, so I thought maybe she took a walk." As she explained her theory, it sounded unlikely.

"Was her coat gone?"

Gennie closed her eyes and imagined Mina's room. "Yes, I'm pretty sure it was. But she had other clothes hanging on pegs, so she didn't pack up and leave without paying her bill."

"Then it's probably as you've suggested. She felt unwell and went for a walk. She may have wandered too far and gotten lost, though. Leave it to me, I'll send someone out looking for her. Thanks, Gennie—and don't worry."

Gennie returned to the dining room, carrying the now-cold coffee, to find eggs, fried ham, and hot biscuits finally on the table.

"Her Highness didn't feel much like drinking coffee

this morning, did she?" Beatrice said. "Give it here, I can find some use for it. Coffee's expensive; some of us know better than to waste it."

"I gather Mrs. Dunmore is indeed unwell?" Horace asked.

"Everything is under control," Gennie said, reaching for a jar of raspberry jam. "This food looks yummy, Mrs. Berg."

"No thanks to that Brother Linus," Beatrice said, but she sounded a shade less surly than usual.

Horace, for once, was not shoveling food into his mouth. He waited for Gennie to swallow and asked, "Would you say that Mrs. Dunmore's condition is serious? Will she be joining us for lunch perhaps?"

"Oh please, could we stop talking about Mrs. Dunmore?" Daisy said. "Let the poor woman alone. It isn't kind to talk about her behind her back."

Horace turned his attention to Daisy. "I do apologize, Miss Prescott. I had no idea you were so fond of her."

"It isn't fondness, just . . . well, it's just bad manners to talk behind someone's back." She kept her eyes focused on her plate while she spoke.

"I heard laughing coming from her room last night, well after midnight. Wouldn't be surprised if she had some company," said Beatrice.

"Dear me, what a thought," Horace murmured.

"More'n likely they was drinkin', from what I could hear." Beatrice held up a nearly empty serving plate. "Anybody want more of this ham? I fried it up real crisp." Horace lifted his hand to reach for it, but Beatrice ignored him, scraping the last bits onto her own plate. "Yep, I reckon I'll find a bottle or two in her room when I clean it."

Though Gennie had lost her appetite, she ate as quickly as she could. She'd forgotten that Beatrice would clean Mina Dunmore's room, which meant she would find it empty except for the port bottle. The rumors would sail through the hostel and into Languor by afternoon. "Shaker Hostel Is Devil's Playground"— that would be the headline in the next *Languor County Courier*. She'd have to swipe the bottle, maybe hide it under her coat, and bring it to Rose. Otherwise, Brother Andrew could wind up in real trouble, maybe even lose his position as trustee, and Rose would not be able to save him.

Sister Isabel went straight from breakfast toward the Sisters' Shop, where she hoped to finish dyeing some fabric before the afternoon worship service. She'd been scheduled to help in the fields, but the soggy ground made that impossible. Isabel was glad. She much preferred plunging her arms elbow deep in a vat of dye to slogging around in mud over her ankles. Besides, she'd be the only sister in the shop, what with Sister Sarah helping out in the kitchen, so she could sneak in a little experimentation. With Rose's permission, she'd bought some commercial dyes in town, and she couldn't wait to see what shades she could create by mixing the store-bought colors with the butternut and golds and browns she made from barks and roots. Wilhelm would frown, of course. He insisted she use only natural, Shaker-made dyes, the colors of the earth. Well, weren't the sky blue and the grass green?

Isabel had to stop and wait at the unpaved path that ran through the center of North Homage. A car and a farm wagon, both full of folks from the world, passed in front of her, heading toward the Meetinghouse. "Just what we need," Isabel muttered, "rowdy ghost hunters invading our worship. Do they think some poor creature will materialize before their eyes?"

She tried to cross the road through a break between two groups on foot, but an arm grabbed her elbow.

"Are you a real lady?" demanded a high voice.

Isabel found a girl of about six hanging on to her elbow with both hands. Her parents walked on ahead, not realizing their child had stopped. The girl examined Isabel's face with suspicious brown eyes. Her gaze shifted to the elbow in her grasp, and she frowned. She unhooked one hand, grabbed a hunk of Isabel's forearm, and pinched hard.

"Ouch!" Isabel yanked her arm away. "I most certainly am real, and it's very rude to go around pinching people."

The girl crunched up her face, sniffed, then let out a howl.

"What's going on here?" The girl's mother and father had circled back to find their errant child. "What have you done to our daughter?"

"She . . . she called me rude," the girl said, between sobs.

Two angry parental faces glared at Isabel. For the most part, Isabel liked children. She sometimes helped Sister Charlotte plan outings for the children being raised by the Shakers. There were, however, exceptions, and this child was one of them. She could not abide ill-mannered behavior. "Your child pinched me," she said. "Kindly remember you are visiting our home, not a circus."

The girl's father took a menacing step toward Isabel,

who stepped back to avoid being too close—or being struck.

"Just because you're a Shaker don't mean you're better'n the rest of us," the mother said. "You're just a spinster lady, you don't know nothing about raisin' up a child."

The day was shaping up badly. Isabel longed to escape, to engross herself in fabric dyeing, away from the world. Best just to walk away, she decided. She turned around and came face to face with Elder Wilhelm. He was close enough to have heard the exchange.

"If thy work in the Sisters' Shop is finished, thy help is needed in the fields," he said.

"I was just on my way to the shop," Isabel said, edging away.

The irate family left, apparently more interested in continuing their hunt than in further threatening a Shaker sister. Or maybe the look on Wilhelm's face told them they might end up as the threatened ones.

Wilhelm fell into step beside Isabel as she headed for the Sisters' Shop. "Thy behavior concerns me," he said. "Consorting with the world is dangerous for thy soul."

"I wasn't consorting, they were—"

"Our Father abhors excuses." With that pronouncement, Wilhelm veered off toward the Trustees' Office, where the community's black Plymouth waited in the central path, its motor running. Isabel was relieved to remember that he and Andrew were heading off on a sales trip to drum up new business for their medicinal herb industry. She'd heard they were going farther south than they ever had before, so they had to leave on

Sunday. With luck, Wilhelm would be so tired when he returned, he'd forget to criticize her behavior to Rose. Not that Rose would pay much heed to his complaints, anyway.

Isabel had never been so happy to step inside the cool, dark Sisters' Shop. She rolled up the sleeves of her loose work dress as she entered her favorite room, which housed the dyeing vats. Loops of yarn, recently dyed in muted gold, rust, and shades of brown, hung from wall pegs, turning the room into an autumn forest. Isabel sighed with pleasure. She was eager to check the wool yarn she'd left soaking overnight in a mixture of green and rust dye.

Isabel was no more than five feet tall, and the vat reached her rib cage. The yarn, heavy with dye, would have sunk to the bottom, so she found a long wooden stick, stained dark by layer after layer of color. She slid the awkward lid off the top, leaned it against the side of the vat, and poked the stick into the dark liquid.

She knew instantly that something was wrong. The water level was much higher than she'd left it. Fabric nearly the same color as the dye floated at the top of the vat. She stood still for several moments, reliving the previous evening's work. Nay, she was sure. She had left yarn soaking, not fabric. She poked at the fabric; it was attached to a solid object. Her hand shook as she reached into the liquid, near the side of the vat, and pulled on the material.

Her hand cupped something soft, just the size of a shoulder. Isabel yanked her hand out of the vat and jumped backward. The liquid dripping from her hand was greenish, not blood red, which gave her only slight comfort. She knew the vat held a body. Almost certainly, the poor soul was dead, but she had to be sure. She would never forgive herself if there was a chance to save someone's life, and she let it pass out of squeamishness. What if this was a sister who'd felt ill while leaning over the vat and somehow tripped into it? Even in Isabel's current state, that sounded unlikely, but still . . .

She approached the vat again, her heart pounding in her ears. Once more, she clutched the soggy curve of shoulder and pulled it until the side of a head appeared. She pulled the shoulder back toward her. The face surfaced. It was bloated and tinted pale green and quite dead.

Isabel hadn't been involved with the Shaker Hostel, but she had seen all the guests, and she knew that this face belonged to one of them. She couldn't remember the name. A widow, she thought. A few days earlier, the woman had just marched right into the Sisters' Shop as if she owned the place. Isabel had been irked and let her know it. She prayed for forgiveness.

Nothing would help the woman now, so Isabel left her as she was and went out into the hallway to phone Rose, then Josie at the Infirmary. As soon as she'd hung up, the strength drained out of her. She couldn't make it to the bench. Her legs gave way, and she collapsed, curling into a bundle on the floor.

NINE

ROSE WATCHED AS SHERIFF GRADY O'NEAL AND DR.
Hanfield, the new young doctor from Languor, squat-
ted on either side of Mina Dunmore's wet body. Mina
lay curled on a sheet that would never again be white.
Her clothes, skin, even her hair showed areas of rusty
green, as if she'd drowned in muddy seaweed. She still
wore the dress she'd worn at dinner the night before.
Gennie had described it as a floor-length gown, several
years out of fashion and meant for a younger woman.
It had been pale blue.

"She might have drowned, but I can't say for sure,"
said Dr. Hanfield. "I don't see any evidence of a
wound. Heck, I can't even tell if she's bruised up. I'll
have to get her cleaned off for a better look."

Dr. Hanfield's round face puckered. Rose had heard
this was his first position, and he'd been in town only a
few weeks. Inexperienced as he was, Languor was
lucky to have him. The town had been limping along
without a doctor for months, since old Doc Irwin died.
He probably hasn't gotten used to ordinary death yet,
Rose thought, *let alone something like this*.

"How long you think she'd been in that vat?" Grady
asked.

"Hard to say." Dr. Hanfield rolled back on his heels and shook his head. "Rigor is well-established, so probably not longer than a day, but we already knew that."

"I'll need to confirm this, but I've heard that a witness claims to have heard her laughing sometime after midnight," Grady said.

"Could have been any time after that. Her body's cold, but she was in cold water. I need to get her to my office fast as possible, then maybe I can tell more."

"Okay, I'll take care of it," Grady said. "Already called Millard to bring his hearse around. You had a chance to meet our town undertaker?"

"Sadly, yes," said Dr. Hanfield. "We've had two deaths of old age, but . . ." He stood and brushed off his pants. "Well, I'll be going back to my office now. Tell Millard to bring her quick as he can."

Rose joined the two men. "Is there any way we can keep this quiet for a while? We've had a hard enough time protecting ourselves from ghost seekers, and we have a worship service scheduled for just a few hours from now."

"I'd cancel if I were you," Grady said.

"I sure won't say anything," Dr. Hanfield said, "but I'll bet word will get out. I've heard that Millard . . . well . . ." He glanced at Grady.

"Millard has a mouth larger than the state of Kentucky," Grady said. "Once he sees the deceased, all of Languor County will know within the hour. Where's Wilhelm? Can't he scare off the crowds for you?"

"Wilhelm left soon after breakfast for a two-day sales trip," Rose said. "He has no idea this has happened." In a sense, having him gone made the situation easier—if he were there, he'd be ranting about the world bringing evil to their village, and he'd surely close the hostel instantly. On the other hand, Wilhelm had decided only the day before to accompany Andrew on his sales trip, and Rose suspected he had done so in hopes the curiosity seekers would turn the Sabbathday worship service into a fiasco. Then he'd have something to report to the Ministry at Mount Lebanon, New York, the leaders of all Shaker villages. Wilhelm never gave up hope that he could get Rose removed as eldress and replaced with someone of his choice—such as Sister Elsa.

Rose glanced down at the sad, wet bundle that once was Mina Dunmore. *Now Wilhelm will have his evidence, with or without a worship service. I should have seen the danger. I should have prevented this.*

"Perhaps we'd best leave it that way for now," Grady said. "If we need him, we can talk to him day after tomorrow. I doubt he saw anything, anyway."

"Thank you," Rose said. And she meant it. Grady understood her difficulties with Wilhelm and had supported her in the past. She guessed Grady wanted to stay in her good graces as well, because he still hoped to marry Gennie.

"Ain't nothin' you could do that'd get me to spend one more night under this roof." Beatrice Berg huddled in a wing chair by the parlor fireplace, glowering at the sheriff and his officers.

"I'm afraid we need to question everyone, Mrs."— Grady consulted a list—"Berg? I want all of you to stay in this room, but please don't speak to each other. These two officers will stay with you." Grady indicated the rest of the Sheriff's Department. Languor County didn't usually need more than three officers to handle the occasional brawl or feud between neighbors. "Don't take offense if they keep you from talking. That's just the way we have to do it."

"Okay, then, Gen—Miss Malone, we'll start with you. Miss Callahan?" Grady turned and nodded toward the dining room. Rose noticed that his cheeks had reddened. The two women followed him.

Grady closed the dining room door behind them and grouped three seats as far as possible from the parlor.

"Grady, I—"

"Don't worry, Gennie, I'll be out of your way as fast as I can. I promised you three weeks away from me, and you'll get them. But this is murder, no doubt about it, and I need to know everything you noticed that might be helpful."

"I understand."

Rose sat very still, her right palm over her left, as if she were waiting for a Union Meeting to begin. Gennie had grown up so much over the past year. She had not sought Rose's advice about the difficulties between Grady and her. Rose felt as if she were intruding.

Gennie stared at her lap as Grady rummaged through his jacket pockets until he found a small notebook and a pencil. "Okay, Gen, just tell me everything that you can remember—anything you think might help us find whoever did this. Don't worry if it's small, even the—"

"Even the tiniest detail can solve a crime, I know," Gennie said.

They gave each other a quick smile, then their eyes were elsewhere. Gennie began with her first introduction to Mina Dunmore and the other Shaker Hostel residents, as best she could remember, and ended with her morning visit to Mina's room.

"There's one more thing," she said. "I hope I haven't ruined the investigation. It never occurred to me that this would turn into murder, or I wouldn't have touched a thing."

"No one expects you to have known," Grady said. "Just say what you need to say."

Gennie ran a hand through her auburn curls, leaving them in charming disarray. Grady's gaze wandered to her hair, then dropped to her face.

"Well, you saw how messed up the sheets were in Mrs. Dunmore's room? That's what I saw when I went to check on her. But there was something I left out. I found an empty port bottle under the blanket. I assumed she'd made herself sick from drinking. Right after breakfast I ran back upstairs and took the bottle." Gennie turned her small palms upward, and Grady's wrists jerked as if he wanted to take her hands in his own.

"I wanted to protect the hostel's reputation," Gennie said. "If it got about that one of the guests had been drinking heavily enough to get sick, everyone would say the Shakers were probably selling alcohol or something, that it was their fault. I was going to hide the bottle under my coat and bring it to Rose, ask her what to do. But I never got a chance. We eat later than the Shakers, and we were especially late this morning. I was just putting on my coat when Hank—when one of your officers arrived to tell us Mrs. Dunmore was dead and we had to stay in the hostel."

"So the bottle is in your room now?"

"Yes. I put it in one of my built-in drawers, under my . . . um . . ."

For the first time, Grady grinned. "Don't worry, we'll find it. I doubt we'll find any usable fingerprints by now, but we can try. Maybe there'll still be some dregs; we'll ask the pharmacist in town to see what he can do with it."

"I'm sorry," Gennie said.

"Oh, I reckon we'll catch the varmint anyway."

Gennie giggled—not quite the way she used to as a child, but close enough.

"And why is the good sister here, may I ask?" Horace von Oswald laced his fingers over his stomach as if he hadn't a care, but his tone was far from casual.

"I've given her permission to listen," Grady said. "Think of her as the police in her own community."

"I'm afraid I can't do that."

"Why not?" Rose asked.

The only sign of personality in Horace's face came from his eyes, which looked like deep, burned holes. "Police care about solving the crime," he said. "The sister cares about saving the reputation of her village."

"Do you distrust all Shakers, Mr. von Oswald?" Rose asked.

Horace didn't answer.

"I do want to save my community," Rose said. "I suspect you would feel that same way if you were in my place."

A faint grimace passed across Horace's face. "I don't care one way or the other about Shakers," he said. "I know very little about them. Stay if you must. I have nothing to hide."

"When was the last time you saw Mrs. Dunmore?" Grady asked.

Horace gazed out the dining room window. "Last evening in the parlor," he said. "We all spent the entire evening together in friendly discussion, sipping port. The gentlemen smoked some rather good cigars. We listened to the storm. That was it. I never saw Mrs. Dunmore again after she retired to her room."

"She left before you did?" Grady asked.

"I believe I indicated so."

"When did you leave the parlor?"

"I left last. I wished to enjoy the fire and have one more cigar in peace."

"In what order did everyone leave?"

Horace closed his eyes, and Rose felt a sense of relief. "I believe that little mouse, Miss Prescott, vaporized first," he said. "Can anyone truly be so demure?"

His eyelids opened, and he looked straight at Rose. She forced herself to hold his gaze, despite a wave of revulsion that swept through her.

"The other gentleman, Saul, left fairly soon after that."

"What is your impression of Mr. Halvardson?" Rose asked.

Horace's mouth formed a perfect semicircle, as artificial as a frosting flower on a cake. "A friendly young man," he said. "Especially with the ladies. He seems to be well-heeled for a traveling salesman in these difficult times. He provided the port and cigars, as well as the coffee this morning. A most generous man—though I suspect it is for a purpose."

"Any idea what that purpose might be?" Grady asked.

"Ah, that would be doing your job, Sheriff."

Grady's jaw clenched, but his face did not betray any irritation. "When did Mrs. Berg leave?"

"Mrs. Berg had secured for herself a coveted chair in front of the hearth. When Mrs. Dunmore left, Miss Malone took the other seat by the fire. The two women chattered for perhaps fifteen more minutes, then left together. It was by then about eleven, I believe. I stayed for perhaps another half hour, then went directly to my room. Does that clear up the murder for you?"

"Did you hear anything—folks talking, for example—when you went up to your room?" Grady asked.

"Not a peep. It was quiet as a tomb." Horace gave no apology for his macabre remark. "That is all I have to tell you, Sheriff, and I am really rather tired. I need to rest. If you will excuse me." He stood and gave Rose a slight bow.

"By the way," he said. "You might look into Mrs. Berg's background. She claimed to have spent her married life in a well-to-do section of Languor, but I happened to be exploring the area and found myself in that very section of town. In the course of a friendly chat with a storekeeper and several customers, I mentioned Mrs. Berg. No one seemed to have heard of her, though they'd all lived in the area for decades. Interesting, don't you think?"

"I ain't talkin' in front of no one else," said Beatrice Berg. "You can call Sister Rose the police if you want, but that don't make it so. I got my rights." Ignoring the empty chair, she crossed her arms over her chest and moved in front of the kitchen door.

"Our hope is to help solve this tragedy quickly," Rose said, "and to keep the hostel operating. If we can't do that, you will lose your job."

"Don't make me no never mind. I can do without gettin' myself murdered and stuffed in a barrel."

"You can't believe that we Shakers had anything to do with this? Why would we?"

"Don't ask me why y'all do any of the things you do. Don't make no sense to me. All I know is, you should be looking at them, not us." She spoke to Grady and tossed her head toward Rose.

"Why?" Grady asked.

"Ask her if she seen that Brother Linus around anywhere today," Beatrice said.

Grady raised his eyebrows at Rose. "What's this about Brother Linus?"

"Andrew assigned him to help with chores here in the hostel," Rose said.

"Well, he sure ain't helped out this morning," Beatrice said. "See this mess all over my dress? It was clean before breakfast, but after I had to haul my own wood, and start my own cooking fire, and lift all the heavy stuff myself, this dress was a mess. Where was Linus, answer me that?"

"I'm sorry Linus missed this morning," Rose said, "but I'm sure he had pressing work elsewhere. The storm last night caused a lot of damage. He is probably out making repairs."

"Oh yeah? Anybody seen him yet?"

"We really haven't been looking for him," Rose said.

"Then maybe you'd better, and that's all I got to say on the matter."

"We'll do that, Mrs. Berg. Thank you," Grady said. Mrs. Berg loosened up enough to take the empty seat across from him. She did not glance toward Rose. Grady flipped back a few pages in his notebook. "As I understand it," he said, "you left the parlor last night with Miss Malone at about eleven P.M. Is that correct?"

"I reckon. I didn't check the clock, just went on up to bed. It was after Mrs. Dunmore, and Miss Prescott, and that flimflam man, Saul Halvardson, already left. That Horace von Oswald, he was still in the parlor, smoking one of those nasty cigars. Soon as I got up, he took my chair and said something uppity to me. I didn't pay him no mind."

"Did you hear anything during the night?"

"I heard fat old Horace clump up the stairs. Didn't hear his door slam, though, like it usually does. Stopped at the washroom, probably. I fell asleep soon as the racket stopped. I work hard all day, don't just sit around primping, like some." Beatrice had thick gray eyebrows that joined over her nose when she frowned. "Now I think on it, I did hear more racket later on, way past midnight. That's when I heard Mrs. Dunmore havin' a good old time with someone in her room. They was laughing fit to wake the dead—well, she was, anyway. Couldn't hear him."

"How do you know it was a man?"

Beatrice snickered. "Who else would it be, that time of night? I'm bettin' it was Brother Linus."

With an effort, Rose kept silent. Beatrice was opening up, and any objection from Rose might stem the flow.

"Why do you think it was Brother Linus?" Grady asked.

Beatrice shrugged and smirked. "Stands to reason.

Mrs. Dunmore waren't no spring chicken, but when she took off her mournin', I knowed she had a hankerin'. She wanted a man."

"Had Brother Linus paid any special attention to Mrs. Dunmore?" Grady asked.

"Not that I saw, but then I wouldn't, would I? Brother Linus, he kept to hisself, like all them Shaker brothers."

"I see," Grady said. "Anything else you remember about last night? No? Then, thank you for your help."

Grady waited for the kitchen door to close behind Beatrice before turning to Rose. "What about Brother Linus? Any idea where he is?"

"Nay, but I'm sure there's a reasonable explanation for his failure to appear this morning." She spoke softly. Beatrice was just the type to put her ear up against the door.

"Nevertheless," Grady said, "I think I'll send Hank out to locate him, just so we can put this accusation to rest." He opened the door to the hallway and poked his head out.

Rose closed her eyes and tried to envision the dwelling house dining room that morning. As always, the Believers maintained silence during the meal, so she wouldn't have heard Linus's voice. The women sat at tables on one side of the room, and the men clustered on the other side, but she'd had a clear view of the brothers as they'd entered single file and stood behind their chairs in prayer. In truth, she could not remember seeing Linus's face at breakfast, nor any other time since the previous evening, when the community had held a brief worship service in the Center Family

Dwelling House. But, then, she hadn't been looking for him.

It was inconceivable that Linus could be involved in this murder. Wasn't it? He had been a wholehearted Believer, as far as she could tell, for all of his ten years in the community. He was quiet, an enthusiastic worker, skilled at finding creative ways to fix buildings and machinery that had seen better days. Wilhelm had never said a critical word about his devotion, nor had Andrew commented on his work with anything but approval. Nay, it was impossible.

"Two interviews left," Grady said, as he returned to his chair. "I've sent for Miss Daisy Prescott. I'm curious; no one seems to have much to say about her."

Daisy Prescott slipped into the dining room and closed the door soundlessly behind her. Without complaint, she sat in the empty chair and waited for Grady's questions.

"Does it bother you if Sister Rose stays?" Grady asked.

Daisy glanced over at Rose, then back at Grady. "No, it doesn't bother me."

"I am interested in everyone's movements from yesterday evening until this morning," Grady said. "Could you tell me what time you left the parlor last night?"

"It was about ten o'clock. I always get to bed no later than ten-thirty. I am not a sound sleeper, unfortunately, so I like to read in bed for a while to make myself sleepy." With a slender finger, she pushed her spectacles up the bridge of her nose. Her nails were well-shaped, but short and free of polish.

"If you're a light sleeper, perhaps you noticed if there were any unexpected noises during the night?"

Daisy licked her lips, which glistened with a pale shade of lipstick. "If you think it will help, I guess I should tell you, though I hate to speak ill of the dead."

"It can't hurt her now," Grady said.

"No, I suppose not. Well, I did wake up around two in the morning, and I heard distinct sounds coming from Mrs. Dunmore's room." Daisy again licked her lips and her gaze drifted over to Rose. "You understand, I would never have revealed this if the poor lady hadn't died. It's so . . . degrading. But I know I must.

"As I said, I heard sounds. Laughing and so forth. She was having a . . . well, a good time, I suppose they call it. There's no other way to say it. She was entertaining a man in her bedroom." Daisy sat up straight, her chin raised in genteel defiance. Rose was growing curious to know what Daisy actually did for a living. A secretary, perhaps, or a librarian?

"You're sure it was a man?"

"I'm afraid I'm quite sure. I heard him laughing."

"Did you recognize the voice?"

Daisy slumped. "No, I'm sorry, I couldn't hear it that well. It was low and gruff, a man's voice. I was far too embarrassed to go out into the hall and listen."

"Of course," Grady said. "Is there anything else you can tell us about last night that might help, Miss Prescott?"

"No, I'm afraid not." Her smile hinted at shy self-deprecation. "You see, I pulled the covers over my head so I wouldn't hear any more. Then I fell asleep."

Daisy left by the hall doorway and was replaced instantly by Hank, the officer Grady had sent in search of Brother Linus. Grady conferred with him, then closed the door and turned to face Rose. She could tell the news wasn't good.

"Grady, surely you can't think—"

"Brother Linus isn't anywhere on the grounds," Grady said. "The brothers helped look. I'm afraid this changes things."

"Nay, I will never believe that Linus had anything to do with this."

Grady said nothing, but he did look apologetic.

"Shouldn't we finish questioning the hostel guests anyway?" Rose asked. "We only have Saul Halvardson left. He might have something important to add." She didn't say it, but she hoped he would know something that would clear Linus of any and all suspicion.

"I'm sorry, Rose, I need all my men. Right now we have to look for Brother Linus, and fast. He's had plenty of time to leave the area. Given what I've heard so far from witnesses, when we find Linus, we might very likely have our murderer."

TEN

"NO, MA'AM, I'M SORRY, BUT THE SHERIFF WANTS Y'ALL to stay put for now. We'll let you know when it's okay to leave." Grady's newest officer was well over six feet tall, with thick black hair that stuck out at odd angles. More black hair curled across his massive arms and broad hands. Since both he and the older officer were named Hank, and he looked so much like a black bear, the staff in the Sheriff's Office had taken to calling him Bar.

Beatrice looked Bar up and down, then complied more readily than usual. "Well, I'll just keep my bag with me, and soon's you say the word, I go out that door." She claimed the settee, placing her suitcase next to her and her pocketbook in her lap. Gennie squashed a chuckle; Beatrice had walled herself in for protection. Grady worried that Bar was too gentle for police work, but with those looks, he could intimidate without moving a muscle.

The guests had settled in the parlor after Grady told them they could not yet leave the hostel. No one seemed inclined to stay upstairs alone. Bar and Hank had scattered the chairs around the room, to keep individuals separate during Grady's questioning. Everyone seemed content to remain as far apart as possible. Even the news that Brother Linus was missing did not allay their mistrust of one another.

It could be anyone, Gennie thought. It would take more than a few hours missing to convince her it was Brother Linus, however. She hadn't known him well when she was growing up—she'd had far less contact with the brothers than the sisters—but she remembered him as cheerful and even-tempered. The idea that he would toss aside his beliefs and deep commitment for a fling with Mina Dunmore was laughable. Even if Linus had found Mrs. Dunmore attractive—which twenty-year-old Gennie couldn't imagine—it seemed out of character for him to have followed through with his feelings. *Besides, Mrs. Dunmore was just . . . well, unpleasant.*

Gennie had been lucky enough to snag a wing chair and one of Daisy's cast-off fashion magazines. Sun streamed through the open curtains. It would have been a perfect day for a worship service followed by a walk through the Shaker gardens. Her mouth watered as she thought about nibbling on tender young spearmint and lemon balm leaves or rubbing her hands against the lavender stalks that had begun to turn from brown to gray-green.

Instead, she was stuck inside with a group of people she'd be glad never to see again. Her quiet weeks of contemplation were not to be. She and Grady had been thrown together again by death. She'd needed to be alone because Grady's presence confused her, stirred her up until she couldn't think straight. Now here she was, stirred up anyway. She swung a crossed leg with unladylike vigor. She flipped the magazine shut, tossed it on a nearby table, and sprang to her feet.

"Ah, the young," Horace von Oswald said. "Such energy." Horace had, of course, appropriated the other wing chair, where he sat like a lump of lard, watching his fellow guests.

Gennie ignored him and paced over to a window. It was hard to tell that the worship service had been canceled—dozens of folks wandered the village, paying no attention to the paths. She let out a startled cry as a man appeared on the other side of the window. Gennie recognized him as one of the men she'd seen with Betty, the ghost watcher she'd met Friday night. He stared at her, then tried to peer beyond her into the room. Gennie yanked the curtain shut. She jumped as she turned and found Daisy Prescott standing right behind her.

"I suppose you can't blame them for being curious," Daisy said, "but it really is rude. Do you think Brother Linus is the murderer?"

"I doubt it," Gennie said.

"Oh? Why not? Just because he's a Shaker?" Daisy's penciled eyebrows arched over her eyes. Gennie noticed that she'd plucked out every last eyebrow hair, which gave her an old-fashioned look, as if she'd come straight from the Roaring Twenties.

"No," Gennie said, "not because he's a Shaker, though I think it makes him a less likely suspect."

"Really? I'd think it would make him *more* likely—all that stifled desire and so forth."

"It's a commitment people from the world don't understand," Gennie said. Aware she was getting testy, she moved away from Daisy and found a rocker set apart from the others. She just wanted to be left alone. She hadn't realized before that Daisy, in her own self-effacing way, could be just as irritating as Horace and the others. Most of the guests seemed to be nursing deep grudges. Including the victim—Mina Dunmore had always sounded like she was angry at the world.

As she considered the room full of potential suspects, Gennie felt her interest quicken. What could have brought such an odd assortment of folks to the Shaker Hostel? None of them seemed to fit there. They had shown no curiosity about the Shakers—worse, they criticized Shaker beliefs and practices. A Shaker Hostel room cost a bit less than a room in the most respectable of the Languor boardinghouses, but North Homage was isolated, and there was only the one old car to provide transportation into town for shopping and entertainment.

Grady hadn't questioned Saul Halvardson. He seemed the most easygoing of the group—was that just a cover? What was he doing there? Certainly not selling fancy undies to the sisters. He didn't seem to have much interest in working, but he had money to spend on numerous bottles of port, cigars, and coffee.

During her brief time in the world, Gennie had learned that men often responded to her with interest. Normally she did not encourage their attentions. She was an engaged woman, and she made sure to keep her ring visible. However, now was not the time to worry about propriety. She caught Saul's eye and sent him a rueful smile, as if to say, *Isn't this a mess? So inconvenient.*

Saul was at her side in moments. He pulled another rocker next to hers and settled down for a friendly chat.

Gennie leaned toward him and gazed up with a trusting expression. She hoped Bar wasn't watching; he might be concerned enough to report her behavior to Grady. "So what do you think, Mr. Halvardson? Did Brother Linus kill poor Mrs. Dunmore?"

"Call me Saul, I beg you. Mr. Halvardson sounds so . . . well, old. And may I call you Gennie? Lovely name—Gennie, that is. Suits you. It brings to mind sweet young maidens picking spring flowers."

Gennie began to understand how Saul sold so much underwear, but she wasn't impressed. In fact, she felt a sudden urge to excuse herself and take a warm bath with lots of soap. Instead, she tinged her expression with shy gratitude and leaned closer. "About Mrs. Dunmore," she prompted him.

"Poor lady. I'm afraid it does look like that brother did it. Otherwise, why would he disappear? Isn't that an admission of guilt?"

Gennie shrugged one shoulder and didn't offer an opinion. In fact, she could think of several reasons Linus couldn't be found, but her aim was to get Saul talking. "But what I don't understand," she said, "is why Brother Linus would do such a terrible thing. Can you?" She tilted her head at him. However, she refused to bat her eyelashes; there were some depths to which she would not sink.

"Men do unspeakable things," Saul said. "Especially when ladies toy with their hearts."

"I had no idea Brother Linus had any interest in Mrs. Dunmore's heart. How did you know?"

Saul gazed into space while an enigmatic smile played around his full lips. It was very effective. "I suppose I am rather attuned to such things," he said. "So when I heard them together in Mrs. Dunmore's room last night, I wasn't surprised. Saddened, of course, but not surprised."

Gennie gasped. "You heard him in her room? In the *middle* of the night?" She was afraid she'd overdone it, but apparently that wasn't possible with Saul.

"Yes, I fear so. It must have been two o'clock, pitch dark, and I was awakened from a deep sleep by lewd laughter. I thought you ladies might be alarmed, so I went out into the hall to find out where the sound was coming from. I was appalled, of course, when I realized it was Mrs. Dunmore's room. I thought she wasn't like that—widow lady and all. She must be at least forty." His appreciative eyes roamed over Gennie's young face.

Gennie had first heard about the man in Mrs. Dunmore's room when Mrs. Berg had mentioned it at breakfast that morning. Saul hadn't said a word about it then. So was he just trying to impress her, using the story to paint himself as the protective male? He was certainly pouring on the not-so-subtle flattery, at poor Mina Dunmore's expense. Chances were he wouldn't have told this same story to Grady.

"I would have been too scared to go out into the hall like that," Gennie said. "What if someone had gotten into Mrs. Dunmore's room from the outside?"

With a well-manicured hand, Saul waved away any suggestion of fear. "Oh, I knew it wasn't dangerous. Like I said, Mrs. Dunmore was laughing, and the man's voice didn't sound threatening, what I could hear of it."

"Could you tell who the man was from his voice?"

Saul rubbed his chin with his index finger. "Now that you mention it, the voice was pretty quiet."

"How did you know it was a man?"

"Because it was so low and deep. Women just don't talk like that. And Mrs. Dunmore's laughter was, well, too friendly, if you catch my meaning." His smile spread slowly, as if he'd drifted into pleasant memories.

"Couldn't it have been someone other than Brother Linus? I mean, what about . . ." She leaned toward Saul and whispered, "What about Mr. von Oswald?"

Saul glanced at Horace, across the room. Before she could stop herself, Gennie allowed her gaze to follow. Horace sat alone, silent, watching them. She told herself he couldn't possibly hear them, but she couldn't shake the conviction that he knew what they were talking about. With his insatiable curiosity, it wouldn't surprise her if Horace knew how to read lips. Just to be on the safe side, she turned away from him, to hide her face. Saul did the same.

"Somehow I just can't believe that Mrs. Dunmore would invite Horace into her . . . No, It's unthinkable," Saul said. "They hated each other from the first moment they met."

"Sometimes hate and passion go hand in hand," Gennie said. Saul raised his eyebrows at her, and she knew she'd blundered. Sweet young maidens could be the objects of passion for men like Saul, but they weren't supposed to have any insights about it. "I mean, what if they actually had met before, maybe when they were young? What if they had been in love, and then they got separated somehow, or one of them went away? When they saw each other again, the spark just ignited." Gennie whispered with as much romantic fervor as she could manage. The notion was ridiculous, but Saul seemed to give it deep consideration.

"Now you mention it," he said, "that could have happened. But wouldn't they have given themselves away before now?"

"Perhaps. It makes more sense to me than the theory that Brother Linus was her visitor. I suppose you didn't notice when they left Mrs. Dunmore's room?"

"Well, actually, I did hear a door opening and closing sometime later, maybe a half hour or so. I was just drifting off again. Whoever it was sure was quiet, though. I didn't hear any footsteps, and if it'd been Mrs. Dunmore and a man, it seems to me they'd be making a racket. They must have been imbibing port for quite some time." He frowned, perhaps regretting his generosity with the port.

"Oh," Gennie said, with a dollop of shocked innocence, "are you quite sure they were drinking together in her room? How do you know?"

Saul's eyes darted sideways. "I'm sure I heard that they were. Someone said so." He sat back and crossed his legs. "I could have heard wrong, of course."

Gennie didn't pursue the matter further, but she knew her digging might have turned up gold, at least a small nugget. Saul might just be creating facts out of Mrs. Berg's speculations at breakfast, but there was another possibility—that he had seen the bottle in Mrs. Dunmore's room. Or he'd given it to her himself.

"I don't suppose you looked out the window?" Gennie asked.

"I was worn out by then. Next thing I remember, it was nearly time for breakfast. What about you? Didn't you hear anything at all?"

"Oh, I sleep like a baby," Gennie said. She had no intention of sharing any information, just collecting it.

Gennie stood at a small window halfway up the hostel staircase, watching the other guests drive away in the Society's huge old Buick. An entire day had passed with no sign of Brother Linus and no progress in finding Mina Dunmore's killer. Now that he suspected Brother Linus of the murder, Grady had told everyone they could leave the village for the afternoon—as long as they were back by evening. Horace had offered to drive. Gennie had decided to stay home, citing the onset of a sick headache. In fact, it had been some time since she'd felt so well—or so full of energy.

She watched the rear of the car disappear down the road to Languor, then waited to make sure the dust stayed settled. She listened for several moments. A faint tick-tock came through the open parlor door, but no other sound spoke of human presence. It struck her how rarely she had been completely alone in a building. For what she wanted to do, being completely alone was essential. Satisfied, she went downstairs to the kitchen. The warm, rich scent of rosemary biscuits baked in a wood-burning oven still hung in the air, making Gennie wish she could linger for a snack, but she didn't dare. She couldn't guess how long the other guests' errands in town might take. Mrs. Berg, at least, would have to be back no later than four o'clock to start fixing dinner, and it was already one forty-five.

Gennie was an observant young woman. She knew that Mrs. Berg had a master key for all the hostel rooms and that she carried it in her apron pocket. When she wasn't wearing her apron, she usually tied the sash in a bow and hung it on a wall peg, leaving the key inside the pocket. Gennie located the apron without difficulty, extracted the key, and hurried upstairs. She stood in the hallway looking at the row of closed doors. Of all the guests, Gennie was most suspicious of Horace von Oswald. If she had time to search only one room, it should be his.

The master key worked smoothly, and she was inside Horace's room in seconds. She closed the door behind her, locking it from the inside. If the worst happened and Horace came back early, at least he wouldn't be put on guard by an unlocked door, and his fumbling with the lock would give her a few seconds to hide—where, she had no idea.

She started at one end of the room and worked her way across, examining everything she could find. His room was neat—by the world's standards, anyway. He seemed to own almost as little as a Shaker brother. His few outfits—all of which Gennie had seen him wear— hung from hangers on pegs. A nightshirt looked like it had been tossed at another peg, probably by Mrs. Berg when she'd straightened the room. Shaving things lay on the desk, along with a pen and some blank sheets of paper. Pretty disappointing so far, Gennie thought. Time to dig deeper.

Like most Shaker retiring rooms, this one had drawers and a small cupboard built into the wall. Gennie opened the cupboard first. It was completely empty. She felt around it just to make sure. That puzzled her. Even Believers normally had small items—books, letters, journals—that stowed easily and neatly in their cupboards. She went on to the drawers. The top one held a small supply of socks and underwear. The sight of men's underwear failed to shock Gennie—not because she was now of the world, which seemed to make some women more squeamish, but because she had done so many laundry rotations that male clothing was no mystery to her.

She moved quickly through the remaining three drawers and found nothing the least bit interesting. Horace didn't even read, as far as she could see. He sounded so literate, though; he had to have books somewhere. Determined to find *something* to justify her mistrust of him, Gennie went through everything one more time. Nothing. Then she remembered a tidbit from her childhood—it was possible to hide small or flat items under the mattress of a Shaker bed.

Mrs. Berg had made Horace's bed, that was clear. No Shaker sister would have left such wrinkles in the bedclothes. Gennie figured she could tear it apart and put it back together, and no one would be the wiser. She flipped the blanket back and dropped it over the foot of the bed, then ripped the sheets away from the mattress. The Shakers, who had many more spare mattresses than covenanted Believers, had piled three thin mattresses on each hostel bed. The people of the world required comfort. Her heart thudding with delighted anticipation, Gennie whipped off the first mattress. All she found was the next mattress. She slid the second mattress onto the floor. Again, she found nothing.

Okay, there was still one last chance. The netting under the bottom mattress surely was tight enough to keep something—a journal, maybe—from falling to the floor. This time she moved more slowly, staving off disappointment. Nothing sat on top of the netting. However, through the netting, Gennie saw a small, dark, rectangular object. Horace had secured it to the bed with lengths of string that almost blended into the pattern of the strong fibers supporting the mattresses.

Gennie cried out in glee, then clamped her hand over her mouth. She reminded herself that Horace was crafty, and he'd been the one driving the Buick. He could show up at any moment. She fumbled at the knots holding the object to the bed, which were so complex they reminded her of a lock. She forced herself to slow down. If she couldn't replicate those knots, Horace would know instantly that someone had been into his secret storage case. She leaned in close and tried to memorize each step as she loosened the strings. She could feel beads of sweat on her forehead; she swiped at them with her forearm without letting go of the knot she was puzzling over. Finally, after the longest five minutes of her life, she undid one knot. She repeated her actions. As the second knot loosened, the dark object slid onto the floor with a light thump.

Gennie crawled under the bed frame and retrieved the prize. It was a small, battered, leather case, just big enough to hold writing paper. The case was too old and inexpensive to have a built-in lock, but Horace had cleverly laced the handles together with more string. *This man has something to hide.* Gennie applied herself to the knot. By now she'd become an expert, so it took only a few seconds to unravel the makeshift lock.

Feeling like it was Christmas morning, she laid the case on the bed and opened it.

Papers. She scooped them out, examined the case, even held it upside down and shook it, but nothing else fell out. She applied herself to the papers. The top page was handwritten, with small, neat letters and lines so straight they must have required a ruler. A centered title topped the page. It was a story—the same story Mrs. Berg had told them Saturday evening in the parlor, about the young Shaker sister who'd inherited a fortune and was killed for it. Gennie scanned several pages. Yes, it was very close, though some of Mrs. Berg's details had been left out. But what did it mean?

She began riffling through the stack of pages, hoping for a clue, but before she could read any more, she heard a rumbling sound outside. A car door slammed, and the rumbling started again. She didn't have to look out the window to know what had happened. One of the brothers must have driven a hostel guest home. Probably not Horace—after all, he'd been driving the others—but she couldn't afford to get trapped in his room.

She selected one page from the middle of the stack, folded it into a small square, and crammed it into the pocket of her sweater. Now came the hard part—putting everything back the way it was. She stuffed the papers back in the case—more or less in the order she'd found them, she hoped. She applied herself to retying the string around the handles. *Concentrate*, she thought, and tried to envision each stage of the knot as it had untied. Before the image could slip from her mind, she retied the string around the handles of the case. She slid the case back into its string holder, and pulled the string ends through the bottom of the bed frame. Her fingers shook so violently that the strings slipped through them, and the case crashed to the floor. Gennie whimpered like a puppy as she crawled under the bed and dragged the case back into position. This time her hands obeyed her. The case stayed in its string container. She found the last set of strings and began the elaborate knot.

The hostel's front door slammed.

With an effort of will, Gennie finished the last knot in record time. She dragged the mattresses back, one by one, and piled them on the bed, wincing as the frame creaked. The tangled bedclothes looked like an impossible mess. She extracted what she hoped was the bottom sheet.

Somewhere nearby, a bedroom door shut. She hadn't heard it open. Maybe, just maybe, she was safe for a time. She'd begun to feel dizzy, so she allowed herself the luxury of a deep breath. She still had to be very quiet, she knew that. Any unexpected noise might trigger curiosity and a knock on the door. Getting away unseen might become impossible. She tucked the rest of the bedclothes into place and stood back to assess her work. The bed looked okay—a bit sloppy, like she'd found it.

She heard a scratching at the door, the distinct sound of a key entering a lock. She must have been mistaken earlier, when she'd assumed there was only one person in that car. Horace von Oswald had returned as well.

The key turned in the lock. She'd lost the knack of ongoing prayer, so she just pleaded for help—inspiration, sudden invisibility, anything. She heard a click as the lock was released. The door creaked. She jumped to her feet and spun around frantically. She could see only one place to hide, and it was behind the opening door. She had little hope she'd get away, but maybe, if Horace was startled enough when he saw her . . .

She held her breath as the door opened toward her and stopped just before it would have bounced off her toes. For several seconds, she heard nothing, no footsteps. The door remained open. She heard a drawer opening and realized Horace had entered soundlessly and gone to his built-in dresser, which meant his back should be toward her. She had a chance. She'd have to slip out soon; Horace would surely close his door for privacy.

She peeked around the edge of the door, into the room. The back she saw didn't belong to Horace von Oswald. It was Beatrice Berg. She bent over an open drawer, pawing through the contents. It was now or never. Gennie took a deep breath and slid around the end of the door. She was fully visible for one agonizing second before her escape was complete. Still afraid to release her breath, she ran on tiptoe down the hallway toward the stairs. She didn't dare go to her room; Beatrice would hear the door open and close. Instead, she hurried to the kitchen, where she dropped the master key back in Beatrice's apron pocket. She slipped out the kitchen door, which Beatrice wasn't likely to hear or see from Horace's room.

Gennie ran and ran, ignoring the mud coating her shoes, until she reached the maple grove behind the foundation of the burned-out Water House. Only then did she stop. Leaning against cool tree bark, she

gasped for breath. Questions swirled in her mind. How
did Beatrice Berg get a second master key—and why?
Was she just snooping around, or did she have a reason
to visit Horace's room while he was gone? What was
she doing back from town, anyway? Had she discovered her key gone from her apron pocket? If so, she'd
surely tumble to the notion that only Gennie had been
home that afternoon. Gennie felt scared, excited, and
guilty all at the same time. Though she had never
signed the Shaker Covenant, she decided it was time
for a confession—to Rose, definitely not to Grady. Not
yet, anyway.

ELEVEN

"AM I STILL GOING TO HAVE A BIRTHDAY?"

Rose resisted the urge to hug Mairin; the child wasn't comfortable with sudden touches, even ones meant to be affectionate and comforting. Instead, she stretched out her hand and silently invited Mairin to take a walk. The ground was still wet, so they followed the path from the Children's Dwelling House to the unpaved central road. It was far from private; people from the world wandered about, seeking thrills of one sort or another. Rose tried not to dwell on their presence. Surely they would lose interest once Mina Dunmore's murder had been solved and the ghost explained away. The sooner they accomplished both, the quicker North Homage could return to peace and worship and hard work.

"Yea, of course you'll still have a birthday," Rose said. "It's just that it will have to be delayed for now, and . . . Mairin, you know that we've been having some troubles lately, don't you?"

"A lady got killed," Mairin said. "And some folks said Brother Linus killed her."

"Who said that?"

"Folks from town. I heard them talking to each other. Did Brother Linus kill the lady?"

141

"I don't think so. I think someone else did, but I don't yet know who. That's why I . . . I might not be able to come to your birthday party."

Mairin said nothing. Rose glanced sideways to find her staring at the ground as she walked. "Do you understand, Mairin? I am eldress of the community; that's like being a mother. Wilhelm is elder, like a father. We have a responsibility to take care of our charges, like a mother and father take care of their children. Sometimes that means we can't do what we'd really like to do."

Mairin's only response was to kick a stone out of her way. Rose felt like kicking, too, but not at a stone. Here she was spouting the Shaker way of living in a family, and Mairin, at about five years of age, had watched her father kill her mother. She'd been neglected much of her short life. Rose and Agatha were the closest she'd gotten to being cared for by loving parents. And now she was being told that she didn't count because the Shakers were Rose's "real" family.

"All the other children will be at your party, and Sister Charlotte. Sister Gertrude is baking you an apple cake. And Sister Agatha wants you to come specially to her retiring room afterward, you and Nora both, to tell her all about the party."

"She's too sick to come," Mairin said. It was a statement of fact and also made it clear that Mairin considered Agatha's excuse valid. "Can I go now? I have to feed Angel."

It took Rose several moments to understand that Mairin was talking about her kitten, not the ghost. "Of course, Mairin. How is Angel doing? Is she getting stronger?"

"Yea, lots stronger. She wriggles a lot more, and her voice is louder. She knows I'm her mama now. Bye."

Rose watched her run on awkward legs, so agile in trees. Mairin headed for the Children's Dwelling House. Perhaps she would become so engrossed in caring for her kitten that she'd forget Rose's bumbling attempt to comfort her.

With less reverence than the book deserved, Rose arranged a copy of *Shakerism: Its Meaning and Message*, by Anna White and Leila S. Taylor, on the shelf in the new library. On impulse, she pulled it down again and opened it to a section that described the reappearance of Sister Caroline Witcher some months following her death. Sister Caroline had materialized as she had been in the flesh, and she had visited the sick, to spread comfort among them. She hadn't roamed around empty buildings, putting on performances that drew the world into her village.

Rose was worried to distraction about her community, and what would become of it if the world came to believe that a brother had murdered one of their hostel guests—and that he hadn't been the first North Homage brother to kill a woman. What would happen to them if the world truly believed the North Homage Shakers had been hiding a murder for a century?

Sheriff Grady O'Neal and his men were combing the countryside, with the help of a group of townsfolk, in search of Brother Linus Eckhoff. They all felt certain that poor, gentle Linus was indeed the killer. A

thorough search of his retiring room in the Center
Family Dwelling House had revealed nothing suspicious. It looked as if he had slept in his bed for at least
part of the night. His wool work jacket and heavy work
shoes were missing, as if he had dressed to go out in
cool weather. Otherwise, his retiring room was as plain
and sparsely furnished as any other Believer's. His
small comb and shaving mirror lay on a table that also
held a basin of water. There was no evidence that he
had shaved that morning.

Linus wasn't a reader—he had no books in his retiring room, but he did keep a journal. It lay in full view
on his pine desk. Rose and Grady both read through it
and found no references to Mina Dunmore. In fact, Linus rarely mentioned people at all. He'd expressed far
more interest in how to repair buildings and objects as
simply and effectively as possible. In his journal, he'd
relived the pleasure he got from finding creative ways
to patch and restore. It was surely not the journal of a
murderer, Rose thought. But Grady was unconvinced.
"People just snap sometimes," he'd said. "He's our
man, I'd bet on it."

When the bell rang for evening meal, Rose made a
desperate decision. She would go, unannounced, to
dine at the hostel. Mrs. Berg would be furious, but that
didn't concern her. She had no appetite at the moment;
she wouldn't eat much. It might be her last chance to
observe and question the hostel guests. If Linus were
found and charged with murder, there would be no reason to keep the guests from leaving.

She dumped her pile of books on a library table and
headed out the door, hoping not to run into worried Be-

lievers arriving from their various work assignments. The last thing she wanted to do was raise hopes that the killer was someone from the world, then find no support for those hopes. Dining at the hostel might easily yield nothing helpful. The guests were on their guard. But she had to try. Wilhelm would be arriving home on Tuesday, and he would blame her for the mess they were in. Not that Wilhelm's opinion concerned her— she was well beyond caring—but he could make her work far more difficult if he believed he could show her to be incompetent. The one consolation to Wilhelm's return was that Andrew would be with him. Andrew would help her to the best of his ability, and that knowledge gave her comfort.

Rose arrived at the Shaker Hostel just as the guests were convening in the parlor for a drink before dinner. Saul Halvardson bounded down the stairs with a bottle of sherry in each hand. He pulled up short when he saw Rose in the entryway.

"I hope you don't mind," he said, holding up the bottles. "I think you'll agree we've all been under a strain." He slid past her into the parlor. Rose decided to let them have their drinks in peace, and she headed for the kitchen.

"Don't expect nothin' fancy tonight," Beatrice said, when Rose told her there'd be an extra person for dinner.

"I promise to eat very little."

Beatrice cracked another egg into a large bowl and whipped the contents as if they were responsible for her being stuck in North Homage.

"Just so's you know," she said, "I'm leavin' soon as I get the word I can go."

"Will you go back home?" Rose asked.

"Don't know, don't care. Anywhere's fine with me, long as it ain't here."

"Where is home, by the way?" Rose tried to keep her tone conversational, but it sounded strained to her own ears.

"No place, just a holler down south. You wouldn't've heard of the place." Her voice softened. "I liked it, though. We was poor, but we managed. My ma could cook up a mess of cornmeal so's it tasted like fried chicken."

For the first time, Mrs. Berg didn't sound bitter, and Rose wanted to keep her in that mood.

"Is that where you learned to cook?"

"Yeah, from my ma. Pa used to say she was the best cook in all Kaintuc. She was somethin', my ma. Bodacious, too—she once took her broom to a black bear that come right up to our door, and she chased that critter down the holler and up the other side. That bear never knowed what hit him." She chuckled. "Never should've left."

"Why did you leave?"

"On account of Mr. Berg, that's why." Her voice had regained its familiar edge. "Right mean, he was. Never should've married him. Ma warned me, but I wouldn't listen." Mrs. Berg's face pinched and puckered as if she were watching an internal film. "Beat me, he did. But he got his comeuppance."

"I beg your pardon?" Rose asked.

Beatrice's head jerked toward her. The eggbeater dripped golden slime on the floor. "I said, I'm fixin' to serve supper in twenty minutes, if I can get some peace."

"Of course," Rose said. "I'll leave you to your work."

"Rose, thank goodness." Gennie was pacing a small circle in the hallway outside the kitchen. "I thought I saw you through the parlor door. I've been dying to talk to you. Come on." She pulled Rose by the elbow toward the stairway, past the closed parlor door.

"I've learned some things, and I just can't wait to tell you," Gennie whispered as she shut the door of her upstairs room. Her eyes sparkled, which lightened Rose's heart and aroused her suspicion. This was the first time Rose had been in her room, and she quickly noted the small touches that showed Gennie had joined the world—the pretty suits and dresses on hangers hooked over wall pegs, the array of perky hats, a lipstick tossed on her desk. She even smelled a hint of perfume, something sweet and flowery.

"You've been investigating on your own again, haven't you?"

"Yes, and I'm good at it, too." Gennie grinned and flopped on her bed. "Although this time I had a narrow escape."

"Oh, Gennie, do be careful."

"Grab a chair, we don't have much time. Saul will probably hand around seconds on sherry, but they've almost finished their first glasses." Gennie told Rose about her conversation with Saul the day before.

"So," Gennie concluded triumphantly, "Grady was wrong not to question Saul. To know there was a port bottle in Mrs. Dunmore's room, he must have been there—or maybe he even gave the bottle to her."

"Could he have been the man in her room?"

Gennie frowned. "Well, he did claim to have heard the man, but he hadn't mentioned it at breakfast, when Mrs. Berg told us about it. He seemed to find Mrs. Dunmore so unattractive—though I guess he could have been pretending. But why wouldn't he throw suspicion on Horace when I gave him the chance?"

"He insisted the voice didn't belong to Horace?"

"It was more that he couldn't believe the possibility," Gennie said. "But I did believe it. That man is so creepy, he's got to be up to something. All the time I talked with Saul, Horace just stared at us with those dead eyes. So I had to see what I could find out about him."

"Gennie, you didn't . . ."

"I did. I sneaked into Horace's room when he went out for a while. I wasn't sure when he'd be back, so I had to hurry, and I was just a bundle of nerves." She grinned again, showing lovely teeth and bubbling excitement.

"But we installed locks on the guests' doors," Rose said, though she wasn't sure she wanted to know any more details than necessary.

"Oh, his door was locked, of course. I just . . . um . . . borrowed Mrs. Berg's master key—she and the others drove to Languor for a shopping trip, so I thought I was safe, at least for a while. I went through Horace's room as fast as I could. As it turned out, he only just returned to the hostel in time for sherry. Anyway, you'll never guess what I found."

"All right, what did you find?" Rose had to admit she'd caught Gennie's excitement. If any evidence existed that could clear Brother Linus's name, she wanted it.

"Papers, scads and scads of them. They were hidden in a leather case strapped to the bottom of Horace's bed, so I knew they were important, if he tried that hard to hide them. Unfortunately, I didn't get much time to read them 'cause I heard a car outside."

"Oh, Gennie—"

"But I skimmed the first few pages, and they told the same story Mrs. Berg did Saturday night—you know, about the young sister looking for her fortune—and it was handwritten, like maybe Horace copied it down right after he heard it. Why would he do that? Anyway, when I heard the car I quick put everything back the way it was, except"—she reached in her sweater pocket and extracted a folded sheet of paper— "I pulled out this one page, so we could study it."

"Gennie, you *stole* something from Horace's room? You invaded the man's privacy, and you stole from him. We certainly never taught you to do that."

Gennie pursed her lips. "Well," she said, "I'll agree that Agatha never taught me such behavior, but you did. How many times have you searched someone's room without their permission so you could prove someone innocent or catch a murderer?"

Rose could think of nothing to say. She had to admit, sometimes she'd bent the rules she believed in for the sake of a higher good. As a result, she'd spent many hours in confession and prayer. Yet in her heart, she'd always believed she'd done what she had to do—that the Holy Father and Holy Mother Wisdom had guided her to the right end, even if the path had been a little crooked.

"You see, Rose, I just can't believe that Brother Linus did what he's been accused of doing. Something else is going on here, I know it."

"I agree. All right, let me see what you've found."

Gennie handed over one sheet of paper covered with handwriting. Rose read it through twice. It sounded familiar. She'd been too busy to read the article in the *Languor County Courier* that Andrew had told her about—the story of the Shaker sister who died from eating rhubarb leaves. This page looked like a segment from the middle of the story.

"I suppose Horace might be compiling Shaker stories, or perhaps ghost stories," Rose said. "Perhaps he's a writer of some kind, maybe a novelist. He is certainly well-spoken."

"In a nasty sort of way," Gennie said.

"I'm not convinced this has anything to do with Mrs. Dunmore's death," Rose said. "Why did you think it might be important?"

Gennie maintained her zeal in the face of Rose's skepticism. "Don't you see? Horace must be hiding some secret life. Maybe he's a blackmailer or something. Maybe Mrs. Dunmore found out who he really was, and he killed her to keep her quiet."

"Gennie, dear, how could he blackmail us with stories that have already been made public?"

Gennie's fervor dimmed, just a little. "I'm not sure," she said, "but that doesn't mean there isn't a good reason. Do you want me to put it back when you're done?"

"Nay, for heaven's sake, stay out of his room."

Rose stood to leave, and Gennie touched the sleeve of her dress. "There's something else, too."

"Now what?"

Gennie spilled out the entire story of Beatrice Berg's visit to Horace's room. Rose dropped back in her chair as if an anvil had fallen on her chest. "You must tell Grady," she said, when Gennie finished.

"He'll kill me."

"Probably not, but he will be angry, and so am I. You violated a guest's privacy and put yourself in grave danger. If you were still in my care, you'd be missing special outings for a year. As it is, you are honor bound to tell Grady everything. It is clear that Mrs. Berg had a duplicate master key made, and I suspect she has used it before. She may be going through everyone's rooms, even yours."

"I hadn't thought of that," Gennie said.

"It also means that Mrs. Berg may know more about the other guests than anyone else. If she is not the killer herself, she may know who is, which would put her in great danger."

"Do you think *she's* a blackmailer?"

"I don't know, but I'm worried."

"I'll keep a close watch on her," Gennie said.

"You are going to stay out of this, young lady. I have the power to send you back to Languor, and I won't hesitate to do so. I'm sure Grady would be glad to move you himself. Do we understand each other?"

"Yes, Rose."

They staggered their arrival in the dining room, so it wouldn't be obvious that they'd been conferring. The other guests had finished their before-dinner drinks and had settled at the table. Rose entered last and chose the end seat, across the table length from Horace von

Oswald. With a shiver, she noted that the seating arrangement was the same as it had been when she'd joined them three nights before. Mina Dunmore's chair stood empty.

The clattering of utensils on crockery was the only sound as the diners filled their plates without speaking to one another. Dinner was simple—eggs scrambled with leftover ham, accompanied by brown bread and Shaker-canned beets. The women, even Mrs. Berg, showed little appetite.

"Off your feed, dear Mrs. Berg?" Horace asked. "I wonder why."

Beatrice neither answered nor acknowledged his presence.

"Are you feeling ill?" Rose asked.

"Why don't y'all just leave me alone," Mrs. Berg said. "I don't want to be here, that's all. Don't feel safe in my bed. Soon as they find Linus, I'm leaving."

"Yet," Horace said, "if the missing brother is found and arrested, won't that make your bed safe once again?" He stabbed a slice of beet with his fork and watched purple liquid drip onto his plate.

Mrs. Berg picked at her eggs.

"I, for one, have no intention of leaving just yet," Horace said. "I'm curious to see how the story turns out."

"I think I'll stay, too," Daisy Prescott said. "I'm sure the police will be successful in catching the man who did this, so I'm not afraid. I like it here."

"Oh, me, too," Gennie said.

"Well, then, it's settled," Saul said. "We'll all stay. I've enjoyed your company, all of you"—he beamed around the table and lingered on Daisy—"and I look forward to many more pleasant times together."

"Y'all are crazy, just plain crazy," Mrs. Berg said. "What if that man sneaks back here and poisons us all before the sheriff finds him?"

"Why do you think Mrs. Dunmore was poisoned?" Rose asked.

"Well, I mean . . . I heard there was nary a scratch on her, so I figured it had to be poison. What else could it be?"

"You know, there's another possibility," said Daisy. She sounded more animated than usual. When everyone turned toward her, she patted her hair and moistened her lips. "What if Mrs. Dunmore actually died of natural causes—say, a heart attack? What if she and Brother Linus were . . . I mean, you know, if they were together, and she simply died? Maybe he panicked and tried to hide the body, so no one would know they'd been . . . together." She cut a tiny slice of beet and ate it.

"You know, I believe you've got something there," Saul said.

"Intriguing," said Horace. His eyes followed Daisy's fork as she raised another minute sliver of beet to her mouth. "And why would he stuff poor Mrs. Dunmore into a dyeing vat? That is what happened, isn't it, Sister?"

Rose chose that moment to take a large bite of bread. Grady had kept quiet about the circumstances of Mrs. Dunmore's death—even she hadn't heard anything about poison—but apparently rumors had spread. At least she could avoid confirming them.

"I suppose people do strange things when they panic," Daisy said.

"Strange indeed." Horace shoveled the remaining scrambled eggs onto his plate, and for once Mrs. Berg didn't chide him. She didn't seem to notice. She pushed aside her half-eaten meal, and Horace eyed it hungrily. "Are you afraid the food supplies are poisoned, Mrs. Berg?" he asked.

Several forks paused in midair.

"Ain't poisoned. I cooked it myself. And don't go lookin' at me like I'm the murderer."

"You are the only one who wants to leave," Horace said. "I find myself wondering why that is."

Beatrice grabbed her plate and wolfed down the rest of her meal. "There, satisfied? And since you're making such a fuss, I'll stay another couple days. Gotta find another job, anyways, and that ain't so easy these days."

"What good news," Saul said. "I'd say that calls for a celebration. Shall we retire to the parlor, and I'll bring down the port?"

Greatly relieved, Rose excused herself. Now that the hostel guests had decided to stay, she had some breathing space, and she wanted to use it fully. She was afraid she'd get little solid information from the guests about themselves. It was time to try elsewhere.

TWELVE

ON TUESDAY MORNING, ROSE RUSHED THROUGH HER before-breakfast chores, lingering only for prayer. Wilhelm and Andrew wouldn't return until late that evening. Rose ran a broom over the floor of Wilhelm's retiring room and smoothed the sheets over his unused bed. He hadn't lived in the room for two days, but it collected dust all the same.

Rose itched to know more about the hostel guests—their backgrounds, jobs, anything at all—and she couldn't sit around and wait for Andrew to return and dig out his records for her. She felt some compunction about rummaging through his desk in the Trustees' Office, but it was the best way to begin. She hurried over to the building before the bell rang for breakfast.

For ten years, Rose had been the community's trustee, and she still missed it. She'd loved the excitement of starting new business ventures, buying and selling land, and watching over the daily work life of the community. Her practical nature had fit beautifully with the demands of the position. Becoming eldress had required more adjustment. She now felt at peace with the change and grateful for the challenges, but it had been a slow process. If she thought too much about

155

it—and she tried not to—she suspected that some of her most satisfying experiences as eldress were those times when the world threatened the village's reputation and sometimes its very survival. This was one of those times. While she had come to embrace her role as spiritual guide for her Children, she had to admit that the call to action always invigorated her. And worried her.

Rose sat at the double desk that had once been hers. She'd always loved its golden patina and economic design. Two trustees could work comfortably side by side without getting in each other's way. Cubbyholes provided organization for smaller items, and generous bookshelves fit on top of the cubbyholes. She ran her hand over the clean surface, remembering its well-used smoothness.

This was no time for sentiment. She sifted through papers, looking for anything Andrew might have written about the Shaker Hostel. Andrew was both creative and well-organized, bless him. He had crammed both sides of the bookcases to the brim with ledger books and journals. Some he'd identified with carefully printed labels on the spines, some were plain. She skimmed over the titles and grabbed one that said "Shaker Hostel." She turned the pages quickly. Numerous pages outlined Andrew's plans for renovating the West Dwelling House. He'd listed sources within the village for furniture, plates, cutlery, kitchen equipment—they'd had to purchase little from the world to complete the project.

Finally she came to his notes about the first set of guests. Andrew had said there wasn't much informa-

tion about them, and he'd been right. However, he'd
scratched some notes that might be helpful. All the
guests had approached him by telephone, and he'd jotted down bits of the conversation. Andrew's handwriting was clear and legible. She took some blank paper
and began to copy.

Horace von Oswald had been the first to call, early
in February. Andrew had noted that his call arrived the
very day the first advertisement had appeared in the
major Kentucky papers; therefore, Horace might have
been staying somewhere nearby. Andrew's notes said:
*Well-to-do, no permanent job, likes to experience new
places. Sounds well-educated. Asked about transport
to Languor. Mentions plain living, wholesome food.
Asked if worship service public. Knows about us??*

No one else called until early March, when the second set of advertisements hit the newspapers, this time
in Ohio and Indiana, as well as Kentucky. Saul Halvardson was next to inquire about a room. Andrew had
written: *Salesman, ladies' personal garments. Travels
often through Kentucky and points south. Wants a
place to rest between sales trips. He asked if women
would be allowed to the share the building. Asked if
furniture authentic—odd.*

Mina Dunmore had called next, followed closely by
Beatrice Berg. According to Andrew, Mrs. Dunmore
had asked several questions about the community. He
had written: *Widow, small inheritance. Needs inexpensive but safe place to stay for a time. Asked who was
elder, eldress? How many buildings? Location?* Beatrice Berg had been brief: *Needs job, place to live. I said
we needed housekeeper who can cook, send refs.* An-

drew had noted to the side that she'd never sent references, but she'd arrived early and demonstrated that she could handle the old kitchen equipment. Andrew's final cryptic note about Beatrice said: *Asked—isolated?*

Daisy Prescott had been the last to call, just two days before the hostel opened. She'd said little. Andrew had written: *Wants vacation. Concerned safety. Soft-spoken.*

Rose turned the page and discovered that Andrew had listed questions for each guest to answer upon arrival. He'd requested a home or last address; telephone number, if available; and source of income, to ensure payment. He'd noted that each had paid for a two-week stay, in advance. She copied down all the information. Horace had given an address in the village of Birdhill, in southern Ohio. Beatrice listed a boardinghouse in Languor; Rose knew the proprietor. Saul and Mina gave Lexington addresses, and Daisy cited Indianapolis as her last address. Everyone except Saul had listed phone numbers; she'd start with those.

She tidied the desk and gathered up her papers. Breakfast would be ending soon, and she was hungry. She missed the days when she could slip into the Trustees' Office kitchen and grab some bread and cheese. She'd swing by the Center Family Dwelling House kitchen and beg some leftovers from Sister Gertrude, then sequester herself in the now empty Ministry House library. The phone hadn't yet been disconnected, so she could make her calls in private.

"Landsakes, you're just going to waste away if you keep missing meals like this," said Sister Gertrude, as she hacked off a thick slice of bread and wrapped it in a towel with a hunk of cheese.

"I expect I'll survive," Rose said, laughing. "I can't stay away from your recipes for long. That dill potato soup I tasted the other night at the hostel was superb."

Gertrude beamed. "Tonight I'm using basil and some of our canned tomatoes to make soup."

"Sounds delicious." Rose stowed the bundle of food in her apron pocket and hurried out the kitchen door to avoid an extended conversation, Gertrude's specialty. Careful to avoid bruising the young oregano plants, Rose cut through the kitchen garden and between the Infirmary and Laundry. She had almost reached the Ministry House when she heard her name called by a high, frantic voice. She turned and saw Nora, Mairin's best friend, running toward her.

"Sister Rose, please, you've got to come right away." Nora ran right up to her and clamped her small hands on Rose's wrist. "Please, now."

"What's wrong, Nora?"

"It's Mairin. You've got to come. I can't—oh, just follow me, please. It's really important." Her voice squeaked with frustration and fear. Rose didn't ask any more questions until they'd reached the Children's Dwelling House.

"Aren't you both supposed to be in school?" Rose asked.

Nora ran into the dwelling house without responding or even waiting for Rose to catch up. By the time Rose got through the door, Nora was halfway up the staircase to the second floor, where the children's retiring rooms were located. Rose followed as fast as she could. She reached the second floor, but Nora was already heading for the third floor, where no one lived. Rose had given Mairin permission to keep her kitten in one of the empty third-floor rooms, to keep it warm and safe but away from the rest of the children. One of the girls being raised by the Shakers had breathing problems, and cats seemed to make them worse.

Nora scurried down the hallway, and, to Rose's surprise, passed right by the room Mairin had been given for her kitten. At the far end of the hall was a narrow staircase that led to a small attic, where the children's out-of-season clothing was stored. Nora turned and beckoned to Rose to hurry. She clambered up the attic stairs and disappeared. Rose climbed the stairs more sedately, having worn herself out.

At the top of the staircase, Nora paused and waited for Rose. Nora took her hand and led her into the attic room. A high window provided minimal light, since it hadn't been cleaned in some time. As they approached a dark corner, Rose heard a tiny cry, which she now recognized as the mew of a kitten.

"Mairin?" Rose asked. "Is that you? What on earth are you doing up here? Are you all right?"

A gasp and a sob joined the kitten's mew. Rose pushed aside a row of winter dresses hung on a horizontal pole. Mairin crouched in the corner, curled against the wall as tightly as a ball of yarn. She held the calico kitten against her shoulder, one hand on its back to keep it from escaping.

"Dear one, what has happened?" Rose knelt on the dusty floor and reached toward Mairin. She expected to be rebuffed. In all the troubled times she and Mairin had shared, she had never heard the child cry with such anguish. In fact, she rarely showed emotion at all. But this time she scrabbled to her knees and threw herself into Rose's arms, wedging the panicked kitten between them.

Rose extracted the kitten and handed her to Nora, then folded Mairin in her arms. She murmured soothing words and stroked the girl's disheveled curls. Mairin sobbed until she began to hiccup. Rose tried to ease Mairin away a few inches, to see her face, but the child clung to her.

Rose gave up and whispered in Mairin's ear, "Can you tell me what has happened?"

For several moments, Mairin's small body remained rigid. Then she pulled back and looked at Rose. Her eyes were red and puffy, and she had the exhausted look of a child at the end of her endurance. She hiccupped and said, "I have to show you."

"All right, then. Can you do it now, or do you need to wait awhile longer?"

"We can't wait." Mairin cast a worried glance in Nora's direction. "I've got to keep Angel safe," she said. "I'm afraid she'll get hurt." She squirmed out of Rose's grip and reached for the kitten. "She's got to stay with me. I have to protect her."

"What if you and I take Nora and Angel to Sister Agatha's retiring room. Will that be safe enough?"

Mairin bit her lower lip. "Okay, but they have to stay there until I get back."

"Agreed," said Rose.

By the time they'd left Nora and the kitten in Agatha's care, Mairin seemed her old self again, though subdued. Rose's heart was pumping with anxiety. Mairin was not a child who allowed much to penetrate her outer reserve. Mairin stared straight ahead, her face set in grim lines, as she led the way across the lawn toward the abandoned South Family Dwelling House. She paused at the cellar door, then seemed to change her mind and led Rose around the side of the building. They arrived at the sisters' entrance. Mairin took Rose's hand and stood in front of the door.

"Should we go in?" Rose asked.

Mairin nodded, but still held back. Fear clamped down on Rose's throat, constricting her breathing. The child seemed terrified.

"Couldn't you just tell me what to look for?" Rose asked. "Then you could stay out here and wait for me."

"Nay," Mairin said, "I'll take you."

Rose had the distinct impression that Mairin was protecting her. She held the girl's hand more tightly and pushed the door open. Mairin stepped in first. When Rose pulled the door shut behind her, the hallway seemed alive with eerie movement. But it was only swirling dust caught in the sunlight. She was allowing her imagination far too much freedom. It was entirely possible that someone was playing at haunting the village, for some unknown reason, and Mairin had found some evidence of the deception. That would surely upset the girl, who had come to believe the ghost was her guardian angel.

Rose followed Mairin through the hallway and downstairs to the kitchen. From the kitchen, another short stairway led down to the root cellar, where Mairin had spent so much secret time—and where she had hidden her kitten. The dank, earthen smell had become familiar to Rose, but she didn't find it pleasant.

She couldn't understand why Mairin was so drawn to the place.

A narrow dirt passageway led all the way to the cellar door. Small storage rooms branched out on either side of the hallway. Mairin stopped at the first entrance on their left, across from the room in which she'd hidden her kitten. She stood in the opening, still and silent. The cavelike room was in near total darkness, so Rose took a step inside. Mairin squeezed her hand as if to stop her, then let go. Rose entered without her. The room's packed earth walls were lined with strong, wide shelves that once had been filled with canned goods. As Rose's eyes adjusted to the dimness, she saw a bundle of clothing on one of the lower shelves at the far end of the room. So she'd been right—this was the ghost's dressing room.

Eagerly, she approached the bundle and knelt on the dirt floor. She reached out to grab it, but the fabric did not give. With instant certainty, she knew what she had touched. Someone was inside those clothes. Someone who did not respond to noise or to touch. No skin was visible because a wool jacket had been draped over the body's head and arms. Behind Rose, Mairin whimpered. For her sake, Rose kept her own reactions under firm control. Though she wanted to leap back, she forced herself to lift the jacket and look underneath.

Open eyes stared back at her. They did not see her, of course. They would never see again. She had found Brother Linus Eckhoff.

Rose dropped the jacket back over his face and stood. She kept her back to Mairin for several moments while she tried to compose herself. Then she scooped Mairin into her arms and didn't put her down until they were out in the sunshine.

"I'm so very sorry you had to see that, little one," Rose said, as they put some distance between themselves and the dwelling house. "I'm going to take you right to Agatha's retiring room. I want you to tell her everything, okay? Will you promise me that?"

"Okay, I promise." Mairin pulled ahead, clearly eager to get to the comfort of Agatha's presence.

"I have to call the police, so I must leave you with Agatha."

"Okay."

Rose wished that she, too, could curl up at Agatha's feet, but her duty lay elsewhere. One of her Children had been murdered.

THIRTEEN

"I WANT TO BE INVOLVED AT EVERY STAGE." ROSE HURRIED to keep up with Sheriff Grady O'Neal as they neared the South Family Dwelling House. His two officers, Hank and Bar, followed behind, pausing now and then to give stern warnings to the crowd collecting behind them.

"I can't promise anything, Rose." Grady said.

"You can promise or not, it makes no difference. Someone is killing our guests and us, too. We have a terrible enemy, and I want to know who it is."

"Don't you trust me to find out?"

"It isn't a matter of trust. I cannot—*will* not—sit idly and let a killer roam free among us. To kill another human being is the most despicable of sins."

"I agree, Rose, and I know that Brother Linus's death is a terrible blow to you, but . . ." Grady reached the sisters' entrance to the South Family Dwelling House and held the door open for Rose. This was not the time to quibble about using separate doors, she decided. She entered and waited for him.

"Which way?" he asked.

Rose led him toward the kitchen.

"Look," he said, "I know better than to try to keep

165

you out of it altogether. Just be careful, okay? And could you keep Gennie out of it, for once?"

Had she felt more lighthearted, Rose would have laughed. "My ability to tell Gennie what to do," she said, "is equal to your ability to tell *me* what to do."

"I can't argue with that. Down here?"

"Yea. In the first room to your left."

Grady flipped on a large flashlight and examined the entire room before shining the light on the sad pile of clothing lying as if tossed on the shelf. Grady lit the floor in front of him and examined it as he approached the body. When he reached Linus, he shone his flashlight slowly over the body before gingerly lifting the jacket and examining the face.

"Has anyone touched anything?"

"Nay. Mairin and I both lifted the cloth over his face, just as you did. I asked Mairin, and she insisted she touched nothing else. Believe me, neither of us wanted to."

Grady looked back over Rose's shoulder. "Hank, get on back to the Trustees' Office and watch for Dr. Hanfield; bring him back here. Bar, you go cordon off all the entrances to this building, and keep folks off the grass. Get them to go home, if you can. I doubt we'll find much in the way of evidence, but the last thing we need is folks trampling everything in sight."

He snapped off his flashlight and rejoined Rose in the hallway. "Did Mairin say what time she found him?"

"I'm afraid Mairin has been wandering around at night," Rose said. "We've tried to get her to stay in bed, but . . . Well, she said that right around two o'clock on

Sunday morning, she went to check on her kitten—it's a long story, but she's watching over a tiny kitten she found near this building. I'm allowing her to keep it in an unused retiring room in the Children's Dwelling House. She played with it for a while, she said. When it went to sleep, she started watching out the window, which faces north and gives her a clear view of the back of this building. She was looking for lights—this so-called ghost, you know. She said she saw the cellar door—down that way, at the end of this hallway—she saw it open upward and someone came out."

"Could she really see much that time of night?"

"She claims the moonlight was strong enough to see the figure, but not who it was. It was wearing a cloak, like this creature who keeps appearing in our buildings at night."

"I've heard about that." Grady turned away, but not before Rose saw him smile. "This figure, was it short, tall, anything noticeable about it?"

"She said it bent over while it ran, so she wasn't sure if it was tall or short, man or woman."

"Ran where?"

"West, from what she said. It could have been going back to Languor," Rose added, with slight hope.

"Yeah, or the Shaker Hostel. Why did she wait until now to tell you?"

"The poor child was trying so hard to do as we'd asked—to stop wandering around where she wasn't supposed to be. She was afraid we didn't want her looking out windows, either, so she resisted admitting she'd done so."

Grady poked his head back into the dank storage

room. "I'm going to take a closer look at him. No telling when Dr. Hanfield will get here, and I can't wait forever. You stay here."

Rose ignored his order and followed him into the room. "Well, at least stand back," Grady said. Rose ignored him a second time.

Linus's body was wedged between the lower and middle shelves, close to a dark corner. Even close up, it was hard to make out any details. Grady left the jacket hanging over the dead face and began an inch-by-inch examination of the rest of the body, using only his flashlight. Finding nothing, he began again, lightly touching areas as he went. He reached the hipbone and something crinkled.

"Here, hold this." Grady handed the flashlight to Rose. "Point it right here," he said. He felt around the hipbone and found Linus's pants pocket. Again, something crackled. Grady reached into the pocket and pulled out an envelope. It had been slit open and held a folded sheet of paper. Grady removed the page and opened it under the light.

"Looks like some sort of official document," he said. "Let me have the flashlight; the print is faded." He held the pages low, with the top folded toward him, so Rose couldn't see the writing clearly enough to read it. Abruptly, he refolded the paper and slipped it into an inside pocket of his uniform jacket. Even in the dim light, Rose could see Grady's jaw muscles tighten. "Did you say that Wilhelm has been out of town on a sales trip?"

"Yea, he's been with Andrew. They are returning today."

Grady nodded, then spun toward the opening to the hallway. He reached the stairs and took the first two in one leap.

"Please, Grady, tell me what's going on." Rose reached toward him, and stopped just short of touching him.

Grady paused but kept his back to her. "I have reason to believe Wilhelm might be involved in these murders."

"*What?* That can't be. He's been out of the village the whole time, and anyway, what could Wilhelm possibly have to do with Mina Dunmore's death? He barely knew her."

Grady turned to face her. The look on his face made her breath catch in her throat. "He may not have known Mrs. Dunmore very well, but he most certainly knew *of* her." He patted his jacket. "What I have here is a birth certificate, dated forty years ago. It's for a girl by the name of Wilhelmina Lundel. Her father was named Wilhelm Lundel, aged twenty-two. Sound familiar? Were you aware that Wilhelm had once been married?"

Rose couldn't seem to form words, so she shook her head and leaned against the cold packed earth of the root cellar wall for support. It smelled like the inside of a grave.

"Aren't you Shakers supposed to confess stuff—like deserting a wife and child?" Grady's voice was cold and hard as Kentucky limestone. He turned on his heel and climbed the stairs toward the kitchen.

With an effort of will, Rose suppressed her shock and hurried after him. As he was about to open the kitchen door, she called, "Grady, wait. Please don't jump to conclusions. I can't believe . . . Surely this is more complicated than it seems. How can you be sure Mina Dunmore really was Wilhelmina? Can't we discuss this before you arrest Wilhelm?"

Grady let go of the doorknob and turned around. "All right, I guess I owe you that. Of course we'll investigate the authenticity of this document, but even if Mina Dunmore was using Wilhelmina's identity, that doesn't mean Wilhelm would have known she was a fake. In my experience, the simplest answer is usually the right one. And this looks pretty simple to me. Mina Dunmore comes here to find her father, maybe to embarrass him, maybe to get money, who knows. Probably not for a happy reunion, though. Wilhelm wants his past kept secret, and he sure doesn't intend to be blackmailed. He wants to get rid of Mina Dunmore. Meanwhile, one of the brothers has gotten involved with her, and he learns Wilhelm's secret, too. Maybe Linus finds Mina's body, or maybe he watches Wilhelm kill her—either way, Linus knows he can identify the killer, so he decides to try a little blackmail himself. He gets Wilhelm to meet with him in the middle of the night and Wilhelm kills him. Wilhelm probably figured it would be weeks or even months before anyone found the body down here. Maybe he planned to return later with a shovel and bury the body. This floor is hard, but it's still dirt, and Wilhelm is a strong man. Anyway, that's more or less how I see it."

"There's a problem with your theory," Rose said. "If Wilhelm killed Linus, why on earth would he leave the birth certificate on the body? You found it easily; why wouldn't he?"

Grady hesitated, but not for long. "Maybe he heard

sounds in the house, so he ran off, intending to come back later. Maybe he heard Mairin coming. As I said, he figured no one would come down here while he was out of town."

Rose shook her head vigorously. "Nay, that can't be what happened. Mairin was still in the Children's Dwelling House, looking out the window, when she saw the cloaked figure leave by the cellar door. And besides, how much effort would it take to extract that envelope from Linus's pocket and take it away? Surely he would have had time to do that, even if he heard noises."

"Maybe, maybe not. He might not have known exactly where the document was, or even that Linus had it on his person. And we don't know what interrupted him; maybe he needed to get out fast."

Rose brushed a curtain of errant red curls off her forehead and poked them under her white cap, as if that would clear her mind. "Are you thinking that our ghost might have frightened him?"

Grady shrugged. "It's certainly possible. Not that I think it's a real ghost, no matter what everyone around here believes. But Wilhelm might have thought it was real and run like the dickens. I'll bet that would make him forget all about searching the victim's pockets for evidence. Anyway, he'd have felt pretty sure he'd have a chance to come back. Look, Rose, you didn't know about Wilhelm's past—his marriage and baby and so forth. You have to admit his behavior has been mighty suspicious."

"I wouldn't necessarily know about Wilhelm's past. He came from another village while I was still a child. He probably confessed to Brother Obadiah, who was elder then, and Obadiah might have kept the details to himself. We used to confess often to the entire community, and many of us still do on occasion, but it isn't absolutely essential. Wilhelm is not acting suspicious, he's just . . . acting like Wilhelm. He keeps apart; he believes that's how an elder should be, so he can lead with authority. It's one of the many things we don't agree on, but it isn't evidence of murder. He is truly a devout Shaker, no matter what you may think of him otherwise. He simply would never kill. I will not believe that he is responsible for these deaths; it's unthinkable."

"I'm sorry, Rose," Grady said. "I disagree. And I can't take the chance of Wilhelm slipping away while we investigate." He ran a hand over his face as if suddenly tired. "One thing I want you to know," he said. "I really believe we'll find all the evidence we need; I'm not just turning on Wilhelm because he's a Shaker. I wouldn't do that. You know that, don't you?"

"I know." Rose felt the strength ebb from her body. For the first time, her determination flagged. At the moment, she saw no way out of this mess, and it might well destroy her village, her home, her Family. Somehow she had to find the strength to keep pushing through the fog until she reached clarity. Even if it meant Wilhelm's destruction. Many times she had wished Wilhelm gone, out of her hair, but not like this. She couldn't let him be blamed without absolute proof of his guilt—and only she would be resolute enough to search for that proof.

"What is the meaning of this? Why was I not told about these killings?" Elder Wilhelm ignored Grady and scowled at Rose as he lumbered toward them like an enraged bear. He and Andrew had returned to the village early, while Grady was still investigating, and he'd come to find them immediately. His thick white hair looked as if he'd just leaped out of bed and forgotten to comb it. A small crowd was gathering around the group, looking for entertainment.

"Wilhelm, perhaps we should discuss this in the Ministry House, where we can be private," Rose said.

"I should have heard the news from thee," Wilhelm said to Rose, ignoring her hand signals to keep his voice down. "Instead, I heard rumors and innuendo, and it was left to Sister Elsa to give me the truth."

"Wilhelm, I urge you—"

"I want your explanation, Sister—*now*."

"You'd best listen to her warnings," Grady said. "We'll talk in the Ministry House—unless you want the world to know your business."

Wilhelm glanced around and saw the growing crowd. Several strangers stumbled backward after one look at his face, but even Wilhelm wouldn't succeed in keeping the world out of earshot. He stalked off toward the Ministry House.

"I'm waiting," Wilhelm said, once they'd gathered in the now-barren Ministry library. Rose left the lights turned off and the curtains closed to deter the curious, giving the room an abandoned feel. The air already smelled stale.

Rose and Grady pulled three ladder-back chairs off their pegs and set them in a circle. But Wilhelm chose to stand beside his chair, his thick arms crossed over his chest, and his wind-roughened lips pressed into a grim line.

Grady and Rose exchanged glances; Rose's eyes pleaded for time. "Wilhelm," she said, "why didn't you tell me you'd once been married and that you had a daughter?"

Wilhelm's face blanched as white as his hair. He collapsed into his chair and stared at the floor. "It was not necessary for thee to know," he said. "It was in my past and none of thy concern."

Rose did not point out that Wilhelm had for years made it his concern to remind her of her own brief sojourn in the world. "There was no need to keep your past secret," Rose said. "Many good Shakers have left their families to become Believers."

Wilhelm raised his eyes to Rose's face. "I should never have married," he said. "I was young, callow. It was sinful of me." He straightened his back. "However, that was many years ago, and I have atoned. I became a Believer and try with all my strength to keep others from committing the same sins. All that is behind me. It can have nothing to do with this . . . this mess you've gotten us into after I've been gone less than three days."

The old Wilhelm was reasserting himself, but for a moment, Rose felt she had seen into his soul. She understood now why Wilhelm's attention always seemed so absorbed by the evils of carnality and the virtue of celibacy. His own sins—or at least, his perceived sins— haunted him. For the first time, Rose suspected there might be a fragile human being beneath Wilhelm's harsh exterior. But she wasn't completely convinced.

"Exactly where have you been during the last two days?" Grady asked. He flipped open his notebook.

Wilhelm's face reddened. "Brother Andrew and I drove south, looking for new customers. Andrew has developed some fine new medicinal herb potions, and we wanted to show them around. I can't recall where we were each precise moment. We would have to check our journals."

"Were you together the whole time?"

"Yea."

"Isn't it unusual for you to go along on these trips?"

"I am an elder, but I work alongside my brothers. That is our way."

"But have you accompanied Andrew before?"

"Nay. I felt it was time. We were exploring new markets, farther away."

Grady glanced up from his notebook and studied Wilhelm's face. "When did you first realize that Mrs. Mina Dunmore was really your daughter, Wilhelmina?"

Wilhelm blinked at Grady as if his question made no sense. His eyes darted around the room, landing for an instant on Rose, then flicking away again. Rose sensed that his mind was working at top speed.

"Well?" Grady demanded.

"Sheriff, I had no idea until this very moment that Mrs. Dunmore was anyone other than a rather irritating guest at our ill-advised hostel."

"Really," Grady said, his voice heavy with disbelief.

"I do not lie," said Wilhelm.

"Yet you had spoken with her on occasion—otherwise, how would you know she was, as you said, irritating?"

"She had an intrusive manner," Wilhelm said. "She wandered through our private buildings without permission. But she never once said she was any relation to me. I would not have believed her if she had."

"We have proof," Grady said. "Her birth certificate."

"I do not believe thee."

Grady pulled the document out of his pocket, opened it, and held it in front of Wilhelm's face. He held on to it tightly so Wilhelm could not take it from him. Wilhelm slid his spectacles from his work jacket pocket and adjusted them on his nose. His hands shook. He examined the document for no more than a few seconds, then bowed his head.

"Do you recognize this birth certificate?" Grady asked.

"Yea. But it does not prove that Mrs. Dunmore was indeed Wilhelmina."

"That should be easy enough to prove," Grady said, slipping the paper back into his pocket. "And when we do, we will have our motive for murder. Wilhelm, you're under arrest for the murder of Mrs. Mina Dunmore—"

"Impossible. I was away from the village."

"—in the early morning hours of Sunday, April 24—well before you left North Homage—and for murdering Brother Linus Eckhoff, which you could easily have done before you left the village. You'll have to come with me." He pulled a pair of handcuffs from a bulging pocket.

"Grady, please," Rose said. "Don't use those; they aren't necessary, and they will only increase the curiosity of all these strangers in our village."

"Go ahead," Wilhelm said, holding his arms straight out in front of him. "Bind my wrists. The world should see that I am being made a sacrifice for the sins of another."

Grady shoved the handcuffs back into his pocket and took Wilhelm by the elbow. "Let's just do this quietly, shall we?"

Rose followed behind them all the way to Grady's dusty brown Buick. She felt a weariness that even one of Josie's reviving teas would not cure. She knew she must believe in Wilhelm's innocence and search for the true killer elsewhere—and she knew that Wilhelm wouldn't be much help. Already he saw himself as a martyr for Shakerdom, rather than a man facing the hangman's rope for two gruesome murders.

FOURTEEN

"DID YOU KNOW ABOUT WILHELM'S PAST?" ROSE SAT IN Agatha's retiring room, sipping some of the peppermint tea Josie had brought to settle the frail former eldress's stomach. Agatha had been unable to eat much for the last couple of days. Rose was concerned that the shock of two violent deaths in the village had further weakened her dear friend.

Agatha nodded slowly. Her pale neck looked so fragile that it seemed to have barely enough strength to complete the action. "Yea, I have known for years. When Obadiah became so ill and stepped down as elder, he recommended to the Mount Lebanon Ministry that Wilhelm replace him. However, he told Wilhelm he would do so only on one condition—that Wilhelm confess to me everything from his life before becoming a Believer. Obadiah believed that elders and eldresses could not guide effectively if we kept secrets from one another. In turn, I urged Wilhelm to reveal his past to you when you became eldress, but I lacked Obadiah's power over him. I did not feel I had the right to tell you myself."

"Didn't it concern Obadiah that he had to threaten Wilhelm to make him open himself to you?"

Agatha gave one of her now-rare smiles. The last stroke had weakened her right side, so the smile was lopsided, yet it made Agatha look younger and stronger. "I have always disagreed with Wilhelm on so many things, but I see him as Obadiah did—a devout Believer who lives his beliefs without compromise. Perhaps I'd prefer for him to compromise just a little now and then. However, I must respect his intentions." Despite the warmth of the room, Agatha pulled her blanket over her arms. "Obadiah saw Wilhelm's secretiveness as his greatest weakness and tried to force him into the light. It did some good, I believe, though it often might not seem so."

"Perhaps you are right," Rose said. "As Grady drove him away after arresting him, Wilhelm turned to look at me. I saw fear on his face—he allowed me to see it, if just for a moment. I suspect part of him welcomes martyrdom, but the rest wants to live."

With her tiny feet, Agatha pushed her chair in a gentle rocking. "I know Wilhelm was deeply ashamed of having deserted his wife and child—the daughter, I believe, was quite young at the time. But he was able to tell Obadiah and then me about it. Now he has finally told you and Grady, as well. Even if I did not know Wilhelm to be a sincere Believer, and therefore a pacifist, it makes no sense to me that he killed his own daughter and his spiritual brother to keep a secret he had already told."

Rose had to agree. Unable to sit still, she paced to the window and peeked through the curtain, closed against rude strangers from the world.

"I am sure that you will find out the truth," Agatha said. "No one is as stubborn as you."

Rose spun around, then laughed as she saw Agatha's

lopsided grin. "I suppose that is one of *my* greatest weaknesses."

"And one of your strengths. Now, before you throw yourself into your search—as important as it is— please do stop by the Children's Dwelling House this afternoon. That's important, too."

"Mairin's birthday party!"

"Yea, we rescheduled it. First one killing, now another . . . Mairin understands, but I didn't want to wait much longer. To gain her trust, we must keep our word. I told Gertrude to bring over a cake at three o'clock, just as the children have finished school for the day. I asked Charlotte to speak with all the parents of the other children, so they might stay for the party, as well. Agatha rocked more vigorously. "Mother Ann is with us; I feel her. You must let her guide you, Rose."

"I will." Rose believed in the messages brought through Agatha's heightened spiritual senses, but she wished that, once in a while, she might hear them first herself.

"You will find the truth," Agatha repeated. "I will keep you and Wilhelm in my prayers." She slowed her rocking. "And Mairin. I am equally concerned about Mairin. I truly believe the child has gifts," she said, "and that she has been sent to us. I see a place for her here, with us."

"I suppose I'm not the best person to show Mairin that adults can be trusted, am I? I do become single-minded—not unlike Wilhelm, I must admit."

"Just be at the Children's Dwelling House at three. After that, you can sleuth day and night. I'll watch over Mairin. I've also asked Gennie to come to the party, and she can help keep an eye on the child."

What will I do without you? Rose didn't say the words. She knew the answer.

With Mairin's party at three o'clock, there was just time for Rose to dig into one or two questions she had about the backgrounds of the hostel guests. She would find the killer among them, she felt sure of it. It was a big job, but she knew Andrew could be counted on to help. They could divide the list of hostel guests between them.

Rose patted her apron pocket, where she'd stuffed the notes she'd made from Andrew's records. He'd be in the Medicinal Herb Shop now. Luckily, the shop was just east of the Center Family Dwelling House, so she left by the kitchen door and cut through the garden. She picked up her pace as she noticed several strangers leave the central path and veer toward her. Word of Wilhelm's arrest had surely spread throughout the county by now. The last thing she wanted to do was field rude questions from the world.

Spring had been drifting into summer all day, though the warmth was still far from oppressive. Bright sunlight and thirsty plants had dried the ground and tinted it with vibrant spring colors. The pungent sweetness of healthy young herbs perfumed the air. If she were not hunting a killer and mourning the loss of a brother, Rose would be singing a Shaker song of praise and gratitude. As it was, she prayed for help, guidance, and a quick resolution to this tragic situation.

Brother Andrew had used his talents to rejuvenate the North Homage medicinal herb industry, which now brought in much needed income. He'd recently lost his most experienced workers, so he spent a fair portion of his time in the Medicinal Herb Shop, training two young brothers who'd shown an interest in learning. All three brothers spent their mornings planting and their afternoons studying medicinal herbs, so they'd be ready to work quickly when the herbs became ready for use. As Rose opened the door to the shop, she was greeted by three startled faces, which relaxed as they recognized their eldress. The odor of unwashed socks told her that one of the ongoing experiments involved a large amount of valerian. She was careful to pull the door shut again behind her. Under normal circumstances, Andrew would have the door and windows wide open, to freshen the air.

"Has the world been intruding today?" she asked.

"Yea, very much so," Andrew said, as he placed a chair next to his tiny, cluttered desk. "I had to ask the last bunch how they would like it if a crowd of strangers walked into their homes without knocking. Apparently it had never occurred to them that this village is our home and doesn't exist simply for their entertainment."

"Perhaps we can do something to help them lose interest," Rose said. She smoothed her long skirt under her and scooted awkwardly onto the chair. She was taller than average for a woman, but this chair had been specially crafted for an even taller man.

"I'll help in any way I can," Andrew said. He closed a journal in which Rose caught sight of scribbled notes about various medicinal herb experiments, and rested his elbow on the desk. He had a thin face, with dark eyebrows that often puckered with intense concentration. Rose felt better because she could share this burden with him. Not for the first time, she wished he were elder.

"I strongly suspect that Mrs. Dunmore's killer and Brother Linus's are one and the same. And I think he or she is one of our hostel guests."

"Are you quite certain it isn't Wilhelm?"

Rose hesitated. She felt sure, but that didn't mean she was right. She had to keep her mind open. "All right, I'm reasonably certain. We must investigate all possibilities. But Grady is sure Wilhelm is guilty, and he won't be scrutinizing anyone else. He won't have reason to look closely at the guests. So we must. Could you free yourself to do a bit more traveling right away?"

Andrew glanced around at his assistants. "Howard and Patrick are learning well. They can work on planting while I'm gone. Where do you want me to go?"

"I want you to track down Saul Halvardson's background—where he's from, whether he is who he claims to be, anything you can find out. Since he's supposed to be a salesman, I thought you might be able to trace his route by talking to your own customers first, and then—I don't know, maybe you can pick up a clue that will lead you to his customers."

"Leave it to me."

"Good. Meanwhile, I'll work on finding out more about Beatrice Berg." She pulled her notes from her apron pocket and spread them on the desk, taking care not to lean in too close to Andrew. "According to your notes—" She glanced up at him. "I hope you don't mind. While you were gone, I went through your desk to find out everything I could about the hostel guests."

"My records belong to the Society," Andrew said.

"Well, you wrote that Beatrice listed a boarding-house in Languor as her previous address. Did she mention anything else, do you remember?"

Andrew leaned back in his chair and pressed an index finger against his lips. "She mentioned she'd been widowed for some time and had only a tiny income. She said that was why she lived in a boardinghouse rather than in her own home. As I remember, she also said she'd grown up in the hill country."

Andrew's memories squared with Rose and Beatrice's conversation in the hostel kitchen. "Did she say how long she'd lived in Languor?"

"I believe she said she married a Languor man and lived in town most of her adult life. She mentioned having a house near the center of town. I think she wanted me to know she wasn't right out of the hollow. Not that I'd have cared, but it seemed important to her."

"Thank you, that helps," Rose said, gathering up her notes. She remembered Horace's contention that Beatrice had lied about living in Languor. It was something to investigate. "Let's get to work, shall we? I suspect we haven't much time."

"I'll phone you if I find out anything that seems important." He swung both their chairs onto wall pegs. "And Rose," he said, turning around to face her, "be careful. If you're right, we're up against someone who doesn't hesitate to kill anyone who gets in his or her way."

"You, too," Rose said. "Be safe."

Impatient as she was to begin investigating Beatrice Berg's background, Rose first went to the Children's Dwelling House for Mairin's birthday party. If she didn't appear, she knew Mairin would be crushed, probably would not show it, and they'd be back where they'd started.

By the time Rose entered the ground floor meeting room in the Children's Dwelling House, the children were seated in a circle and chattering wildly, as if they'd already consumed more than enough sweets. Rose counted—only the seven children being raised by the Shakers were present. Sister Gertrude, Sister Charlotte, and Gennie were piling plates and forks at a side table. On the table they'd set a lovely cake with thick white frosting. Normally, Gertrude would have sprinkled powdered sugar on a dried apple cake, but for the children, she'd splurged. Rose suspected the frosting would be flavored with rosewater, and her mouth watered. She'd meant to skip the cake, leaving all of it for the children, but perhaps a small sliver . . .

Mairin caught sight of Rose and ran over to her. She grinned up at Rose, the copper flecks sparkling in her green eyes. "Come on," she said. "Sister Gertrude is going to let me cut the cake."

When they reached the table, Sister Charlotte drew Rose aside. "I haven't had a chance to tell you," she whispered. "None of our students from the world have come to school this week. Their families don't have telephones, so I haven't been able to contact them yet."

"It's because of the murders, I'm sure," Rose said. All the more reason to solve them quickly. The world would not be patient for long. If the murderer turned out to be someone staying at the hostel, the Shakers might lose the business, but at least the children would probably return to their school. However, if the killer turned out to be a Believer . . .

"Does Mairin understand?" Rose asked.

"Yea, I think so. I explained to her that their absence has nothing whatsoever to do with her, and I think she accepted it, though it's hard to tell sometimes. She does seem thrilled about her birthday, even so."

Gertrude was holding Mairin's hand to steady her as she clambered onto a wooden stool, so she'd be high enough to slice the cake. Mairin took the knife from Gertrude, then looked around until she saw Rose. "Come on. It's time to cut the cake," she said, a note of command in her voice.

Rose and Charlotte obeyed. With intense care, Mairin sliced thirteen more or less equal pieces. "One is for Sister Agatha," she said. To Rose, she said, "I want you to take the other extra one to Brother Wilhelm. Maybe it will cheer him up."

The children's prattle didn't diminish as they jostled one another for the best positions in line, but the three adults grew still. Gertrude wiped her eyes with the edge of her apron. *As always, Agatha is right,* Rose thought. It was a rare twelve-year-old who had such compassion. Perhaps Mairin would someday be a Shaker, and a gifted one indeed.

As Mairin, with Gertrude's help, slid each piece of cake onto a plate and handed it to the next child in line, Rose made her way to Gennie's side.

"You look more cheerful," Rose said. "I do hope it isn't murder that has raised your spirits."

Gennie chuckled. "I know it's just terrible, but I suppose the excitement does distract me from my own problems. I'm awfully sorry about Brother Linus, though. He always seemed so kind."

"Yea, he was. Are you truly not sorry about Mrs. Dunmore?"

"Oh, of course I am. No one should die like that. But she was a frightful woman. She was so bitter all the time, and she made everyone else suffer for it. I guess we know why now, don't we?" Gennie glanced toward the children, half of whom were still waiting for their plates of cake. "Rose, do you want me to try to find out more about Mrs. Dunmore?"

The eagerness in her voice sparked fear in Rose's heart. "Nay, I'm sure Grady will do that as he builds a case against Wilhelm, and he has far more resources than we do."

"Then what shall I do? I want to help."

Rose thought fast. Telling Gennie to stay out of it was tantamount to a dare. It might be best to give her an assignment—one that sounded adventurous but wasn't too risky. "After the party, I'm going to Languor to look into Mrs. Berg's background. Has she said anything to you that might be helpful?"

"Nothing that I can remember," Gennie said, with regret. "Do you want me to—"

"Nay, Gennie, please don't search Mrs. Berg's room." Rose patted Gennie's shoulder to soften the warning. "But if she says anything, pass it along. And there's one more thing you could do for me, if you would."

"Anything."

"When she's settled down from her party, ask Mairin to tell you every single place she has seen the ghost. Make her think it through night by night. We know she has followed the creature through buildings, but she's afraid we'll be angry with her, so she tells a little at a time. Convince her we won't punish her and that she's helping us by telling everything."

"Sure, but why? Do you think a *ghost* is killing people?"

"At the moment, I haven't any idea what's going on, but this so-called ghost just happened to appear right when we opened our hostel. I'm betting there's a connection. I want to know what it's doing wandering around our buildings at night."

The last child was reaching for her slice of cake, so Rose and Gennie walked back toward the party. The noise level had declined now that the children concentrated on eating. The smallest two had frosting smudged faces, which Gertrude and Charlotte were attempting to wipe off with their aprons.

"Gennie, one more thing," Rose said, before they were close enough for Mairin to hear them. "Ask Mairin if she has seen the ghost in the last few days."

"You mean you think Mrs. Dunmore might have been—"

"I have no evidence one way or another," Rose said. "I haven't heard any reports since Mrs. Dunmore's death, so I just wondered."

"But why would she do such a thing?"

"Well, think about it. You said yourself she seemed bitter, and she had good reason to hate the Shakers. This ghost has brought us nothing but problems—our village is overrun with people from the world hoping to catch sight of the ghost, so they were right on hand when the murders occurred, making everything more public and more complicated for us. Mrs. Dunmore might not have known how much trouble she would cause—surely she didn't expect her own murder—but, if she was the ghost, she has certainly exacted revenge on us." Rose didn't add that she hoped Mrs. Dunmore had indeed played at haunting the village. It would be so much simpler that way.

With Andrew off sleuthing in the community's staid black Plymouth, Rose had been forced to borrow Gennie's roadster. The car was smaller and showier than anything Rose had ever before driven, and she had to admit to a smidgen of guilty pleasure. Given the current situation, she was glad the car would make her less recognizable as a Shaker, at least while she drove down Languor streets. North Homage's relations with its neighbors were generally peaceful, even friendly, except during periods like this—when hard times combined with fear, rumor, and suspicion.

The dirt road from North Homage to the town of Languor got bumpier every spring. There was no money to maintain it or most of the other roads in rural, poverty-stricken Languor County. Rose felt the ruts even more in the smaller car. Yet the countryside exploded with vivid greens, the intense purple-pink of redbud trees, and the subtle white of dogwood flowers. In nature, there was no poverty.

Only when she reached the outskirts of Languor, the poorest section of town, did Rose see the effects of interminable Depression. Each spring, the shacks looked shabbier and their inhabitants thinner. A few curious heads swiveled toward her as she drove through the shantytown area, but she sensed no antagonism. Perhaps they were now too hungry and dispirited to care.

Rose stopped first outside the county courthouse,

which housed the Languor County Sheriff's Department. The courthouse had once been an elegant building, and would be again if its limestone façade ever got cleaned. She found a parking spot right at the bottom of the worn stone steps. Normally she would park a block or two away to enjoy the elm-tree-lined walk to the building and the chance to run into old friends from the world, but today she was in a hurry—and she was nervous about the town's reaction to the murders at North Homage.

Inside, the first-floor rotunda was dark, cool, and empty. She climbed the staircase to the second floor, where the Sheriff's Department door was wedged open. Grady's predecessor, Sheriff Brock, had kept the department as inaccessible as possible to anyone but his patrons and friends. Since Grady had become sheriff, the department had opened up and become responsive to all, earning Rose's fervent gratitude.

Still, thought Rose, *if Grady can so easily conclude that Wilhelm would kill two people, then he doesn't truly know us.*

With a surge of determination, Rose barged through the open door and nodded to Hank, who glanced up in surprise. She burst into Grady's office without knocking.

"I don't care what you think," she said. "I know Wilhelm is innocent, and I mean to prove it. I want to know all the evidence you've collected, and then I want to see Wilhelm."

Grady's startled expression turned to amusement. "Whoa, you're loaded for bear today. Sit down, Rose, please. Whether you believe me or not, I want you to be right. Okay now, you asked to know what evidence we've collected, and I'll tell you. As you predicted, we found nothing in Wilhelm's room to prove that Mina Dunmore had contacted him personally. However, in her room, we found this." He held out a small leather-bound book. Rose took it.

"As you can see," Grady said, "it's full of references to Wilhelm. The lady would have made a fine investigator. She'd uncovered just where Wilhelm was and what he was doing every year back to nine years after he'd left her and her mother."

Rose skimmed the pages, which contained precise notes along with the rantings of a vengeful woman. The first few pages, though short on details, made it clear that Wilhelm had not gone directly from hearth and home to the Society. That was a problem. It looked like he'd simply deserted his family, roamed around for a number of years as if he hadn't a care—or a responsibility—in the world, and then joined the Shakers. He did not, apparently, leave his wife and child to serve a higher purpose.

"You are welcome to read it all," Grady said, "but I can save you time by summarizing. Wilhelm took off in 1905, when little Wilhelmina was only seven years old. Wilhelm was twenty-nine—plenty old enough to assume adult responsibilities, I'd say. In 1917, he enlisted at the ripe old age of forty-one and served six months in the war. Most un-Shaker-like, I'm afraid. He was sent home, wounded and suffering from shell shock. He spent some time in a hospital in Lexington, then checked himself out and disappeared for almost a year. In the fall of 1918, he showed up at North Homage, wanting to become a Believer. Don't y'all call that a 'Winter Shaker'?"

Rose skimmed through rest of the journal. According to this account, Wilhelm did indeed look like a bread-and-butter Shaker—one who arrives in the autumn, professing conversion to the Shaker faith, then leaves in the spring after using the Society for room and board. Yet many Shakers had lived less than admirable lives before finding their way to Mother Ann. These notes, assuming they were true, did not prove Wilhelm's faith to be false. However, they might make him look suspicious to the world.

"What else have you found?"

Grady consulted some papers on his desk. "We have statements from several folks who've been spending time in North Homage recently." He glanced up at Rose, who waved her hand impatiently. She knew full well what these witnesses had been doing in her village. "Anyway, several of them claim they saw Mina Dunmore enter the Ministry House shortly after Wilhelm on Saturday afternoon." Rose was another witness, but she didn't admit it. Grady took her silence as disbelief.

"They described her perfectly—middle-aged woman, slightly stout, dressed in bright pink. That's her, right?"

Rose nodded.

"Which puts them in the same building at the same time. And yet Wilhelm denies having met her. Why would he do that if he had nothing to hide?"

"He might not have seen her in the Ministry House. Perhaps he was cleaning out his own retiring room with the door closed."

"Perhaps. To be honest, we don't have any witnesses

to a conversation between them. Still, the Ministry House isn't a large building, and according to most everyone, Mrs. Dunmore barged in just about anywhere she pleased."

Rose said nothing. It was true, of course, that Mrs. Dunmore had seemed fearless when it came to intruding upon the Shakers' lives, but Rose felt no need to add weight to Grady's suspicions.

"How did Mrs. Dunmore and Brother Linus die?" she asked.

"Ah, now that's interesting." Grady tipped his chair back on two legs, making Rose anxious for his balance. Perhaps it was the strain of the past few days, but she had to stifle a giggle. She remembered stories of some of the first rocking chairs fashioned by the Shakers—in an effort to create an efficient design, the carpenter had made the curved bottom pieces shorter than usual, and Believers had routinely rocked themselves into a back flip.

"Mina Dunmore was poisoned. There wasn't a mark on her body. She was already dead when she was stuffed into that dyeing vat, as was Linus when his killer shoved him onto that shelf. But Linus was strangled. When we moved Linus's body, we found a skein of a sort of brownish-colored yarn, like what was hanging around the room where we found Mina Dunmore. Doc Hanfield said it could have caused the bruises around Linus's neck."

"Could Dr. Hanfield determine when Linus was killed?" Rose asked.

"He said a day or two was as close as he could get. Rigor was complete, he said. We figure that Wilhelm killed them both early Sunday morning. Mina Dunmore's death seemed planned. There was nothing unusual in the port bottle Gennie took from her room, but somehow Wilhelm got her to ingest poison—maybe he met with her in the Sisters' Shop and offered her another drink. After he'd stowed her in the vat, he grabbed a skein of yarn and met with Linus in the root cellar. Or maybe he hadn't intended to kill Linus; maybe Linus surprised him."

"Then why would he take the risk of carrying Linus into the South Family Dwelling House? There were more vats handy in the dyeing room."

Grady shrugged. "Heck, there could be lots of scenarios that make sense. Maybe Wilhelm convinced Linus he'd pay hush money if Linus would meet him a little later in the root cellar."

"Wilhelm had no money of his own."

"Gennie has told me something of Shaker history," Grady said. "There have been occasions, haven't there, when elders or trustees have absconded with Society funds?"

Rose's fingers cramped, and she realized she'd been clutching the sides of her chair. Grady's speculations seemed so logical, but they made no sense when they were about Wilhelm and Linus. How could she convince him? She couldn't, not without evidence.

"Both murders would have taken some strength," Grady continued, "and Wilhelm is plenty tough, even against a younger man."

"I'll bet I could accomplish both those feats," Rose said. "The shelf we found Linus on was quite low. Someone could have lifted his lower half onto it, then his upper half. It wouldn't take excessive strength. And Mrs. Dunmore wasn't really very stout; I could surely have tipped her into the vat."

"You'd have splashed green dye all over you, wouldn't you?"

"Yea, I suppose so. But if I were wearing a dark-colored Dorothy cloak, it probably wouldn't show much once it had dried. You haven't found such a cloak, have you?"

"Nope, but it's a good idea. I'll send Hank over to look."

"What poison did the killer use?" Rose asked.

Grady's chair landed on all four legs with a clunk. "That's the part that makes me so suspicious of Wilhelm. During the autopsy, Dr. Hanfield found some tiny bits of a plant, ground fine enough so Mrs. Dunmore could have ingested them in a glass of port. When we emptied that dyeing vat, we found some rags that might have been used to clean up after someone who'd been pretty sick."

"Poor woman," Rose said.

"Yeah, it couldn't have been much fun."

"You said all this made you suspicious of Wilhelm. Why, just because of the plant?"

"Dr. Hanfield called in a chemist he knows in Lexington. His best guess was she was poisoned with monkshood. Only place I know of where that's grown is right here."

"It's all over, if you know where to look," Rose objected. "Besides, it's too early to harvest monkshood."

"Yeah, but I checked with one of the brothers in your Medicinal Herb Shop—Howard, I think it was.

Andrew was gone. Howard said they keep some dried monkshood leaves and roots in the shop, clearly labeled as poisonous."

"Anyone could have taken that."

"But only Wilhelm had a reason to. As elder, he can go where he pleases, when he pleases. Sorry, Rose, but it all adds up."

FIFTEEN

BEFORE VISITING WILHELM IN HIS CELL, ROSE WANTED to start her investigation with at least one interview. Maybe she'd have something hopeful to report to Wilhelm. She drove through the center of town and parked half a street down from Winderley House, the most respectable of Languor's boardinghouses, located just a block away from the town square.

Winderley House had once been an elegant Victorian mansion, owned by the wealthiest family in the county. One Winderley still remained, a middle-aged spinster named Ida, but the family fortune had vanished even before the onset of the Depression. Ida had never lived anywhere but in that house, and she had no intention of giving it up, so she'd turned it into a boardinghouse expressly for genteel persons in limited straits. Beatrice Berg claimed to have lived in the house for several months. Luckily, Rose knew and liked Ida, who often ordered eggs and woolen blankets from the Shakers.

"I wondered if I'd be hearing from you one of these days," Ida said, once Rose had explained the reason for her visit. "As a boarder, Beatrice was perhaps less refined than one might have hoped. Do come into the parlor. I have the kettle on for tea, and I've baked some currant scones." As a child, Ida had traveled extensively in England, and the effect had never worn off. Despite limited funds, she somehow managed to obtain a steady supply of tea, sugar, and cream to keep the illusion alive. Rose knew better than to refuse.

While Ida was in the kitchen preparing afternoon tea, Rose wandered around the formal parlor, letting the atmosphere quiet her mind. The furniture dated back to the previous century, but Ida had refinished and recovered in lighter hues to alleviate the oppressive effect of Victorian décor. A settee and two wing chairs of pale blue velvet clustered around a mahogany tea table covered with a white lace cloth. Andrew might do well to consult Ida about sprucing up the Shaker Hostel parlor—if it remained in operation long enough for him to do so.

"Here we go, Rose. Now, you just settle down and sip some tea before we speak of unpleasantness."

Ida had made chamomile tea flavored with lemons—Rose could smell the apple-lemon scent as she took the offered cup. She treated herself to a spoonful of sugar in her tea and a scone, which felt warm, as if it had just come out of the oven. After all, she told herself, with all this sleuthing, she might easily miss the evening meal. For just a few moments, as she chewed the fresh scone and sipped her sweet fruity tea, Rose felt her tight shoulders relax. With a sigh, she put her empty cup and plate on the table and tackled the "unpleasantness."

"Ida, you said you were expecting me. Was Mrs. Berg a problem for you?"

Ida poured them both another cup of tea, adding sugar to the cups. "Yes, I'm afraid she was quite difficult. Impolite to the other guests, rude to visitors, always complaining about this or that—no one liked being around her. I'd spoken with her about her behavior on many occasions, but she couldn't seem to learn. You know how difficult it is for me to send anyone away"—in fact, Rose knew Ida's spine was pure iron clothed in antique lace—"but I was just about to tell Beatrice to find other accommodations when she announced she'd be moving to the Shaker Hostel. She made it sound as if she'd been invited, even urged to come, but I knew her too well to believe that. I considered calling you, but I thought perhaps she'd be happier with you."

Rose sipped her tea and said nothing. Ida was a wonderful woman and very determined to make a success of her boardinghouse. It was more likely that she hadn't wanted the Shakers to send Beatrice back.

"Can you tell me anything about Beatrice's background? She told us only that she was widowed and had a small inheritance."

Ida took a bite of scone and chewed with deliberation. By the time she swallowed, she seemed to have come to a decision. She put down her plate and cup, folded her hands in her lap, and tilted her head at Rose. With her cap of hair, dyed black, and her tidy gray suit, she looked like a curious chickadee, peeking in the window during dancing worship.

"I had my suspicions about Mrs. Beatrice Berg," Ida said. "So I did a little investigating of my own."

A chickadee with the soul of a fox, Rose thought.

"You might recall that I have an old friend in the newspaper business," Ida said. Rose did recall. The man's name was Mr. DeBow—Ida never referred to him by his first name. Rose remembered that he had asked Ida to marry him. Ida seemed quite happy as a spinster, running her own business. Somehow she'd managed to turn the man down, yet retain his everlasting friendship.

"I asked him to find out anything he could about Beatrice." Ida stood and brushed a wrinkle out of her skirt. "If you'll excuse me a moment, I'll show you what he found."

She returned in moments, carrying a sheaf of papers that looked like newspaper articles. Without comment, she handed them to Rose. As Rose read through the pile, Ida straightened the tea things, then sat again and waited in silence.

All the articles but one came from a Lexington newspaper during a six-month period in the spring and summer of 1932. However, the top article was from a four-page weekly, published in a small town Rose had never heard of near Hazard, in southeastern Kentucky. Both the prose and the printing were amateurish. The author wrote with glowing hyperbole about a town father named Darryl Berg. Toward the end of the article, Beatrice's name was mentioned as the "little wife." Darryl had just given the town several thousand dollars, a huge amount in those early years following the stock market crash, to rebuild the town hall, which had been destroyed by fire. He'd also, on several occasions, given money to local businessmen to keep them from losing their businesses. There was to be an ice cream social in his honor, followed by a special town meeting at which folks would be invited to publicly declare their gratitude. Someone had suggested naming a street after him.

Rose put the article aside and turned to the next. Dated a year later, it reported, in the more professional tones of a big-city paper, that Darryl Berg was dead, apparently poisoned. His wife, Beatrice, had been questioned but not arrested. She claimed she'd been sick, too, so somebody was trying to kill both of them. She had no idea who the culprit might be.

All the remaining articles traced the evolution of the investigation into Mr. Berg's death. At first, a local handyman was suspected after Beatrice reported that her husband had refused to give him money to pay his gambling debts. "Darryl would give the shirt off his back for a good cause," said the grieving widow, "but he had his limits. Gambling is a sin, no doubt about it." The reporter had cleaned up Mrs. Berg's grammar, yet Rose recognized her distinctive tone.

There followed several articles, each presenting a different suspect, all suggested, in one way or another, by Mrs. Beatrice Berg. The police did not seem to find this suspicious, stating only that a wife would know best whom her husband had riled. For Rose, however, the pattern fell into place.

"So you think Beatrice Berg poisoned her husband?" Rose asked, raising her gaze to Ida.

"Well, I have no proof, and I certainly wouldn't accuse someone out of suspicion alone. But it does seem to be a reasonable conclusion. More tea?"

"Nay, thank you." Rose gathered up the articles. "May I keep these for a while? I'll be glad to return them to you."

"You may keep them forever," Ida said. "I am finished with Beatrice Berg."

"I'd better be on my way," Rose said. She folded the pile of articles and stuffed them into her apron pocket, beside the small, napkin-wrapped slice of cake Mairin had insisted she take to Wilhelm.

"Do drop in again, Rose, perhaps on a cheerier errand."

As Ida swung open the heavy front door, Rose thought to ask, "By any chance, did your newspaper friend know what poison killed Darryl Berg?"

"Mr. DeBow heard from another Lexington reporter that the police never figured out what poison was used. The poor man showed symptoms of some kind of poisoning—you know, dreadful sickness and so forth." Ida's mouth puckered with distaste. "So they were convinced he had somehow eaten something he shouldn't have. He had a great interest in gardening, Mr. DeBow said. He simply wouldn't have eaten anything poisonous, not knowingly. Mr. DeBow and I strongly suspect Mrs. Berg of murdering her husband."

Rose was inclined to agree.

"Wilhelm, you must eat." Rose sat on a small stool Grady had provided for her, since the jail cell held only a hard, narrow bed.

Wilhelm knelt on the stone floor, his head bowed, mumbling incessant prayer. He raised his head just long enough to shake it once before resuming. Uncertain what to do or say next, Rose offered a few prayers of her own, both for Wilhelm and for guidance.

"Please, Wilhelm," she said, after sending a special plea to Holy Mother Wisdom, "we must talk about this

•

situation. You are in danger. I want to help, but I need to hear anything you know that might lead me in the right direction. I'm quite sure you are not responsible for these deaths. I mean to find out who is. We can set this right; I know we can."

Wilhelm squeezed his eyes shut and continued praying. Rose couldn't watch anymore. She gazed around the cell and her spirit sank. Near the ceiling, weak light entered through one tiny north-facing window and painted stripes on the cement floor in front of Wilhelm. Mold grew in malignant clumps along the bottom edge of the wall. The chilled, fetid air sickened her. Shaker retiring rooms were always kept fresh and clean. She wasn't used to such squalor. She wished she'd brought her cloak along to pull tightly around her; she could have left it with Wilhelm.

"Wilhelm, I respect your desire to pray, but I believe the Holy Father would understand if you pause a few moments."

Wilhelm ignored her.

"All right, then, I'll tell you what I've learned so far, and what I need to know from you. If you feel guided to do so, please answer my questions. It will make my task easier and get you out of this terrible place that much sooner." She listed every piece of information she had gathered, speaking slowly so Wilhelm might interrupt at any time. He did not comment.

"And here's what I need you to tell me," Rose continued. "Did you ever speak with Mina Dunmore?"

"Nay, I did not."

She hurried to her next question, hoping to keep him talking. "I myself saw you enter the Ministry House just after Mrs. Dunmore had gone in—on last Saturday afternoon. Are you saying that you two did not run into one another?"

Wilhelm stopped praying. He stared at the floor in a silence so long that Rose wondered if he'd gone into a trance. Then he raised his eyes to her face. They were bloodshot and underlined with puffy, bluish circles.

"I saw her that day, but I did not wish to speak to her. Her demeanor struck me as unpleasant. My own daughter. I found an old chair, closed myself into my old retiring room, and wedged the chair against the door." Wilhelm's normally ruddy face, now pale from hunger, twisted in unmistakable pain. "She walked around the building calling out 'Father, Father.' I thought perhaps she knew about Mother Ann and was using the information to mock us, naming me father instead of elder or brother. I was enraged, wanted to order her out of the village. That is all. I never spoke with her, never saw her again." His voice picked up power as his personality reasserted itself, at least for a moment. "I did not kill her, nor did I kill Brother Linus. These foolish police; they have no understanding. I would sooner cut off my own arms than kill another."

"I know," Rose said. "We have had our differences, but be assured that I will never stop searching until I have discovered who *did* kill Linus and Mrs. Dunmore. Now, I beg of you, eat—and rest. You need your strength. I hope you won't have to be here long, but—"

"Nay, leave things as they are."

"What?"

"I did not kill my daughter in the physical sense. But I killed her spiritually. I am responsible for the woman she became. I deserve to stay here, in this hell on earth, until the Holy Father, in His mercy, ends my misery."

Rose took the somewhat smashed bundle of birthday cake from her apron pocket and placed it on the bed behind Wilhelm. "Mairin insisted you have this," she said. "She is concerned for you. We all are."

Wilhelm did not respond.

Rose rubbed her forehead with her thumb and index finger. Wilhelm always seemed to trigger a headache—even now, when hardship had brought them closer than she'd ever believed they could be. She would continue, of course. There was no other choice. But Wilhelm would be little help, most likely would never thank her for her efforts. She called for Grady to let her out. She was not about to let Wilhelm hang to atone for his sins. He would just have to find another way.

It was late afternoon when Rose left Wilhelm, and the Kentucky spring was at its glorious best. After being in Wilhelm's dark, damp cell, she paused outside the courthouse to breathe in the balmy air. A sweet breeze brushed her face with warmth, and color surrounded her. She was tempted to walk to the town square, maybe sit on a bench under a magnolia tree, and think through everything she'd learned. Yea, that would surely clear her mind. She turned toward the square and nearly ran into two men of the world—businessmen, by the look of their pressed suits. They stared at her for several moments. She flinched with discomfort, aware of her long loose dress, tied to her waist with a white apron; the white lawn cap covering her hair; and the plain black shoes that gave comfort rather than glamour. One of the men slowly raised his dark blue trilby and nodded a silent greeting. The other did not.

Once the men had passed by, Rose reconsidered her visit to the town square. Since Grady had taken over as sheriff, the townsfolk had shown less animosity toward the Shakers. Relations between North Homage and the world were friendlier than they'd been in years, and the Shaker businesses were thriving as best they could during such painful economic times. But when something went wrong at North Homage, the world was still quick to blame. Because the Shakers strove to establish a heaven on earth, outsiders expected them to be perfect in every way.

Rose settled herself back in Gennie's car and pulled her notes from her well-used apron pocket. She realized immediately that Beatrice Berg had lied to Andrew about her past—if Andrew was remembering correctly, and Rose trusted him to do so. Beatrice claimed to have lived her married life in a house near the center of Languor, yet it was clear from the newspaper articles about her husband that they had lived in a small town, probably near the hollow where she'd grown up. Clearly, Beatrice wanted to hide her past, but her lies were stupid. Did she assume the Shakers were so unworldly that they wouldn't know how to check the veracity of her answers? Everything Rose had uncovered so far placed Mrs. Berg firmly on the suspect list. Her lies, the possibility she had murdered her husband, the apparent use of poison in two cases—all pointed to Beatrice Berg.

Rose skimmed the rest of her notes, searching for another avenue of investigation. She paused at Horace von Oswald's name. He'd given Birdhill, Ohio, as his most recent address, but he had responded to the first advertisement for the Shaker Hostel—the one that appeared only in Kentucky papers. Granted, he could have gotten the news through friends or relatives or any number of other sources. Yet he had phoned Andrew the very first day the advertisement appeared.

Daisy Prescott—no one knew much at all about Daisy. She seemed to fade into the walls when anyone else was in the room. Rose closed her eyes and searched her mind for memories of Daisy. The images emerged in shades of gray and brown. No wonder she seemed invisible. Yet Rose recalled her stance as she walked into the dining room, how she slid onto her chair as if her body were made of silk. Her tall, slender figure and heart-shaped face promised great beauty, yet somehow the promise was never fulfilled. Why? Was she a woman who cared nothing for outer beauty and so ignored her own? Yet Gennie had mentioned that Daisy spent an entire evening reading women's magazines. Did she wish for beauty and not realize that she already possessed it?

Was Daisy Prescott playing a role? Why?

Rose moved on to Mina Dunmore. Investigating the victim might shed some light on why she died. According to Andrew's notes, Mrs. Dunmore had asked some questions about North Homage that made more sense in retrospect. She'd wanted to know who were elder and eldress, probably to make sure she'd found her father. Her question about how many buildings the village had might have been a crude attempt to assess how much money she thought she could extort from Wilhelm.

Otherwise, they had no information about Mina Dunmore except a phone number. Rose had scribbled the number too quickly, and now she couldn't make it out. A shadow blocked the light from entering the car's small side window. The number looked like a Languor exchange, but she couldn't be sure. She held the paper close to the window to catch what light she could, and the shadow moved. It was a person. Several people, in fact. A small crowd had gathered next to her car. It moved closer, and a dirt-streaked face appeared at the window. Two other faces materialized behind the first. All three were boys around fifteen or sixteen years old. What Rose could see of their clothing looked stained and tattered. Ordinarily, Rose would greet such an audience with kindness and generosity, but something told her to stay safe inside the car. She crammed her notes back in her pocket, rammed her foot on the starter button, and drove off before the crowd could move around in front of the car. She looked back and saw the boys standing in the street, watching her speed away.

SIXTEEN

BY THE TIME SHE HAD DRIVEN FROM LANGUOR BACK TO
North Homage, Rose's heart had settled back to a normal rhythm, and she was a bit ashamed of herself. The
boys who'd frightened her probably meant no harm. It
occurred to her that in Gennie's roadster she might
have seemed an unusually prosperous—and ostenta-
tious—Shaker. Perhaps the boys had only wanted food
or a little money to buy some bread. She could at least
have given them the dollar she always carried with her
in case of emergency. When everything was back to
normal, she would take some food and clothing—in
North Homage's conservative black Plymouth—and
seek out those boys.

She had about half an hour before the bell for the
evening meal, so she parked Gennie's car next to the
hostel and went directly to the Trustees' Office. She
plucked the page from her notes that listed all the hostel guests' former telephone numbers. She began with
Daisy Prescott. The operator put through her Indianapolis call, which was answered after two rings with
the precise and unmistakable tones of a butler, probably hailing from Boston. Rose was taken aback and
stumbled over her words. The butler waited politely

until she managed to ask if Miss Daisy Prescott was at home.

"I'm afraid madam must have the wrong number," he said. "This is the Carswell Houghton residence. Miss Prescott does not live here."

"Oh, I must have been misinformed," Rose said. "Perhaps Miss Prescott has been a visitor at the Houghton home at some time? I was told I could reach her at this number."

"Ah. Madam is surely referring to Mr. Houghton's secretary. She has worked here on occasion, but she does not make her home with the Houghton family. I believe she has several such appointments. She has not been here for several weeks."

"Do you know the names of any of her other employers?" Rose asked.

"No, I'm sorry, madam, I do not. Is there anything else I can do for you?"

Rose almost said, "Nay," but stopped herself just in time. "I'm sorry to have bothered you," she said.

"Not at all."

Rose jotted down the results of her call, then selected Mina Dunmore's number to try next. The call went unanswered, and Rose made a note to try again later. She might have just enough time between dinner and the evening worship service.

She skimmed her list again. Saul Halvardson she would leave to Andrew. Next came Horace von Oswald, who both repulsed and intrigued her. She connected with the operator and prepared to wait. Within seconds, the operator came back on the line.

"I'm sorry, ma'am, this number isn't in use. Are you

sure you got it right?" She repeated the number Rose had given her.

"Perhaps I was given the wrong number," Rose said. Interesting. Horace might have invented the number. Maybe he thought Birdhill, Ohio, was such a tiny dot on the map that no one would care to check it out. What he couldn't know was that Rose had a friend in Birdhill, Terrence Smythe, rector of St. James Episcopal Church. Terrence had spent a summer in North Homage several years earlier, while Rose was serving as trustee. He thought he might be called to become a Shaker, but in the end he decided the life was too restrictive for him. He and Rose still corresponded, though. It was time for a chat.

"Horace von Oswald? The name sounds familiar, but I can't place him," Terrence said, after expressing his surprised pleasure at hearing from her. Rose tried to keep her friendly greetings brief but sincere. "Funny, too—Birdhill is still quite small," Terrence continued. "I know most everybody, even the Southern Baptists. Let me ask around and call you back tomorrow. Why do you want to know about him?"

"Could I explain that tomorrow, as well?" The last thing she wanted to do was tell anyone, even a friend, that Wilhelm was sitting in jail accused of murdering two people. She doubted even Terrence could keep such a juicy story to himself. "You and I will catch up then, too," she said.

"I look forward to it," Terrence said, a hint of concern in his voice.

Just as she hung up, the bell rang for the evening meal. And rang and rang. It was the alarm bell, and it hadn't rung like that since the Water House burned down. Rose sprinted down the Trustees' Office steps and across the lawn, praying fervently, "Oh please don't let there be another killing. This really is too much."

Believers were coming from all directions and converging on the Meetinghouse lawn, where the alarm bell stood. Sister Isabel, tiny and frantic, was yanking the bell with all her strength.

"Isabel, what on earth—" Rose was panting so hard she couldn't force out another word.

"Thank heavens," Isabel said. "I didn't know where you were, and I had to find you fast. Come on." She grabbed Rose's hand and nearly jerked her arm out of her socket. "Elsa is at it again."

"Holy Father, Holy Mother Wisdom, we pray you, reveal the killer to us. Send us a sign, we beg you." Sister Elsa Pike flung out her arms and began to spin, faster and faster. Her normal walk could shake a room, but when she danced, her feet seemed to hover above the floor. She had removed her apron so her loose, brown dress billowed out around her like a chestnut. She had claimed the middle of the Shaker Hostel parlor for her performance. The hostel guests had pulled the furniture out of her way and sunk into their seats looking dazed and a little dizzy.

"Oh dear," Rose said, under her breath. She considered her choices. If she stopped Elsa and dragged her off, it would announce to the world that she believed the sister to be a charlatan. Elsa certainly had a checkered history when it came to dancing worship, but it was unfair to assume the worst of her. Was it out of the question that Mother Ann might communicate with Elsa? As eldress, Rose could not let herself believe that Mother would find Elsa forever unworthy. On the other hand, Elsa was inclined to misinterpret messages, at times believing them to come from angels when in fact they came from her own hopes and ambitions. She might easily create havoc.

Rose decided to let Elsa dance but keep a close watch on her. If the situation got dangerous, she would step in. Meanwhile, perhaps she could learn something by observing the guests' reactions. The guilty party might just give himself or herself away. She motioned Isabel to take a chair facing the hostel guests, while Rose positioned herself so she could watch the audience's faces yet step in quickly to subdue Elsa, if necessary.

Elsa's lips were moving, and Rose guessed she'd begun to speak in tongues. The hostel guests all appeared fascinated. No one betrayed any hint of guilt. Elsa stopped twirling and stood motionless, her arms straight out from her sides. Rose's immediate and less than kind thought was that she was trying to regain her balance. Elsa's arms dropped to her sides and stiffened, as did her whole body. She began to hop up and down like a wooden doll with springs for legs. Every few jumps, she lurched toward the hostel guests. After a minute or two, Rose realized she was pointing at the guests, one by one, with her entire body. Was she asking the heavens about each individual? Perhaps she was offering her body as an instrument, hoping to feel a surge of certainty when she pointed to the guilty one? She included Gennie in her ritual. Surely she couldn't believe that Gennie had anything to do with these murders, could she? Rose took a step forward, ready to call a halt, trance or no trance.

Elsa stopped of her own accord. She stood still, her eyes closed. She leaned her head one way, then another. Her face twitched, as if she might be listening to the voice of an invisible messenger. Her white indoor cap had come loose at the nape of her neck; one side hung down from her ear, revealing thin, gray hair pulled back from her face in a tight bun. Rose scanned the guests' faces and saw Horace von Oswald smile. For the first time in her memory, Rose felt protective of Elsa. She wanted to retie Elsa's cap and replace her apron. Most of all, she wanted to protect Elsa from Horace's mockery.

Elsa opened her eyes and announced, "I have heard the angels speak, and I know the truth. It was all of thee!" She swept her arm before them in a gesture that included all the guests, even Gennie. "Thy guilt is known to the Holy Father, and not even the intervention of Mother Ann can save thee from thy fate." Whenever Elsa fell into a trance, her speech lost its coarseness and became cultured, even faintly British. This was one reason Rose often hesitated to declare her trances to be false.

Horace chuckled, then threw his head back and shook with laughter. Smiles broke out among the audience. Even Gennie cracked a grin before raising her hand to cover it. Horace shook his head and took a deep breath to quiet his gasps of mirth. "I must hand it to you, Sister, that was a masterful performance," he said. "Everything looked so authentic, just like the old days. You had us all gripping the edges of our seats. My goodness." He again dissolved into laughter. He drew a handkerchief from his pants pocket to wipe beads of sweat from his forehead.

The tension in the room had broken. Guests began chatting with one another and moving about. Elsa seemed oblivious to the loss of her audience. Once again, she closed her eyes and began spinning, this time slowly. The guests turned their backs to her but kept their distance. Only Gennie kept watching Elsa, as if she knew the show wasn't over.

Elsa raised her arms above her head, reaching for the heavens, and let out a cry like a wounded wolf. The effect was instantaneous. Conversation ceased. Heads swiveled back toward her. Elsa clenched her fists and pulled them downward. Her muscles strained and her jaw clenched; she seemed to be hauling a wild and struggling creature down to earth. She lowered her fists all the way to the floor, opened them as if releasing an invisible demon. With another cry, this time more like the bark of a dog, she leaped into the air and stomped the spot where she'd placed the unseen creature. Rose felt confused—she was familiar with the stomping movement, had done it herself a few times to symbolize stomping out sin. But what was this horrible thing Elsa had dragged down to earth? What was her dancing supposed to show?

Elsa stomped over and over with such force that a vase on the fireplace mantel teetered and crashed to the floor. Elsa didn't flinch. She kept stamping the ground, even though shards of glass punctured the soles of her soft summer shoes.

"That's enough, Elsa," Rose cried, running toward her. "Stop this instant. You are hurting yourself."

Elsa ignored her. She hurtled herself at the offending but invisible creature as if she must destroy it even if it killed her. Saul Halvardson hurried over and reached toward Elsa.

"Don't touch her," Rose said. "I'm sorry, I know you mean to help, but you must leave this to me. The rest of you," she said, raising her voice, "please leave the room at once." Her only hope of controlling Elsa was to deprive her of an audience. Isabel herded the guests toward the parlor door, and everyone was more than happy to comply. Within moments, only Rose and Gennie remained. Gennie closed the door. It didn't make any difference. Elsa just kept right on stomping. Sweat rolled down the sides of her face, her indoor cap had fallen off, and blood dotted the floor.

"Stop it, now!" Rose grabbed Elsa's shoulder and bore down. Rose was strong and also tall, which gave her a small advantage. Gennie tried to help by clasping Elsa around the waist. But Elsa was in a spell that gave her unnatural power. She easily threw off Rose's grasp and continued to stamp the floor, dragging Gennie behind her like a weightless doll. Rose could think of nothing to do but wait her out. Surely she couldn't last much longer. Gennie let go of her just in time to avoid getting slammed down on top of broken glass. The two women collapsed on the settee.

While they waited, Rose pondered why Elsa might have come to the Shaker Hostel, trapped everyone in the parlor, and gone into an apparent trance. She suspected she knew the answer. Elsa was deeply committed to Elder Wilhelm—she believed as he did, followed his instructions over Rose's, and always went to him for guidance. This episode was, more than likely,

Elsa's way of saving Wilhelm. In the past, Elsa's so-called trances always seemed to benefit Elsa herself—in particular, they enhanced her importance in Wilhelm's eyes. Perhaps that explained the unusual intensity of her trance; this time it was life or death—Wilhelm's. For the same reasons, Rose had to admit that the trance might be real. Perhaps angelic visits were more likely when the recipient was acting for the welfare of another.

Elsa leaped and barked for another five minutes or so, until Rose felt ready to drop from the exhaustion of watching. Then the strength seemed to leave Elsa's legs, and she slipped to the floor. She lay still, breathing rapidly, her face flushed and damp with sweat. Rose knelt beside her.

"Elsa? Are you back among us?"

Elsa groaned and pulled her knees up against her chest. She opened eyes brimming with tears. "My feet," she whispered. "What's wrong with my feet?"

"You stepped on broken glass. Don't try to stand up. We'll get Josie over here to wrap your feet, and we'll use the hostel car to take you back to the dwelling house." Rose scanned the walls and saw no broom to sweep away the glass. Plenty of empty hooks, but no broom. "Gennie, could you find something to clean up this mess with?"

Gennie reappeared with a broom and dustpan and soon had cleared an area so Elsa could sit up.

"Elsa, try to remember—what were you told in your trance?" Rose knew she'd learn nothing if she expressed doubt about the truth of Elsa's experience. Indeed, it seemed a truer trance than Elsa had ever displayed before.

"What're you talkin' about? *What happened to my feet?*" She pulled off her shoes.

"Please, Elsa, I know your feet hurt, but try to concentrate. You were in a trance. You listened to angels, you said, who told you that all the hostel guests were responsible for the killings we've had here. Then you pulled something down from the sky and stomped on it. What did all that mean? It's important. You could help a great deal." She looked into Elsa's confused eyes. "You might help Wilhelm greatly if you could just remember."

Elsa's eyes took on a familiar cunning glint. Rose could only pray that she found the truth in her memory before she began making up stories just to help Wilhelm. "I'm mighty distracted when I have a trance," Elsa said. "I usually figure the folks around me'll remember better'n me what I said."

"Well, most of what you said was incomprehensible," Rose said.

"To ordinary ears, anyway." Elsa grasped one of her feet and turned it over to inspect the sole. She grimaced and laid it back on the floor, apparently hoping it would hurt less if she didn't see it. "Well, let me think a spell. Sometimes it comes back to me in pieces." Rose sat back on her heels and waited. "I don't rightly remember who all was talkin' to me, but it seems like there was a whole passel of angels flyin' around. They was speakin' different languages, but I could understand them." Her tone had turned haughty, but Rose chose not to suggest humility just then. Later, definitely.

"I do remember them sayin' how everyone at this hostel is heavy with guilt. 'Heavy with guilt'—that's what they said exact." Elsa nodded to herself. Her cap was long gone and strands of straight damp hair hung like gray strings around her face.

"But the angels didn't say that all of the guests had committed murder?" Rose asked.

"Nay," Elsa said, "Nay, they didn't." She dragged herself across the floor toward the settee. "My back hurts. This here's no place to have a trance, that's for sure." Rose helped her raise herself onto the settee. Gennie made a quick visit to the kitchen and found a clean rag to spread under Elsa's feet. The soft soles of her shoes had absorbed most of the pressure of the broken glass, but some pieces had cut through to her skin. Elsa lifted her feet up onto the settee and lay back against the arm. She looked about to drift off to sleep.

Rose pulled up a delicate chair with a round padded seat, embroidered in bright colors. "Elsa, do you remember, in your dance, leaning toward each hostel guest, one by one?"

"Yea, reckon I do. Seems like one of the voices told me to do that so's I could tell what was in their souls." She shook her head and noticed the hair swing in front of her face. "Where's my cap? Get me my cap, it's over there," she said. Rose bent to retrieve the cap, hoping she hadn't given Elsa time to make up a dramatic lie.

"I got a bad feeling from most of 'em. But that man, though, he was the worst—the fat one with the pasty face. Never did a lick of work in his life, I'll bet."

"You mean Horace von Oswald?"

"Don't know his name, don't want to. He's a demon in human form. Well, near human, anyways. Where's Josie? My feet are killin' me."

"Is there anything else you remember, especially anything about the individual guests?"

Elsa shrugged. "They ain't what they seem. Not a one of 'em. Exceptin' Gennie, she was okay."

"Why were you stomping the floor? What did you pull down from the heavens?"

Elsa's hazel eyes, which could burn with zealotry, looked tired and faded. "Don't remember," she said, with obvious regret. "Maybe it'll come to me in a dream."

She pulled herself up straighter against the side of the settee. "I could always try again," she said. "The angels'll understand. Maybe Mother will come next time—to help Wilhelm."

Rose said nothing. She had no intention of encouraging another display, yet . . . For the first time, she found herself believing in one of Elsa's trances. Elsa couldn't know much, if anything, about these people, yet her conclusion that none of them was what he or she seemed matched the information Rose had gathered so far. The notion that they were all somehow guilty—if not of murder, then of something else—was intriguing. On the other hand, Elsa's information, if it qualified as information, didn't get them much further. Rose still had to sort out who among the guests had killed two people, and she didn't have much time to do it.

SEVENTEEN

A CIRCLE OF LIGHT POOLED ON ROSE'S RETIRING ROOM desk, turning the pine a mellow gold. Rose felt immense gratitude that, simple as their lives were, the Shakers never shunned a useful new invention—they'd been the first in the entire county to install electricity, and it had given them many more hours to finish their work. As a consequence, they had more time for worship. Having attended the evening worship service downstairs in the large meeting room, Rose felt free to organize her jumbled thoughts on paper.

She sipped the warm, fragrant tea Sister Josie, bless her, had brought to her room. Josie had tended to Elsa's wounded feet and put her to sleep with some peppermint-valerian tea. Knowing her eldress would be at her desk for some time, trying to sort out the details of the past few days, Josie had brewed a pot of Rose's favorite rose hip and lemon balm tea to "help her think." For energy, she'd added a dollop of honey from the Society's own hives.

Rose scribbled nonstop for twenty minutes, listing each hostel guest, followed by what she knew about him or her. To be fair, she'd included Brothers Wilhelm and Linus, as well as the reputed ghost, Sarina Hastings. She sat back to read her notes. Interesting patterns jumped out at her, as did the holes in her knowledge. Growing excited, she wrote down her questions. She took out a fresh sheet of paper and began again, this time listing what she knew and what she needed to know. When she'd finished, she went back to the top of her list and considered ways to get the information she needed. There was no time like the present.

She'd begun with the first victim, Mina Dunmore. She had written : *We have evidence she was Wilhelm's daughter and might have come to the Shaker Hostel to blackmail the father who abandoned her. Was she the "ghost"; was this disguise part of a plan to punish Wilhelm and the Shakers? Who was the man in her room the night she died? Did she have previous or hidden relationships with anyone else staying at the hostel?*

Next she'd listed Horace von Oswald. *He was very eager to stay in the Shaker Hostel, he knows a bit about the Shakers, and he dislikes us. So he came here with a distinct purpose in mind—perhaps to gather information about us, or to hurt or embarrass us in some way. He has copies of stories about our "ghost," which he takes care to hide. Are these stories part of a plan? Find out—What has he done to earn a living? Does he have a previous connection with the Shakers? Or with Mrs. Dunmore?*

As an afterthought, she turned the paper sideways and added a question to Horace's segment. *Why did Elsa claim that Horace was particularly evil, compared to the others? Did the angels speak, or does Elsa know something she isn't revealing?*

Daisy Prescott was a cipher in many ways, but Rose had at least some information. *She apparently worked as a secretary. She had given Andrew a phone number for one employer—probably not her most recent— rather than for her home or a family member. Why?*

Saul Halvardson. *He lied about seeing the advertisement for our hostel in the Cleveland paper. Did he lie about his sales route, as well? He said it went north; Andrew thought he remembered it went south. What is his purpose in staying here? Did he lie about hearing a man in Mrs. Dunmore's room? Where does he get the money to be so generous?*

Beatrice Berg had several strikes against her, yet her past might have nothing to do with the current situation. *If she murdered her husband, and it looks likely that she did, then she has experience with poisoning, which ties her to Mrs. Dunmore's death and to the* Languor County Courier *story in which Sarina Hastings was reported to have been poisoned. Is this just coincidence, is it evidence, or does someone else know about Beatrice's history and is using it to cast suspicion on her? She claims to have seen the (plump) ghost in the hostel, and she told the story of the ghost looking for jewels. She had a spare master key made, which she used to search Horace's room. Is she just a snoop? A blackmailer? Did she get her story from Horace, or did he get it from her?*

About Brother Linus Eckhoff, she could write little, except that he didn't deserve to be killed. He had never shown any inclination to violate his beliefs, had seemed happy and at peace in North Homage. If he had been the man in Mrs. Dunmore's room—and she could not believe he was—then why was he killed? All Rose could write under his name was: *Did he witness Mrs. Dunmore's murder, and was he killed to silence him?* It was the only conclusion that made sense.

She shook her head sadly when she reached Wilhelm's name. He had been so irresponsible, and now it had come back to punish him. He had abandoned his wife and child, not to become a Believer, but to roam the world. He had served as a soldier, something no Believer would have done. But his real foolishness was in hiding his past. Had he been more open, he might have felt full forgiveness. If he'd been concerned for the welfare of his child, the community would have encouraged him to locate her, make sure she was cared for. Still, despite his wish to hide, he had told his elder and eldress everything. He had been able to bend his pride. Blackmail was not a real danger. For a devout Believer, a pacifist who valued all life, to murder his own child and then one of his spiritual Children—such an act would require a powerful motive, which just wasn't there, as far as Rose could see. Under Wilhelm's name, she wrote: *In the absence of new information, he cannot be the culprit.* She did, however, ask one question. *What brought Wilhelm to us?*

Finally, Rose had listed the "ghost" of Sister Sarina Hastings. Somehow she—or it—was connected with the opening of the Shaker Hostel and with its guests. Rose had been treating the ghost's appearance as a nuisance. Now she intended to discover everything about it she could. She listed several questions. *Was there really a Sarina Hastings here in North Homage? In any of the other Shaker villages? Is the "ghost" plump or pregnant—or disguised as either? Has the ghost disappeared since Mrs. Dunmore's death?*

Rose rubbed her eyes and stretched. With her thoughts neatly organized on paper, her mind had finally slowed down. She saw her direction more clearly.

Sleep sounded delicious. She forced herself to wash her face and brush her teeth; exhaustion was no excuse for slovenliness.

"Rose. Rose, please wake up. This is our chance." Gennie's urgent whisper interrupted Rose in the middle of a lovely dream about—well, now she couldn't remember anything except that it had been delightful. She groaned and tried to pull the bedclothes over her head.

"Oh, I know you're tired, but truly, Rose, this is important."

"It had better be." Rose opened her eyes a fraction of an inch. She could barely see Gennie, the room was so dark. "What time is it?"

"Three o'clock," Gennie said. "Yes, I know, it's the middle of the night." She reached over to Rose's bedside table and turned on the lamp.

Rose moaned and flipped her pillow over her head to block the light. She was awake, whether she wanted to be or not. She heard the muffled sound of a chair scraping next to her bed, followed by an exaggerated sigh.

"I'm only here," Gennie said, "because you always fuss so much about how I go out on my own and put myself in danger, but if you'd rather sleep while I investigate by myself, well, that's just fine with me."

Rose peeked out from under her pillow. "That wasn't fair."

"And this is really important."

Rose sat up, hugging her blanket around her. "All right, what's so important?"

"Remember you asked me to find out from Mairin if she'd seen the ghost in the past few days—you know,

since Mrs. Dunmore's death? Well, I had a long talk
with her, and she insisted she hadn't seen a thing. First
she said she'd stayed in her room, but then she admitted she'd looked but hadn't seen any lights or the
ghost."

"This couldn't wait until morning?"

"There's more," Gennie said. Her whisper was
breathy with excitement. "It was just last evening that I
talked with Mairin, in her room after supper. I made
her promise on her honor that if she looked out and
saw a light again, she wouldn't go outdoors without
coming to get me. Nora was stern with her and insisted
she keep her promise, so I sort of believed her."

"You told Mairin to walk alone to the hostel at night
to get you?"

"Oh. Wait, I'm getting ahead of myself. No, I decided to spend the night camped out on the third floor
of the Children's Dwelling House. Mairin's little kitten, Angel, is so darling, I stayed in her room. To be
honest, I could see more of the village from the
dwelling house than from my room in the hostel,
which faces south. I wanted to keep a closer eye on
Mairin, too."

"I gather Mairin or you saw something?" Lack of
sleep had turned Rose irritable, and she couldn't
muster the strength to pray for patience.

"Yes! Mairin kept her promise. She came knocking
on my door a little while ago. I'm afraid I'd fallen
asleep. Anyway, she told me she'd seen a light in the
Meetinghouse. She was really excited, thought maybe
her guardian angel had gone there to dance and worship. We went to another room to look out, and the

light was still on. It was upstairs—you know, in those rooms the elders and eldresses once used for . . . oh, I don't remember, offices or something."

Rose was now fully awake. She threw off her blanket and pulled a loose work dress over her nightgown. "Let's go," she said. She didn't bother to tell Gennie to stay back; it would be pointless. Gennie was already holding the door open for her. Besides, Gennie had proven she could be resourceful in a touchy situation.

"You see?" Gennie whispered. "It's sort of faint, but it's up there." Clouds hid the moon and stars, so the light in the upper Meetinghouse stood out more than it might have in a brighter night. Gennie and Rose stood at the southwest corner of the South Family Dwelling House, watching the Meetinghouse next door.

"That light is moving," Rose said. "I think it must be a flashlight. Didn't the ghost always turn on the building lights? I don't see any movement in the window, either. Maybe this is something else. Those rooms haven't been used in some time. Why would anyone be up there?"

The room went dark. "Look!" Gennie pointed to the room next to it, where the wavering light had reappeared.

"There she is! There's the ghost. Come on, over here." The shout came from a voice Gennie recognized—Betty, the ghost hunter. She and a group of seven or eight other folks from the world came trampling through the grass from the north. They hadn't seen Rose and Gennie, who jumped back out of sight behind the back of the South Family Dwelling House.

The visitors gathered on the Meetinghouse lawn and watched. At once, the window filled with light. A hooded figure with its arms raised in the air twirled across the window without stopping. Several seconds passed, and the figure twirled back the opposite direction. The room went dark.

"Well, that sure ain't worth waitin' for," Betty said.

"Maybe she went 'round to the other side," someone else said. The group took off at a run to circle the Meetinghouse.

When the last stranger had disappeared, Rose said, "Come on, we're going in. I've had all I can take from this . . . whatever it is."

They took a cautious peek around the corner and found that no one was watching the front of the Meetinghouse, so they were able to slip in one of the doors. They stood quietly in the large meeting room where for decades the North Homage Shakers had sung and danced in Sabbathday worship. Rose was glad for the absence of moonlight; they'd be less visible to outsiders who might peer in the large windows lining the walls. To their right was a cast-iron stove beside a closed door, which led to small offices and a staircase.

"Follow me," Rose whispered. "Keep as quiet as you can. If she's here, I want to surprise her." Rose knew the Meetinghouse, its creaks and corners, the way Gennie knew the Herb House. She led the way up the narrow staircase to the top floor. They paused at the landing and listened. Gennie's young ears had picked up a sound, and she gestured for Rose to follow her down the hall toward two small offices that once had been used by elders and eldresses. The rooms had been empty—and uncleaned—for years. Both doors were ajar and no light shone out.

The hallway had one small window at the end, so it got little natural light. Rose and Gennie tiptoed, sliding along the wall for guidance. They were within about twenty feet of the offices, when something large and dark swooshed through the far doorway, barely moving the door itself. Rose and Gennie flattened themselves against the wall. The whole second story needed a good cleaning and airing. The walls smelled musty; humid summers and lack of air circulation had caused some mildewing.

For a moment, the figure looked up at the ceiling, then down the hallway, apparently missing the two women in deep shadow. It moved to the hallway window and looked out. Rose wished for just a moment of moonlight to clarify the silhouette, but it remained nothing more than a dark clump. A slight ridge around the shoulders and the shape of the head told her the figure was wearing a Dorothy cloak, so it must indeed be Sarina Hastings, whoever she or he really might be. She was tall, probably agile, perhaps strong—especially if she was a he—but Rose believed she and Gennie between them could subdue her, if they could catch her off guard. Rose grasped Gennie's hand to get her attention.

If ever Rose needed proof that dirt chased away good spirits, this was it. Gennie sneezed.

Without even a split second of hesitation, the figure whirled around and ran past them, toward the staircase. She had disappeared down the stairs before Rose or Gennie had managed to budge. Gennie took off first, but Rose grabbed her arm and pulled her toward the observation room, which had a window overlooking the large meeting room below. Elders and eldresses sometimes used the room to watch over worship services. Perhaps in other villages, observers tried to catch private, forbidden looks between a brother and a sister, but Agatha and Rose had used the room to keep an eye on the visitors from the world. It provided an almost complete view of the worship space below.

"We'll never catch up," Rose said. "I want to watch as she leaves the Meetinghouse. Maybe we can learn something."

They reached the observation window just as the figure emerged from the stairwell into the meeting room. She seemed to know exactly where to go. Upstairs she had looked out a west-facing window—perhaps she had noticed that the area was free of ghost watchers. She ran to a window next to the west doorway and looked out, taking no more than two seconds. Watching her movements, Rose saw impressive speed and agility. The ghost demonstrated superb awareness of her surroundings and quick reflexes. In another two seconds, she was out the door. Rose and Gennie rushed back into the hallway and to the west window.

"There she is—over there behind the South Family Dwelling House," Gennie said.

Despite the moonless sky, Rose was able to identify the running figure. The long, dark cloak flew out behind her. It looked like she was heading toward the Shaker Hostel, but she disappeared before Rose could be sure.

"Shall we chase her?" Gennie asked. "I could go back right now to the hostel and search everywhere. I'd

bet anything one of the guests has been playacting—
that was no ghost that ran past us. A ghost wouldn't
even have to run, it could just dematerialize, right?"

"Right," Rose said. "Let's go."

They searched the hostel inside and out as best they
could without alerting the sleeping guests, but they
found no sign of anyone, substantial or otherwise.
Rose had run out of strength. "I can still get about two
hours of sleep," she said, "and I intend to do so. I'd ad-
vise you to do the same."

Before falling into bed, however, Rose pulled out
her notes and found the section on Sarina Hastings.
She had the answers to a couple of her questions. Nay,
the ghost had not disappeared after Mina Dunmore's
death. Rather, she seemed to be keeping a low profile.
And the ghost looked neither plump nor pregnant. It
was still possible that Mrs. Dunmore had masqueraded
as a ghost, the plump one several folks had reported
sighting. But the one Rose had seen tonight . . . She—
or possibly he—was quick, light-footed, and bent on
some purpose of his or her own that might have nothing to do with embarrassing North Homage.

Rose pulled her dress off and, for the first time in her
life as a covenanted Shaker, left it in a heap on the
floor. Her last conscious thought was that she really
was getting too old for all this.

EIGHTEEN

"I HAVE SUCH JUICY TIDBITS FOR YOU, ROSE. I COULDN'T wait for you to call me back." Terrence Smythe, Episcopal priest though he was, delighted in a good story. He'd never been a grim sobersides. For that reason, Rose had always enjoyed him, and Wilhelm had made his time with them as miserable as possible.

She'd been feeling tired and confused after the adventure of the previous evening, and she had settled in the new library after breakfast to think. The bright morning sunlight spilling in the dwelling house windows helped buoy her spirits. When she heard Terrence's excitement, her hopes soared.

"You've found out something about Horace von Oswald?" Rose asked. She grabbed some paper and a pen from the library desk and pulled a chair over to the phone.

"Have I ever. As it turns out, I didn't know him because he lived here during the year I spent with you all in North Homage. By the time I returned, he was gone, but the bad memories lingered." Terrence chortled, a sound Rose remembered with fondness. She could picture his hollow-cheeked face with its long, white beard, so impressive in the pulpit, where no one could see the glint of humor in his blue eyes.

"I spent breakfast and lunch yesterday at the Chickadee Diner here in town, asking all and sundry if they'd ever heard of Horace von Oswald. I got quite an earful. Seems he was quickly and universally disliked. He had a sharp tongue and a habit of asking personal questions. The folks around here are friendly, but not that friendly.

"Anyway, he wangled a job on the *Birdhill Bystander*, our local rag, as a reporter, which made the situation worse. I made a point of talking to the old editor of the *Bystander*—Fred Strauss, finally retired last year at seventy-nine, but his mind's still sharp as ever. He said Horace von Oswald was a damn good reporter—his words, not mine—but he had a chip on his shoulder a mile wide. Fred, as you know, was another damn good reporter—my words, I'm afraid—so he decided to do some digging, as only reporters can do. I didn't ask how he did it, but somehow he found out that Horace was from Massachusetts. A small town somewhere near Pittsfield, I believe."

Rose's heart picked up speed. "And near the Hancock Shaker Village?"

"Precisely."

"Was he ever a Shaker or a novitiate?"

"That isn't clear. He'd left his little Massachusetts town as a young man, just after the turn of the century, and he was in his late forties when he lived here, so the trail was pretty cold by the time Fred got interested. Fred said he called the Hancock Shakers, but they didn't recognize the name. Then he called an old newspaper buddy in Pittsfield, who said that Horace had moved to Pittsfield as a young man. He'd been handsome in those days, quite the dapper man about town.

Bright, too, with a rosy future. He got himself engaged and enrolled in Harvard. Then everything fell apart. Harvard changed its ivy-draped mind, for reasons no one ever knew—or no one would tell. His fiancée chose a public setting to throw the ring in his face. And then Horace disappeared."

Rose had been scribbling notes on her lap as fast as she could. "Do you know the girl's name? Did Fred have any suspicions about why Harvard refused him?"

"I'm sorry, Rose. That's all I could get." Rose heard genuine regret in Terrence's voice. "Shall I keep digging? I do have a sermon to prepare, but this has been great fun."

"Don't neglect your own work," Rose said. "I can take it from here. This information is helpful indeed."

"Any time."

Rose spread all her notes on the library desk and bent over them, resting her chin on her palms. Now she could answer a couple of her questions about Horace von Oswald. He'd worked as a newspaper reporter. He was from the area near the Hancock Shaker Village, which meant he almost certainly had knowledge of them, if not contact. She added another question:*Does he resent the Shakers because of something having to do with the break-up of his engagement?* She still couldn't explain his handwritten Shaker stories, but it was possible he'd been copying them from newspapers and meant to use them to hurt the Shakers somehow. Maybe he hadn't yet figured out of what use they might be. She also wondered why he hadn't given a more recent phone number. She suspected he didn't want Andrew to call and find out what he'd been doing the last couple of years.

She moved down her list to Daisy Prescott. Finding out more about her might prove almost impossible. From what Rose had observed of her, direct questioning likely wouldn't work. Daisy kept her private life a secret. She seemed to be hiding something, but what? If she wasn't exactly what she presented herself to be, then she had perfected her role. She wouldn't make a mistake, not unless Rose could surprise her, catch her off guard. To do that, Rose would need some knowledge Daisy wouldn't expect her to have. How to get it, that was the question.

Rose paced the full perimeter of the room, thinking. She wound up back at the phone. She picked up the receiver and rang the Shaker Hostel. Beatrice answered and grudgingly promised to find Gennie.

"Rose, shouldn't you still be sleeping?" Gennie sounded more cheerful and alert than she had any right to be.

"Can you come over to the library? Right now? I need your help."

Gennie arrived so fast, Rose suspected she'd galloped. In flat shoes and a comfortably loose light blue dress with two long pleats down the front of the skirt, she looked fresh and ready for anything. Rose put aside her qualms. Gennie was a grown woman; it was time to stop treating her like a half child. Besides, Rose needed the help of someone who could mix more easily with the world's people.

Rose went over all her notes with Gennie, then sat back while Gennie went through them again.

"Looks like you need some help with Daisy," Gennie said, handing the pages back to Rose. "What can I do? Shall I search her room?"

"Nay, I don't think we'll have to do that. We have a source of information about the contents of everyone's rooms, if we handle her carefully."

"Mrs. Berg!"

"Precisely. I believe we have enough information about her to throw her into a tizzy. She'll be only too glad to cast suspicion on everyone else in the hostel."

"So what do you want me to do?"

"I want you to tell Mrs. Berg to meet me here. Don't alert any of the other guests. Then stay in the hostel and try to keep anyone from slipping away to wander around the village. If someone does leave, follow him or her—at a discreet distance, of course. I don't want anyone to know I'm talking to Mrs. Berg. I'm very afraid the killer will become suspicious and run."

Gennie's small face puckered. "You know, there's something I don't understand. If one of the hostel guests is the killer, why hasn't he or she left already?"

"I can think of a couple of reasons," Rose said. "The other guests are staying, and the killer can't be the only one to leave—it would look suspicious. But I think the more important reason is that the killer still hasn't fulfilled his or her purpose. The killings might be part of the plan, or they might have become necessary because Mrs. Dunmore and Brother Linus learned too much."

"Which would put Mrs. Berg in danger."

"It would put everyone in danger."

Rose was not one to sit on her hands. While she waited for Mrs. Berg to show up, she closed the library door and made a series of brief phone calls to newspapers in and around the Lexington area. She checked her notes again and decided she needed more information about the self-effacing Daisy Prescott. She placed another call to the number Daisy had given when she'd moved into the hostel. This time she asked to speak to the lady of the house, Mrs. Carswell Houghton.

"Mrs. Houghton, I have rather a strange question to ask you," Rose said, after she'd explained who she was.

"I don't mind strange," Mrs. Houghton said, "as long as it's brief."

"Of course." This time, rather than using the name Daisy Prescott, Rose described her in detail.

"The more you say about the woman," said Mrs. Houghton, "the more she sounds like that person our son was engaged to briefly five or six years ago. The hair was different—black, as I remember, though I never thought it was her natural color. But she carried herself just as you describe. At first we thought she was a lovely girl. She was polite, well-spoken, well-dressed. She seemed to hail from the right part of society, and she certainly presented herself as well-to-do. We must be careful, you know. All sorts of unsuitable women have pursued our son simply to get their hands on our money."

Mrs. Houghton didn't seem to require any answering comments, so Rose remained silent.

"I'm afraid I've forgotten her last name—there have been so many women, you know—but I seem to remember her first name was Clarissa or something like that. When they announced their engagement, my husband, Mr. Houghton, had the girl's background investigated. Well, you can imagine our shock when we discovered she was nothing but an *actress*. She wasn't wealthy and well-born at all; she was just playing a part. We got rid of her quickly, of course. Haven't heard a word about her since then. Is that all? I'm in rather a hurry."

"Just one more question. Your butler mentioned your husband has a secretary named Daisy Prescott."

"Off and on, when he requires her services. He hasn't needed her for a while, though. I believe she keeps busy with other clients."

"How long has she worked for your husband?"

"Oh, at least ten years," Mrs. Houghton said. Impatience showed in her voice.

"What does she look like?"

"Tall, thin, lightish hair. She always wears her hair pulled back in a practical style, most appropriate for her station. Is that all?"

"That's very helpful," Rose said. "Thank you so much for your time."

Mrs. Houghton broke the connection without any further niceties.

So, thought Rose, *our Daisy might easily have known the real Daisy Prescott. Perhaps they'd become friends. But why assume her identity?*

Beatrice Berg still hadn't arrived, and Rose suspected she was dawdling out of innate distrust. Rose had just begun to rearrange a few books on the new library shelves when the telephone rang. Worrying that Mrs. Berg might be getting ready to flee, she grabbed the phone. To her delight, the operator put through a call from Brother Andrew.

"How good to hear your voice, Andrew."

"Yours, too. I have interesting news about Saul Halvardson. May I speak freely now?"

"Yea, but I might have to cut you off. I'm expecting Mrs. Berg to drop by. I have some tough questions to ask her."

"Wish I could be there. I'll be brief. Saul Halvardson lied to you about his route. What he told me originally was the truth. Perhaps he thought of us as so unworldly he had no need to lie—until he met you, that is. He told you he traveled north, all the way to Cleveland, but according to several of our customers, he had a regular southern route, down to Lexington, at least. That's as far as I've checked—or need to. Several folks told me the same story. Saul had a habit of romancing the ladies to whom he sold lingerie."

Knowing the world all too well, neither Andrew nor Rose was embarrassed or shocked by the topic of conversation. So neither wasted time on cries of disapproval.

"Finally he romanced one woman too many. He left a young woman with child. About a month ago, the woman confessed everything to her husband, including the name of the child's father. The husband gathered together a band of friends, and they took off to find Saul and punish him. There was talk of a lynching. Saul disappeared right around the time our advertisement appeared in the Lexington paper. He reappeared at our hostel, apparently thinking no one would look for him there."

"I'm a little surprised he used his own name."

"From what I've heard about Saul, he greatly exaggerates his own abilities. He was often heard to say that he'd always been blessed with 'the most wonderful luck,' so it might not occur to him to question the wisdom of any plan that might pop into his head."

Rose heard a belligerent knocking on the library door. "I must hang up now," she said.

"I understand. At the risk of sounding like Saul, good luck with Mrs. Berg. I'll see you very soon."

"Would you close the door behind you, Mrs. Berg? It seems a bit drafty today."

"I got lunch to get ready, can't set around jawin'." Beatrice Berg edged into the library and stood halfway between the door and the desk. Rose had quickly ordered a pot of spearmint tea and requested a few of the cinnamon cakes Gertrude had whipped up as a treat for the children. Mrs. Berg shifted her weight from foot to foot as if she couldn't decide between the safety of the hallway and the allure of those cinnamon cakes.

"Thank you for taking time from your busy schedule," Rose said. "This won't take long. Have some tea and a cake." She used her firmest eldress voice, so Mrs. Berg would assume she didn't really have a choice.

"That tea—spearmint, ain't it? My gram used to collect spearmint from the hills and make up tea for us chillen when we took sick. She used to put a heap of molasses in it, said it'd give us strength."

"Will sugar do?"

"Reckon it'll have to." Having made her decision not to bolt, Mrs. Berg wasted no more time. She stirred three heaping teaspoons of sugar into her tea, dipped a cinnamon cake in it, and ate crouched over the cup so the liquid would catch the crumbs. Rose watched quietly as she gobbled up the cake, then drained the cup.

"More?" Without waiting for an answer, Rose filled Mrs. Berg's cup and offered the plate of cakes.

With no apparent diminution of appetite, Mrs. Berg

began the process again. As she chewed her second bite, Rose spoke. "It has come to my attention," she said, "that you have been less than open with us about your background. Because of that, and given the recent tragedies in our hostel, I have become increasingly alarmed."

Every muscle in Beatrice Berg's body froze. Her stare held more surprise than cunning, which had been Rose's aim.

"So this is what we will do—first, I want the truth, all of it. I know already that you lied about where you lived before coming here. You never owned a home near the center of Languor. Before living in Winderley House, you lived near Hazard, Kentucky. Your husband died of poisoning, which you very probably administered. He was a violent man, but he beat you in secret, and he gave away money that should have been yours. So you killed him."

Mrs. Berg opened a mouth still full of partially chewed cinnamon cake. "That's a lie," she said. A few crumbs spilled out into the teacup. She swallowed quickly. "I never poisoned him, never."

"The evidence seems clear," Rose said. She had been trained all her life not to lie, so she chose her words carefully. In fact, the evidence did seem clear—just not conclusive.

"Who you been talkin' to? It's that woman, ain't it? I heard Brother Andrew left all of a sudden—you sent him down to check on me, didn't you? He talked to that woman, didn't he? Well, she's lyin'. She thought he'd leave me and she could get ahold of his money, but—"

"But you killed him first." Rose said it as a statement, though she knew it was a guess. If she were wrong, she could lose her temporary advantage.

Mrs. Berg's gaze jumped around the room, landed for a split second on Rose, then jerked away. But not before Rose saw the fear in her eyes. Her guess had been right. Mrs. Berg would never admit to killing her husband, but she had done so all the same.

"If I kilt him, how come I ain't in jail?" Mrs. Berg asked. "Answer me that one."

Rose poured herself a cup of tea and took several sips, to give herself time. She had driven tough bargains with businessmen from the world, stood her ground against Wilhelm, convinced recalcitrant sisters to confess, even tracked down criminals before. But she had never used her training and skills to manipulate a liar and killer into trading information for silence. It was wrong in so many ways, yet she saw no other way to get what she needed, as quickly as she needed it. Wilhelm's life hung in the balance, and perhaps other lives, as well.

"I know, too, that you had a second hostel master key made, so you could search the other guests' rooms. You made it obvious you left the original key in your apron pocket. That way, everyone would know where it was. If the others suspected their belongings had been gone through, you could say the key was there for anyone to borrow when you weren't around. It also means that if we asked you to leave at some point, you could sneak back and get into all the rooms. Were you just thinking ahead, or did you have a plan in mind? Did you think you might leave, then come back and kill Mrs. Dunmore and Brother Linus?" Rose knew she

was on shaky ground, since she had no evidence to indicate Mrs. Berg had a motive for the killings, but one
more hard push might loosen the woman's tongue.

"I never—that's a damn lie. All right, I did make a
key. But I never kilt nobody." She flapped her hand at
Rose as if to dismiss the importance of the whole discussion. "It's just a game, that's all. I'm right curious,
always have been. 'Specially when folks is uppity—
that type usually's got a heap of secrets."

"And knowing their secrets gives you power over
them." Rose was starting to feel tired and a little sick.
More than ever, she was deeply grateful to be a Believer. Believers were fully human, of course, and
therefore capable of every evil, but they were blessed
with Mother Ann's guidance and the Shaker way of
life to show them the path of goodness. Mrs. Berg was
of the world—the worst of the world. Mrs. Berg began
to eat again, more slowly, and Rose knew she hadn't
much time to press her advantage.

"I should call Sheriff O'Neal right away," Rose said.
Mrs. Berg watched her warily. "But I will not, on one
condition."

"What?" She held the cake in front of her mouth but
stopped eating.

"You must tell me everything you have discovered
about your fellow guests, every little detail."

Mrs. Berg's eyes narrowed. "Oh yeah? And you a
Shaker and all. Aren't you supposed to be against
killin' and gossip and all that?" She put down her un-
finished cake and leaned back in her chair. "You must
want that information *real* bad. Mind you, I ain't admitting nothin', but seems to me, you want this bad

enough, you should give me a whole lot more. I want to get out of here, home free, no callin' the police after me, and I want some money, too—enough to take care of myself for the rest of my life."

Rose might be new at this type of negotiation, but she wasn't naïve to the ways of the world. She'd anticipated that the wily Mrs. Berg might try to raise the stakes. "Perhaps you are right," she said. "Violating my beliefs is too high a price to pay. I'll call the sheriff right now." She stood quickly and walked to the phone. Picking up the receiver, she turned her back on Mrs. Berg and spoke clearly into the horn.

"Ring the Languor County Sheriff's Office, please."

"Wait." As Mrs. Berg stood, her chair scraped back and fell over. She laughed nervously. "Don't pay me no mind, I was just joshin' you. Can't blame me for that."

Without replacing the receiver, Rose turned to look at her.

"Hang that thing up. I'll do like you asked." She looked genuinely frightened. Rose had won, but she did not feel elated. She prayed silently and very hard for forgiveness, for guidance, and for the eventual arrest of Beatrice Berg for murdering her husband. Rose knew she had no firm proof of that murder, but she knew in her bones it had happened, or Mrs. Berg would not now be so willing to talk.

"All right," Rose said. She replaced the receiver. "Pick up your chair and sit down again, then we'll talk." She kept her voice firm, edged with impatience, to maintain control of the situation. When they were seated again, Rose said, "Begin with Horace von Oswald. What do you know about him?"

Mrs. Berg shook her head. "Not much. He's a mean

one—I wanted to know why, that's all." Her glance darted to Rose and down to the floor. Rose did not reply. "Writ a lot, he did, but he tore the pages into little bitty pieces, so's I couldn't read even a word when I cleaned up his room. Every now and again, he'd take the car away without askin' the rest of us, till Daisy took him to task. So then he'd offer rides to us, and sometimes we'd go with him."

"Where did he go?"

"Don't know. He'd drop us off where we asked, then he'd drive off to somewheres and come back for us later. Sometimes we had to wait a spell." She crunched her iron-gray curls with one hand. "Knew lots about the Shakers. All that about y'all being against killin'? I learnt it from him. He told us about how y'all don't have babes or famblies like normal folks, and you let the women be in charge just like the menfolk. He said y'all go crazy when you dance, like that Sister Elsa did, and then you see ghosts." Mrs. Berg now seemed to have forgotten her fear.

"What exactly did Mr. von Oswald say about ghosts?" Rose asked.

"Just that they was real to y'all, even if we couldn't see 'em, and maybe they was really real."

Rose was surprised. She'd expected Horace to make fun of the Shakers, the dancing worship and trances. "I heard that you told a story last Saturday evening about the ghost of a young sister who searches for some jewels."

"Yeah?" The guarded look returned to Mrs. Berg's eyes.

"Where did you get that story? Was it from Horace von Oswald?"

"No, he never told that story."

"You didn't read it in his room?"

"Told you. He tore everything up in little pieces. Waren't nothin' to read."

So Mrs. Berg hadn't found Horace's hiding place under his bed. "Then where *did* you get that story?"

"It was in a newspaper," Mrs. Berg said. She picked up her cup and began to sip with intense concentration.

Rose realized that Mrs. Berg wanted to keep as much information to herself as she could manage. More than likely, she still had hopes she could use some of it for her own benefit. "What newspaper?" Rose asked.

"Don't remember. It was just some newspaper story, what does it matter?"

"It surprises me that no one in North Homage has seen it. Since you came here from Winderley House, in Languor, how did you see a paper no one else has seen?"

Mrs. Berg's shoulders dropped. "Oh, all right. I got a cousin in Owensboro. The story showed up in the paper there, and she wrote and told me about it."

"I see. Let's go on then. What have you learned from Daisy Prescott's room?"

Mrs. Berg grinned. "She tries to hide things behind her undies in that little cupboard in the wall. If she wanted to hide things, she should've stayed somewheres else."

"What else did you find there?"

"A whole passel of stuff, like a carved wood box, prettiest thing I ever did see. Inside she had paint for her face and a spare set of spectacles and so on. Funny thing, though—those spectacles, I'd swear they was clear glass. Nothin' got fuzzy when I looked through 'em. Ain't that what's supposed to happen?"

"Perhaps her eyes need only a little correction," Rose said. Mrs. Berg was cunning; if she hadn't already figured out that Daisy Prescott was playing a role, it was best not to encourage her.

Mrs. Berg was eyeing the last cinnamon cake. "Do take it," Rose said, holding out the plate. "I had a full breakfast."

"I work mighty hard," Mrs. Berg said, grabbing the cake. "I need my victuals."

I imagine ransacking other people's belongings takes a great deal of energy, Rose thought. This time, she did not request forgiveness for an uncharitable thought.

"All right," Rose said, "Tell me what you found in Saul Halvardson's room."

"Hah, that flimflam man. He sells more than women's undies, I can tell you that." She bit into the cake and washed it down with tea. Rose felt stuffed just watching. "Did you know he's been collectin' things from all over the village? I thought that'd get your attention. Yeah, I found bits of this and that, mostly small stuff, like those funny round boxes with the lids, some small baskets, those pegs y'all screw in your walls. Keeps 'em all in a big, beat-up, old suitcase under his bed. I reckon he's gonna sell it all after he leaves. Wouldn't surprise me none if he stole that hooch he's been so free with."

"Did you see anything else in Mr. Halvardson's room?"

"Nope. He's got mighty fine clothes for a traveling salesman, but he probably stole them, too. Nothing else you'd be interested in."

"And Mrs. Dunmore?"

"I didn't kill her, didn't have no reason."

"I'm not accusing you. I want to know what you found out about her, that's all."

Mrs. Berg smoothed the wrinkles in her dress, which looked homemade, and not very skillfully. "Didn't find nothin' there," she said.

Rose watched Mrs. Berg in steady silence, a tactic that many had found unnerving—especially when they were trying to hide a lie. Mrs. Berg fiddled with the cloth tie around her waist. Rose waited. She had a strong hunch that, once she pierced Mrs. Berg's resistance, she wouldn't find out anything new; Mrs. Berg had probably seen Mina's journal with her notes about Wilhelm. However, she wanted to make it clear, without revealing that the police had the journal, that the opportunity for blackmailing Wilhelm or the Shakers was long gone.

Under Rose's scrutiny, Mrs. Berg caved in. "Well, now I think of it," she said, "I remember seeing some old notebook lyin' around Mrs. Dunmore's room. It just had notes in it. I guess they was mostly about that elder of yours, that Brother Wilhelm. Seems like she knew him."

"We know all about that," Rose said. She didn't elaborate. Mrs. Berg looked crestfallen. Apparently she couldn't read all that well, or she would have gleaned a great deal more from Mina's journal. "Anything else?"

Beatrice shrugged. "That's it, I'll swear to it on a stack of Bibles. You gonna keep your word? You won't go callin' the sheriff on me?"

"I always try to keep my word." With any luck, justice would tap Beatrice Berg on the shoulder without Rose's direct help—though she might have to find a way to nudge it along.

NINETEEN

"WHAT NEXT?" GENNIE'S CHEEKS WERE PINK WITH excitement. Unable to contain her energy, she'd sped ahead of Rose as they hiked through an overgrown, secluded area just west of the Trustees' Office. A century earlier, the North Homage Shakers had designated the spot their holy hill, which they had named the Empyrean Mount. The mount itself was a grass and weed-covered hill, the only part of the area that enjoyed any sunshine. Since Agatha's health had become so delicate, Rose had taken to coming here to think. Once, long ago, Believers had celebrated feast days on the holy hill. They had fasted, marched, and danced. From visiting angels, they had received celestial food and gifts, which they enjoyed using mimed movements. When she sat on the hill, Rose always felt the presence of those long-dead Shakers, guiding her as she thought through difficult decisions or problems.

The little-used path was thick with brambles, which caught at their ankles. Gennie didn't seem to mind when a thorn pricked a hole in her stocking. She found a sunny spot on the hill, plunked down on the grass, and waited for Rose to catch up.

"Well, what do we do next?" she repeated impatiently.

"Let me catch my breath, for heaven's sake." Arranging her long skirt under her legs, Rose settled next to Gennie. "It's clear to me that I've been doing too much traveling and sleuthing, and too little good physical labor."

"Oh, you're strong as a horse," Gennie said. "Come on, show me your notes again."

Rose extracted her growing pile of notes from her apron pocket and handed them over. "As you can see, we're finding answers to my questions, yet I *still* have no sense of who the killer is. The hostel guests all seem to have secrets, but I can't link them to the murders. I have yet to find prior connections between Mrs. Dunmore and any of these people—except poor Wilhelm, of course."

"So maybe that isn't it," Gennie said. "Maybe they are all up to something, but those somethings aren't related. Maybe Mrs. Dunmore found out about one of them and that's why she was killed."

"I agree that's the most logical solution, but . . ."

"You do have suspicions, don't you?" Gennie asked. "Just tell me, we can talk it out."

"All right." Rose readjusted her legs to release a kink in one knee. "Let's start with Horace von Oswald."

"Goody, I knew he was bad."

"I think Horace is actually deeply bitter. I called several Kentucky newspapers and found that the story Mrs. Berg told you all appeared in two of the papers just two days after we placed our first advertisement for the Shaker Hostel. We know that Horace has a handwritten copy of that story, and we know he has a stack of papers that might be many more stories about our so-called ghost. I searched our records, including the Covenant, and I found no sister named Sarina Hastings. I found several Brother Joshuas, but none during the period described in the articles."

"So they're made up," Gennie said.

"They might be real, I suppose, but actually from another village. That would be difficult to find out, since so many villages have closed in the past century. However, Eldress Fannie at Hancock Village—and Horace lived in Pittsfield, remember—assured me no such brother and sister lived there at that time, either. She found no Sister Sarina Hastings at all in their records."

"You think Horace is responsible for the articles?"

"It looks so to me. That would explain his regular trips to Languor and his desire to avoid being in Languor with the other hostel guests for a period of time— he might be wiring stories to various newspapers.

"His life fell apart while he lived in Pittsfield. My suspicion is it had something to do with the Hancock Shakers, and he blames all Shakers for his losses. When we opened our hostel, he saw his chance to publicly embarrass a Shaker village, so he began to plant these stories, knowing they would bring the world pressing in on us. He came to stay because he wanted to watch and, I suspect, to foment disaster."

Gennie gave a little bounce of excitement. "So Mina must have found him out somehow. He was always goading her, probably trying to get her to leave because she was suspicious of him. Finally he must have killed her to keep his plan quiet."

Rose shook her head slowly. "Nay, Gennie, that isn't

enough. If Mina had figured out his plan, he had only to leave and try again somewhere else. There was no reason to kill her."

Gennie's shoulders slumped. "Grady is always talking about motive," she said. "You're saying that his motive wasn't strong enough?"

"Exactly."

"Well, I'm not ready to give up on him," Gennie said. "I know! I'll call Mrs. Alexander in Pittsfield, remember her? I stayed in her boardinghouse when we visited Hancock last winter. She was a wonderful gossip. If anyone will know what happened to Horace in Pittsfield, she will. I just have to call her before she starts pouring the sherry."

"Good idea. Perhaps his motive is more serious than I've imagined." Rose took her notes from Gennie's hand and shuffled through them until she found Beatrice Berg's name. "I strongly suspect Mrs. Berg had a hand in her husband's death," she said, "or she wouldn't have given me all that information she discovered from searching the hostel rooms. But I have no real proof. I promised to say nothing to Grady about my suspicions, but if it turns out that she is the culprit . . ." Rose sighed.

"Well, you didn't promise to say nothing to *me*, and I haven't promised anything at all. Don't worry, if we find evidence she's a killer, I'll take it straight to Grady."

Rose still felt uncomfortable with her ploy to extract information from Mrs. Berg, but allowing Wilhelm to be wrongfully convicted of murder would have been unbearable. "Mrs. Berg, I suspect, came to the hostel because she had little money and wanted a safe, out-of-the-way place to stay. She has acted like a blackmailer, yet there's no evidence she has used any of the information she's collected. She even knew that Mina had tracked down Wilhelm, but she kept it to herself. My guess is she was simply protecting herself. She must feel enormous guilt—"

"I think you give her too much credit," Gennie said, laughing.

"Well, then, she must feel threatened, always in danger of being discovered. Finding out about her fellow guests might be a way to protect herself. If one of them is there to follow her, to find out about her, she needs to know so she can get away."

"Which means none of the guests is a detective or policeman or anything like that," Gennie said. "Otherwise, Mrs. Berg would be long gone."

"Good point." Rose checked her notes again. "It concerns me that poison keeps popping up. If Mrs. Berg killed her husband, she did so with poison. And Mrs. Dunmore was poisoned."

"Oh goodness, I just realized." Gennie put her fingers over her mouth. "We've been eating Mrs. Berg's cooking!"

"No one else has complained of being ill. It's unlikely she would poison anyone now, knowing she has come to my attention. To be on the safe side, I won't eat at the hostel again. I'm the only one she might try to get rid of."

Gennie pulled up her knees and curled her arms around them. Rose couldn't help smiling. Gennie had learned to dress and hold herself well in the world, but that didn't mean she wasn't still the same eager, adventuresome girl who'd brightened all their lives.

"If I can't have Horace as the killer," Gennie said, "my second choice is Mrs. Berg. Remember she was the only one packed and ready to leave after the murders. I'll bet she only stayed 'cause it would look suspicious if she tried to leave. If Mrs. Dunmore found out she'd killed her husband, that would sure be enough of a motive, wouldn't it?"

"Definitely," Rose said. "But if I couldn't find out for certain, how would Mrs. Dunmore?"

"It might have been enough just to *say* she knew for sure, even if she didn't."

"I don't know," Rose said. "After all, Mrs. Dunmore was completely focused on one mission—to locate and probably punish the father who abandoned her. Did you ever see her show much interest in anyone else?"

Gennie rested her chin on her knees. "No, I suppose not. I think she was a little sweet on Saul Halvardson, from the way she looked whenever he flirted with Daisy, but she never asked questions about anyone or even really held a conversation with anyone." Gennie sighed with her whole body. "Okay, who's next?"

"Let's tackle Daisy Prescott."

"She's a tough one," Gennie said. "She likes fashion magazines, although her clothes aren't terribly smart. She just seems like a spinster typist or something."

"Yet she never talks about herself or her life, does she?"

Gennie's spine straightened. "You're right. Never. And I've noticed that she's really graceful when she walks, like a dancer."

"I'd noticed that, too. Adding together our observations and Mrs. Berg's, I suspected she is playing the part of spinster typist, or something along those lines. I didn't have a chance to add it to my notes, but I made a second call to the number Daisy listed as her last residence. This time I spoke with Mrs. Houghton. When I described the Daisy we know, without mentioning her name, Mrs. Houghton said she sounded like a woman her son had once been engaged to. She said the woman had been unsuitable for her son because she was an actress."

Gennie giggled. "I'm lucky Grady's people aren't quite so uppity."

Rose recounted Mrs. Houghton's description of Clarissa.

"Sounds like our Daisy," Gennie said. "Seems odd she'd be staying here. If she's looking for another rich man, she isn't likely to find him among the Shakers."

"Nay, but it might seem a good and inexpensive place to practice a new role—or wipe out the last one. At any rate, even if Mrs. Dunmore had recognized her from somewhere, perhaps the stage, that doesn't seem enough motive for Daisy to kill her. I do wonder, though, if Miss Daisy Prescott might be our ghost."

Gennie drew in her breath in a gasp of delight. "Oh, do you think so? Is it more playacting, do you suppose? Maybe she got the idea from one of the articles and thought it would be fun to see if she could be convincing."

"That's possible, but we don't yet know enough about her. I intend to find out more." Rose glanced down at the notes in her lap. "The only one left is Saul

Halvardson." She relayed what Andrew had learned about Saul.

Gennie listened with avid interest. "So maybe he *was* the man in Mrs. Dunmore's room."

"Quite possibly. It would be in character. And you said she seemed taken with him. But it doesn't seem in character for him to kill her. Even if she threatened to reveal his apparent stealing or his past, all he had to do was pack up and run."

"Motive again," Gennie said, sounding tired.

"Yea, motive again. We still need to know more. Let me know what you learn from Mrs. Alexander."

"I do have one more piece of information for you," Gennie said. "You asked me to find out from Mairin where she has seen the ghost. Mairin claims she's been staying indoors more now, but she admits to looking out the windows when she's checking on her kitten. She said she's seen the ghost in every building except three—the Laundry, the Infirmary, and the Herb House."

"Good, that might help," Rose said.

Gennie stood and brushed off her skirt. "How is Wilhelm doing?"

"He won't speak to me. When I phoned this morning, he sent the message through Grady that I must stop any attempts to free him. He said it is up to the Holy Father to determine his fate. I mustn't interfere."

Gennie merely nodded.

"I feel the answer is very close," Rose said. "I will pray for it to come in time."

"Ida? It's Rose again, calling from North Homage. I'm sorry to bother you again so soon, but I wondered if I could ask a favor of you?" Rose glanced around the hallway nervously. She'd decided to make her call from the second floor hallway of the now-deserted Ministry House because she wanted absolute privacy, but she thought she'd heard a noise.

"Rose, dear, if I can help in any way, I will—except, of course, I'm afraid I simply couldn't allow Beatrice Berg back in Winderley House. I'm sure you understand."

"And I would never ask you to do so," Rose said. "My request has nothing to do with Mrs. Berg."

"Then ask away."

"I'm hoping this won't put you in an awkward position . . . I was wondering if you might ask your newspaper friend, Mr. DeBow, to investigate another name for me?"

"Oh, my dear, that's no problem at all. Nothing awkward about it."

Rose felt free to smile, since no one would see her amusement. Ida Winderley took her ardent friend's devotion for granted and never felt beholden to him, no matter what he did for her. "It may be rather complicated. I have only a first name and a physical description, and both might have altered many times over. However, I do know that five or six years ago she was an actress on the stage." She gave Ida every detail she could think of about Daisy Prescott.

"This should be quite fun for Mr. DeBow. Since he retired, he hasn't known what to do with himself, poor dear. Now, don't you worry about a thing. I've written everything down, and I will call Mr. DeBow just as soon as we finish speaking. How are you faring?"

The question, Rose knew, was Ida's delicate way of asking about the murders in North Homage. "When this is all over, Ida, I will make a special visit to Winderley House and tell you everything. I promise."

"Lovely. We'll have high tea. Do take care—I'm counting on that visit."

Rose replaced the receiver and stood very still. She was sure she'd heard another noise, a clattering somewhere downstairs. She told herself to relax. With Wilhelm in jail, one of the brothers was probably gathering up the last of the items to be moved to the Center Family Dwelling House. They'd almost finished the downstairs before the murders, but the upstairs had hardly been touched yet. Since she was here, she might as well pick up a few things herself. She'd left some small items in her old retiring room and in the workroom she'd set up and barely had a chance to use.

She opened the workroom door and gazed around in confusion. The room had been stripped down to the furniture. She'd left several projects—mending and so forth—lying around, intending to finish them before packing up the tools. They were gone. Her sewing basket had disappeared, along with all her needles, pins, her shears, and the lovely calico pincushion old Brother Hugo had made for her shortly before his death.

She hurried across the hall to her old retiring room. It, too, was empty, except for the bed and the desk. She'd been studying North Homage's past and had left several old journals on her desk. They were gone. She'd taken her own journals and her mattress and bedclothes with her to her new retiring room, but nothing else. Her favorite blanket, the one in which she wrapped herself when she spent the end of a winter evening reading in her rocker, had disappeared—along with the rocker itself.

No Shaker brother had been asked to pack up her rooms. She'd left strict instructions that she wanted to do that herself. And no brother would have taken it upon himself to disobey her orders. Besides, the brothers were far too busy with spring planting to worry about whether the Ministry House had been emptied yet. Crops took precedence.

Two names popped into her mind—Horace von Oswald and Saul Halvardson. She hadn't been too concerned when Mrs. Berg had mentioned finding a valise full of small Shaker items under Saul's bed. One valise wouldn't hold enough to hurt the village financially. She'd intended to make sure it stopped, but she wasn't worried. But what if he was carting off everything he could get his hands on, intending to sell it all for his own profit? Collectors had begun to discover and appreciate Shaker designs and would probably pay well for good examples. Her cheeks burned with fury at the thought that Saul Halvardson might be taking advantage of them in such a way.

And then Horace von Oswald—the theft of journals looked more like his handiwork. She wouldn't put it past him to be combing the journals written by decades of North Homage Shakers for stories he could embellish to humiliate them. Were both Saul and Horace involved in this outrage? She had a mind to burst into their rooms and search them, inch by inch. As she paced back and forth across her now-empty retiring room, she fumed and refused to pray for calmness.

Eventually calm arrived, unbidden. A thought

stopped her in mid-pace. If her thinking had any validity at all, it was the first link she had even suspected between two of the hostel guests. She could be wrong, of course. Saul might just be stealing everything he could pick up and carry, then hiding it somewhere until he could take it away, perhaps to another room in Languor. But what if he was stealing the journals because he knew Horace wanted them? And what if Horace was helping him transport the items off Shaker property? Horace might view it as one more way to hurt the Shakers.

Rose walked outdoors and circled the Ministry House. Hiding a load of furniture called for a safe, deserted area. The village had its share of abandoned buildings, but it was unlikely anyone could drive up to any of them, load up with furniture, and drive away, all without being seen from someone's window. So the pickup place must be closer to the edge of the village. Not in the fields, though—too open, too many brothers working in them. The orchard? The southeast end of the orchard hadn't been tended in years. A car probably couldn't make it, slogging through the fields, but a wagon could. With so many ghost hunters roaming the village, one more wagon wouldn't attract attention. Saul and his confederate could fill it with Shaker goods, cover everything with a blanket, and drive right through the middle of the village, with no one the wiser.

She headed back to the central road and walked west. Saul, if it was Saul, also might have selected a pickup spot somewhere on the west edge of the village. That's where the hostel was located, and it was the quickest way out of the village. She passed the aban-

doned South Family Dwelling House. Nay, surely that
wouldn't work. So many people had been in and out of
that building lately, what with Mairin's nighttime wan-
derings and finding Linus's body, that it was an unsafe
place to hide anything. She kept walking until she had
passed the Shaker Hostel, right on the west edge of the
village and close to the road leading to Languor. On
her left was only open countryside, to her right the
Empyrean Mount. She'd surely have found anything
hidden in the east end of the holy hill; besides, neither
a car nor a wagon could get in there. The west side
would work, though. North of the holy hill was the old
cemetery, unused for decades, with a drop-off on the
west edge. North of the cemetery were woods, dotted
with shade-loving plants Brother Andrew grew for medicinal herb experiments. Andrew and his helpers
checked the area regularly.

"Rose! I've been looking all over for you." Gennie
came running up behind her, her curls flying around
her face. "I made the phone call—you know, to Mrs.
Alexander in Pittsfield," Gennie said, as they fell into
step together. "I think she'd already started nipping at
the sherry, but all it did was loosen her tongue. She
gave me an earful about Horace von Oswald." She
lowered her voice as they passed in front of the hostel.

"Let's go back to the dwelling house," Rose said.

Once they'd closed themselves into the library, Gennie said, "What your friend found out about Horace
was true. Mrs. Alexander told a similar story without
any prompting from me. Then she told me more.
Sounds like Horace was way too big for his britches.
He wanted to be a newspaper reporter, but not just any

reporter. He was sure he was going to be the best news-
paperman in the country. Mrs. Alexander said she'd
once heard him lay out his whole life—first he'd write
for the *New York Times*, reporting on all the important
stuff, like politics and war. Then he'd take all his experiences and write books and become very famous.
Folks got scared to be around him, 'cause he always
scribbled in a notebook whenever they said something.
Mrs. Alexander said he mostly seemed interested in
digging out peoples' secrets, which is funny coming
from her."

"What happened with Harvard, did she know?"

"Well, she'd heard rumors. He bragged that he was
going to Harvard to study politics and literature, that
they'd begged him to come, gave him money and
everything. That's when he got engaged to the daughter of Pittsfield's most prominent businessman. They
were going to marry right away, so she could go with
him to Boston. It was supposed to be a huge, expensive
wedding, and everybody was talking about it."

Gennie's expression sobered briefly, and Rose wondered if she were thinking about her own wedding,
whether it would ever take place. "Anyway, as we already knew, his fiancée threw the ring in his face. According to Mrs. Alexander's story, Horace was tricking
everyone. It was true that he'd been admitted to Harvard, but they hadn't pursued him. He'd been applying
for years, that's why he'd been hanging around Pittsfield working on the newspaper. When he finally got
accepted, he realized he didn't have the money to go,
so he came up with a plan to get it. He courted a rich
man's daughter and lied about his own success to get

himself accepted by the family. His idea was that once he'd married the daughter, her father would foot the bill for Harvard just to save face."

"Why didn't it work?"

"Harvard wanted a chunk of money ahead of time, before the wedding had taken place. Horace put them off as long as he could, but Harvard finally told him it was too late and they'd given his spot to someone else. His fiancée found the letter in his room. She ran out, he followed her into the street, and she threw the ring in his face. And that was that."

Rose sat in silence, digesting the information. It certainly provided a reason for Horace's bitterness—he wasn't the sort to blame himself for his fate—yet the story wasn't complete enough to help her in the current situation.

"Terrence and the *Birdhill Bystander* editor weren't able to find out most of these details. How did Mrs. Alexander know?"

Gennie smirked. "Because Horace's room was in her boardinghouse. She watched the whole thing. She'd been dying to tell the story for years, but Horace's almost father-in-law was rich and powerful and had no intention of allowing everyone to know he'd been duped. He swore her to secrecy, and she was scared of what he could do to her if she broke her oath. She was afraid he'd buy up her boardinghouse and kick her out on the streets. So even under the influence of sherry, her fear kept her quiet."

"This is wonderful work, Gennie. Thank you so much. But there's still one problem with the story."

"What?"

"It seems to have nothing to do with the Shakers."

Gennie clasped her hands together and held them against her lips. At first, Rose thought she was praying, but then she saw the corners of Gennie's mouth twitch, as if she were trying mightily to contain her excitement.

"You saved the best for last, didn't you?"

Gennie nodded. "It seems the future father-in-law was good friends with the Hancock Shakers. He was a shrewd businessman, and he respected how well the Shakers conducted their business affairs. He was always telling people how honest the Shakers were, how their products were such good quality. His daughter had spent many happy days visiting the Hancock sisters, while her father chatted and did business with the trustees."

"Let me guess," Rose said. "The daughter became a sister."

"Yes! And her parents made it known that they had changed their will, leaving their entire fortune and their land not to their daughter, but to the Hancock Shakers. Mrs. Alexander said Horace was furious and left town soon after."

"Are the parents still alive?"

"Yes, but the daughter died of pneumonia after about five years with the Shakers. Once she was gone, her father talked about changing his will again, but Mrs. Alexander doesn't know if he ever did so. She said he's still pretty powerful in town, so she made me swear I wouldn't tell her story to anyone in Pittsfield. She doesn't want me calling the father. She's really scared of him."

"But you believe her story is true?"

"I do." Gennie slid to the edge of her chair and

leaned forward. "And there's one more truly wonderful part to the story. The daughter's name was Sarah Haskins."

"Sarah Haskins. Sarina Hastings." Rose relaxed against the slats of her chair. So she'd been right about Horace. After his disgrace in Pittsfield, he must have gotten as far away as possible, taking a series of jobs on small newspapers. He surely felt humiliated, and it was his character to blame others for his failures. He believed the Hancock Shakers would get the money he felt was his. It explained so much about him and provided several pieces to the puzzle. Without doubt Horace had planted the Sarina Hastings articles in newspapers, starting just after the announcement that North Homage was opening a hostel. Had he gone so far as to appear as the ghost? He was plump—was he the "pregnant" ghost several witnesses had reported?

However, several issues remained unresolved. Rose was quite sure that the ghost she and Gennie had seen in the Meetinghouse was not Horace von Oswald. It had been tall, quick, and definitely not pregnant. It could have been Saul or Daisy—or an outsider brought in by Horace to enhance the credibility of his ghost stories. And the most pressing question still begged an answer—granted Horace was a mean, bitter, vengeful man, but why would he kill Mina Dunmore and Brother Linus?

TWENTY

LIGHT RAIN DRIZZLED DOWN HER RETIRING ROOM WIN-
dow, but Rose barely noticed it. She rocked unevenly,
pausing now and then as she followed a trail of
thought, and pushing hard again when the trail led
nowhere. The knock on her door distracted her, for
which she was grateful.

Petite Sister Lydia, one of the Kitchen sisters, poked
her head inside. "Sorry to bother you, Rose, but there's
a telephone call for you. Someone named Ida? It
sounded important."

Rose jumped up from her chair and left it rocking on
its own. The phone hung on the hallway wall, but Rose
was too impatient to find a more private setting. Lydia
seemed to be the only sister about. Lydia would spread
no rumors.

"Ida?"

"Oh good, you're there." Ida's genteel voice was
faintly tinged with a Kentucky twang, a lapse that Rose
suspected was due to excitement. "I've just had a most
intriguing chat with my friend Mr. DeBow, and I was
sure you'd want to know immediately."

"Bless you, Ida."

"Thank you, my dear. It is Mr. DeBow who deserves

the blessing. I must say, he threw himself into his task with only the little information you were able to provide, and I believe you will be delighted by the results. Now, you asked about an actress named Daisy Prescott—or perhaps Clarissa—who might have been on the stage five or six years ago. Mr. DeBow, as it happens, once followed the theater for his newspaper work, though he had retired by the time you asked about. He had never heard of a Daisy Prescott. He contacted all his old friends in the theater—those who were still living, of course—and asked about her. No one remembered her. However, when he mentioned a Clarissa and described what she might have looked like in those days, the memories emerged."

"Wonderful! Could you hang on a moment, Ida? I forgot paper and pen." She returned with a chair, as well.

"As I said, the name Clarissa rang a number of bells," Ida continued. "Several people remembered a Clarissa Carruthers, who was unusually tall, quite slender and graceful, and an extraordinary actress. She performed on the stage and is still known in theater circles for her brilliant performance as Desdemona. It was widely thought she would eventually go to Hollywood and become famous."

"But she didn't?"

"Here is where the story becomes fascinating. Some of Mr. DeBow's friends assumed she had gone to Hollywood, but they couldn't recall a single film in which she'd appeared, not even with a bit part. With her talent and beauty, they thought she'd have no difficulty. Two actresses who used to be friends with Mr. DeBow"—

Rose detected a slight emphasis on the phrase "used to be"—"said that they had heard Miss Carruthers had given up acting to marry a wealthy man, but they never heard more about it. It seems that Miss Clarissa Carruthers simply vanished. Not one person remembers so much as a glimpse of her waiting for a bus. I find that extraordinarily interesting, don't you?"

"I do indeed," Rose said. "Did Mr. DeBow hear any other stories or rumors about her—perhaps about other activities she might have been involved in while she was still on the stage?"

"Not really. Several of his friends confided that they'd never found her to be friendly or easy to get to know. She kept to herself. By all accounts, though, she was a stunning and quite serious actress. Very ambitious, too. Everyone Mr. DeBow spoke with was surprised to realize that she must have given up acting altogether. They'd thought she would die first."

Rose replaced the receiver and sat in the hall for several minutes. *Everyone thought she would die before giving up acting.* Perhaps, in a way, she had.

Rose's head was swimming with questions to which she almost had the answers. Patience had never been her greatest strength, which made it tough to wait several hours for night to fall. She had plans for the dark. Even more frustrating, a light rain had settled in. Rain might force her to wait another day to implement her scheme. Meanwhile, it was time for the evening meal, which Rose had no intention of missing. She would need her strength.

She gathered with the other sisters in a small room

just outside the dining room. Putting aside her own agitation, she led the sisters in prayer, then single-file into the large dining room. The brethren entered from another door, also in silence and a much shorter line. The Believers stood at their places, the sisters across the room from the brothers, and prayed silently before seating themselves. The only sound was the scraping of chairs. In recent years, long benches had been replaced by rows of chairs, in deference to aging Shaker backs. The change had created more noise, but it was necessary.

Out of habit, Rose glanced around the two tables where the sisters sat. As eldress, she liked to keep an eye on her charges. At meals she could often tell if a sister was ill or unhappy, or if some squabble had caused rifts in the community. She sensed a general nervousness among the sisters—sideways glances and grim expressions, especially among a small group of younger sisters. All too many times, it was Sister Elsa who caused such discontent. This time, however, she couldn't tell if Elsa was responsible. Her chair was empty.

Shaker meals tended to be quick, so Believers could return to work. No one seemed inclined to dawdle this evening, despite Gertrude's wonderful fare. The spring vegetable soup, with its delicate lemony fragrance, disappeared in no more than two minutes, as did the ham and potato hash. Gertrude surprised them with lemon pie, Rose's very favorite dessert, tart and sweet at the same time. She almost forgot to smile her thanks to the Kitchen Deaconess, who watched her expectantly.

When the meal ended, Rose led the sisters out of the

dining room and pulled aside the two sisters, Lottie and Frieda, who had looked the most uncomfortable during the meal. She waited for the other Believers to scatter toward their evening chores before asking, "All right, what do you two know about Sister Elsa's absence from evening meal? Where is she?"

Lottie and Frieda gazed at her in awe. They gave each other another of those irritating sideways glances.

"I do not hold you accountable for Elsa's behavior," Rose said, "but I have many tasks still to do before the evening worship, and I have very little patience."

"Of course," Lottie said. She cleared her throat. "Sister Gretchen asked if Frieda and I could help her a spell in the Laundry after the noon meal, and Sister Sarah said we could leave our sewing, so we went. When we got there, we found out that Sister Elsa had left without permission, soon after the noon meal."

"Perhaps her feet were hurting," Rose said, remembering Elsa's dancing in the Shaker Hostel.

"Sister Gretchen didn't think so," Lottie said. "Sister Josie said she wasn't hurt that badly, and Gretchen said she was walking fine." Lottie clearly had little sympathy with Elsa's injuries.

"Why didn't Gretchen tell me Elsa had left her rotation?"

"She said you had your hands full with these awful killings. Frieda and I got the work done fast, and it had started to drizzle. Gretchen said we should go out and look for Elsa, in case she'd fallen ill. Mind you, Gretchen didn't think she'd been the least bit ill. She had called Josie at the Infirmary, and Josie said Elsa hadn't been there. So we all figured Elsa was, well, acting like she does sometimes." Again, Lottie and Frieda exchanged glances, this time accompanied by smirks.

"And did you find her?"

"Yea, we did. We called all the other buildings and finally Brother Archibald said he'd been coming in from the north herb fields, and he saw Elsa heading right toward the old cemetery. It was raining by then, and we thought she'd probably gone indoors, but we decided we'd better check anyway."

"Wise choice," Rose said.

Hearing the impatience in Rose's voice, Lottie became tongue-tied. Frieda took over. She had a sweet, soft voice and a gentle manner; it was tougher to be openly irritated when Frieda spoke.

"We found her in the old cemetery," Frieda said. "She was kneeling before Brother Ezekiel's marker, praying really hard."

"She must have been soaked. She really could become ill. I assume you put her to bed?"

Frieda nibbled her lower lip. "We tried, truly we did. But she pushed us away and shouted at us to leave. She said we would be responsible for Wilhelm's death if we interrupted her prayers."

"So we had to leave her there," Lottie added. "I mean, the bell was ringing for the evening meal, and we . . . We're truly sorry. We should have tried harder."

Rose said nothing. They should indeed have tried harder, and would have for anyone but Elsa. They had behaved badly and she would take them to task for it. Yet she understood—and was saddened. Elsa was a trial for all of the sisters. Perhaps that was why she had been sent to them. It was something to ponder. Later.

"Is she still out there?" Rose asked.

"As far as we know," Frieda said.

"We'll discuss this further some other time."

After confirming that Elsa had not returned to her retiring room, Rose fetched her long cloak and pulled the deep hood over her head. The cloak was really too heavy for the warm evening, but one sister soaked to the skin was enough. Thank goodness the days were lengthening. She had a clear view of the cemetery as she reached the limestone wall surrounding it on three sides. Elsa was kneeling, her head hanging down, just the sisters had described. In no mood to waste time, Rose approached her. As she drew close, she realized that Elsa was no longer praying. Her shoulders heaved with sobs.

"Sister Elsa," Rose said, more gently than she'd intended. "I've come to bring you indoors. You've prayed enough. The Holy Father has surely heard you." Rose held out her hand. Elsa raised her head and looked up. Rain and tears dribbled down her round face, and her eyes were red, puffy, and miserable.

"I gotta keep prayin'," she said, "else Wilhelm will die."

"Not if I have anything to say about it," Rose said. "Come along now. Your voice is nearly gone. You've probably caught a chill. I seriously doubt our Mother and Father expect you to sacrifice yourself to save Wilhelm." She tried to grab Elsa's arm to pull her up, but Elsa plunked backward on her rear.

"Don't expect *you'd* understand," Elsa said, sounding a bit more like her petulant self. "It don't matter if I die. I'm ready to go anytime, and if it'll save Brother Wilhelm, I'll go right this instant."

Rose began to sympathize more with Lottie and
Frieda's decision to leave Elsa in the rain. However,
Elsa was Rose's responsibility, and she was coming indoors if Rose had to drag her. Elsa seemed to sense the
imminent struggle and crossed her arms tightly over
her generous bosom.

"I believe in Wilhelm's innocence," Rose said, "and
I will prove it. But I can't if my sisters insist on dis-
tracting me by putting themselves in danger. Every
minute I spend here arguing with you is a minute I
can't use to find the real killer."

Elsa's arms dropped to her sides, and her stubborn
expression dissolved into anguish. "It don't matter
what you do," she said. "It's gonna be too late. I called
over to the Sheriff's Office this afternoon to talk to
Brother Wilhelm, cheer him up. The sheriff said Wilhelm couldn't talk no more. Sheriff said he's refusin'
food, but I'll bet they're starvin' him, just like what
happened to Mother Ann. I wanted to go and slip him
some food, like Brother James did for Mother Ann
when she was thrown in prison for weeks without food
or water. But there ain't even a car around here.
Brother Wilhelm's gonna die, I know it."

Rose knelt down in the wet grass in front of Elsa.
"I'll tell you what," she said. "If you come back with
me now, I'll take you myself to see Wilhelm. Then perhaps you can persuade him to eat."

Rose saw something in Elsa's eyes that she'd never
seen before. Gratitude. It was soon replaced by suspicion. "You're just sayin' that."

Rose swallowed her anger at being accused of lying.
"I promise you," she said. "However, if you become ill,
we will be forced to wait until you recover, which

might be too late. We'd best get you into dry clothes. You may skip the evening worship and go straight to bed. I believe you have prayed enough for one day."

Elsa accepted defeat. She rolled back on her knees and struggled to her feet, grunting and panting. Rose attributed her docility to sheer exhaustion, and that was fine with her. Elsa was unlikely to cause more distractions this evening. As they reached the path that cut through the center of North Homage, Rose realized the rain had stopped and streaks of blazing pink glowed through widening cracks in the clouds. Rose's suspicions had begun to crystallize. With diligence and a heavenly boost, this night would prove her right.

TWENTY-ONE

"MORE PORT?" SAUL HELD UP A BOTTLE AND POINTED TO the label. "I got an especially good one for this evening, as a farewell and thank-you for your pleasant company. I'll be moving on tomorrow morning. Must get back to work, you know, and with these murders solved, there's no reason to stay."

Though the rain had stopped, all the hostel guests had gathered in the parlor after supper, choosing the cozy room over walks outside in the gloom and damp. Everyone accepted Saul's offer with eagerness and surprising good cheer. Gennie allowed Saul to fill her glass to the brim and returned his smile with a coquettish glance up through her lashes. Daisy Prescott wasn't the only one who could act a part.

"Let's drink to something," Saul said, holding his glass aloft.

"By all means," Horace said. "Shall we drink to your departure?"

Saul lowered his glass a fraction. He never seemed to get angry, Gennie noticed. "Let's drink to your future success," Gennie said, lifting her glass toward Saul. The atmosphere relaxed again. Gennie pressed her glass against her lips but did not drink. She watched the others. Daisy seemed lost in her magazine, unaware of the entire interchange. She hadn't touched her drink. Mrs. Berg drained her glass, which Saul quickly refilled. Horace took a gulp and raised his eyebrows in appreciation. He sipped again, then asked to examine the bottle's label. Saul drank very little. Now that she thought about it, Saul had always busied himself filling everyone else's glass. Apparently he wasn't much of a drinker himself.

While the others were distracted, Gennie arose from her rocking chair, carrying her glass of port, and sauntered over to a small table centered before a window. The table held a potted begonia Saul had bought from the Languor Flower Shop to "brighten the room." Gennie positioned herself directly in front of the table and leaned forward, as if to check the view through the window. Instead, her gaze slid downward as she carefully poured most of the contents of her glass into the flowerpot. The poor begonia probably wouldn't appreciate the fine quality of the port, but Gennie intended to stay alert.

Before turning around, she raised the nearly empty glass to her mouth and simulated drinking. She waited another few seconds, then turned and ambled back to her seat. No one seemed to be watching her movements. She slipped back into her chair and placed her glass on a nearby candle table.

"Your glass needs filling," Saul said, striding toward her.

"Oh no, I couldn't," Gennie said, with a tiny giggle. "I'm feeling a bit tipsy already. But I see Mrs. Berg could use a refill."

Saul spun around and headed toward the fireplace, where Beatrice Berg curled in a wing chair, holding her glass close to her chest. The room grew quiet. Gennie forced herself to look relaxed, though she tingled with excitement. She and Rose had guessed the hostel residents would spend the evening in the parlor, given the weather earlier and the availability of free drinks. So Rose had given Gennie an assignment to carry out when the time felt right. Always impetuous, Gennie had a hard time waiting for that right moment. But she must, so much depended on completing her task without raising suspicions.

Horace held out his glass for a refill. "Perhaps I will depart tomorrow, as well," he said. "Now that the excitement has dimmed, I'm finding the isolation here tedious. And I must say, the Shakers themselves have disappointed me. Imagine, an elder killing his own daughter. It seems these Shakers are not the saints they present themselves to be."

Gennie swallowed her ferocious response to Horace's comment, and she was sure she'd bitten her tongue sharply enough to make it bleed. She could ruin everything if she drew attention to her fondness for the Shakers. However, the right moment to speak had better come soon, or she'd explode and give Horace a piece or two of her mind.

"I've had my bag packed since Sunday." Beatrice said. "One ghost was bad enough, but this place is fillin' up with 'em. Pretty soon there'll be more ghosts floatin' around than there is Shakers."

Daisy finally looked up from her magazine. "I'll be leaving, too," she said.

"Tell me, Miss Prescott," Horace asked, "what will you be going back to?"

"Oh, just my same old life, of course. I lead quite a dull existence, really. This has been an exciting time for me."

"Do you have a job?" Horace asked.

Daisy's lips curved in the gentlest of smiles. "Yes, I've been very lucky, I've been able to keep my position through these terrible times. And you, Mr. von Oswald? I don't believe you've ever discussed what you do for a living."

"Who cares what anybody does," said Beatrice, clanking her empty glass on a nearby table. "We're all leaving, we ain't likely to see each other again, and that's all that matters. I'd leave now if I had a way. It ain't safe. I keep tellin' y'all, there's more'n one ghost now. Mina Dunmore and Brother Linus—you think they're gonna rest peaceful in their graves? No, sir. They'll be out there tonight and every night till they get justice." She suddenly jumped out of her chair and pointed to Horace. "Here you, change chairs with me. I ain't sittin' another minute in Mina Dunmore's old spot. Gives me the shivers."

Everyone except Horace refrained from snickering. Beatrice grabbed a handful of his sweater and yanked. "Stand up." Horace complied.

"Far be it from me to torture a guilty conscience," he said, as he switched seats with her.

Now is the moment. Gennie cleared her throat. "You know, maybe the ghost of Sarina Hastings will leave soon, too." She paused until she knew she had everyone's attention. "I heard another story about her—I think it must have been in some newspaper, but I'm not sure. Anyway, this story said that Sarina was a sister who came from somewhere far away from here, maybe back East. She'd come from this really rich family and was beautiful, and she got engaged to a man who had looked like he was going to be successful. But her fiancé betrayed her, I think it was by courting another woman, so Sarina just up and left town. She took all her gorgeous jewelry with her to use for money. She got on a train and ended up in Languor, where she heard about the Shakers."

Gennie feared she was rushing the story, but when she gazed around the room, her audience was riveted. Even Beatrice seemed to have forgotten her nerves. Rose had carefully constructed the story, and Gennie was determined to repeat it perfectly. She wished Rose had confided her suspicions, but she understood why she hadn't. It was important Gennie not know yet. If she knew, she might give something away with just a look or a word, and then the trap wouldn't work.

"Sarina's heart was broken," Gennie continued. "She didn't want anything to do with men or love anymore, so she decided to join the Shakers. But that isn't a very good reason to become a Shaker, I guess. She knew right away that she wouldn't stay forever, so she took all her jewels and hid them in one of the buildings. She figured she could take them with her when she was ready to leave. By then it was winter, and she decided to stay until spring, when it would be easier to travel. Besides, she liked working in the Herb House, and she couldn't right offhand think of a job she'd like better." Gennie was tempted to explain about "Winter

Shakers," but she stopped herself. That would be knowing too much.

"Then a terrible thing happened," she continued. "A deadly influenza swept through Languor County and next came to North Homage. Sarina caught it. Even though North Homage had its own doctor in those days, there was nothing he could do. Sarina got weaker and weaker until she died."

Horace leaned forward in his wing chair and stared at Gennie. "What an odd story," he said.

"Ain't odd," Beatrice said. "It's practically like what I heard. That ghost is lookin' for her jewels. She died before she could get 'em back."

"Yet in this new story, she told no one of the jewels' whereabouts," Horace said. "So how does the author of the story know about them?"

Gennie was ready for him. Rose had guessed that Horace, knowing he had not written the story, would pick holes in it. "Because," Gennie said, "she did tell someone. She'd made friends with another young sister, who wrote about it in her journal. After Sarina died, this sister looked and looked for those jewels. Whenever she could, she searched the buildings, but she never found anything. She said so in her journal. She—this other sister—stayed with the Shakers for many years, but then she left with one of the brothers—Brother Joshua, I think his name was—so she took her journals with her and never told the Shakers about the jewels. She died soon after, and no one really read her journals until recently, when all these stories started about Sister Sarina."

Horace said nothing more. Gennie was sure his

blank face hid a desperate attempt to figure out what
was going on. She took stock of the other guests. Beatrice looked like her old self—bad tempered and crafty.
Saul and Daisy's expressions showed polite interest.
Saul turned away and began to fill empty glasses. Beatrice was the only one to reach for her drink.

Gennie waited for more questions, but none came.
She hoped the hint had been clear, yet not too obvious.
She'd find out soon enough.

Rose could barely make out Gennie and Brother Andrew's faces in the faint moonlight, the only light in
the empty Medicinal Herb Shop, but she knew they
were determined to help. The hostel guests, savoring
the last night of their stay, had stayed unusually late in
the parlor. Rose and Andrew had waited with growing
impatience for Gennie to change into her darkest, most
comfortable outfit and make her escape. Now they had
to move fast or lose their opportunity. *Wilhelm would
be furious if he knew we were doing this*, Rose thought,
without guilt. *But it is for him that we are doing it—at
least in part.* She did, however, feel fear and heavy
doubt about the wisdom of involving Gennie and Andrew in her plan. They were up against a murderer who
killed without conscience. The danger was real. Yet she
could not do this alone.

Grady had been no help. When she had suggested to
him that he and his officers try to set a trap for the
killer, he'd replied that the killer was already trapped
in jail. He would come if they got into trouble, of
course, but it might then be too late. However, if her
plan worked, Grady would already be in the village
when the crucial moment arrived.

"If my suspicions are correct, we have very little time," Rose said.

"What *are* your suspicions?" Gennie asked in a hoarse whisper. "I've done my part, can't you tell me now?"

"I wish I could, Gennie, but there just isn't time. You and Andrew must go immediately to the west side of the village, over to the far side of the holy hill. Andrew already knows what to do."

"Where will you be?" Gennie asked.

"Here, for the most part."

"But—"

"Gennie, I promise you will understand very soon— if I am right."

"And if you aren't right?"

"Then we'll change our plans. Even if I'm wrong about who the killer is, I think the right person will fall into our trap. Now *go*."

Brother Andrew led the way out the back door of the Medicinal Herb Shop and into the night. They ran without speaking, several yards apart. The rain clouds had disappeared, turning the moon and stars into infinite bright searchlights trained on the earth. The danger was that a brother or sister suffering from insomnia would gaze out a retiring room window just as one of them passed by—or visitors from the world might hear the rhythmic squishing of their shoes in the rain-soaked ground, and follow them. It could happen at any stage in their journey. They had to risk it.

They reached the eastern edge of the holy hill without hearing shouts or an alarm bell, so they slipped under the cover of some trees and stopped to catch their breath. Gennie longed to ask questions, but she was afraid her panting was loud enough to wake the dead, not so far away in the old cemetery. Before her breathing had returned to normal, Andrew whispered to follow him.

Andrew must be able to see in the dark, because he managed to find a path that was reasonably clear of brambles. However, by the time they'd crossed the little crick and reached the southwest corner of the holy hill, Gennie knew her sandals had perished in the line of duty. She didn't care, as long as they held up through the night. As they approached the end of the tree cover, Andrew put out his hand to tell her to stop.

To their left was an open area about the width of the Trustees' Office, and beyond that they could see the narrow rutted road that linked North Homage and Languor. Gennie followed Andrew's example and peeked out beyond the trees toward the road. She saw nothing—no people, cars, or wagons. On the other hand, she wasn't sure what she was supposed to be looking for. She was just about to whisper the question to Andrew when he turned and headed north, staying inside the tree cover. She followed. He walked slowly, crouched down like an animal stalking its prey. She imitated his stance, even though his crouching only brought him down to Gennie's normal standing height. He seemed to be searching for something.

They both saw it at the same time. Just outside the tree line, about a third of the way along the western edge of the holy hill, heading north, they spotted what looked like a hillock, a small mound probably no

higher than Gennie's knees. It blended into the undergrowth and probably wouldn't be noticeable from the
road, even in the daylight.

Again Andrew gestured her to stay where she was.
He stepped outside the tree cover, looked in all directions, then went quickly to the small mound. He lifted
what looked like a tarp. It was too dark for Gennie to
see what was underneath, but she thought she knew
anyway. Rose had told her about the items missing
from her old retiring room and workroom in the Ministry House, though she hadn't shared any speculations
about who might have taken them. Perhaps this was
where the items were being stored.

Andrew's head jerked to the side, and he drew back
into the woods. Gennie knew he'd heard something.
They moved farther north and hid themselves behind
two thick trees. Sure enough, a rattling sound grew
louder and louder. A whinny marked the object as a
horse-drawn wagon. Every muscle taut, Gennie listened from her hiding place. The rattling stopped and a
horse snorted. She couldn't bear it; she peeked around
the tree trunk and saw a farm wagon stopped beside the
mound. Two figures sat on the wagon seat. One of
them, dressed in a simple shift, held the reins. The
other one looked like a Shaker sister. She wore a
Dorothy cloak with the hood pulled over her head. She
stood up, hopped off the wagon, and strode to the
mound. The other woman waited a moment, then
scrambled down awkwardly and joined the first.

"Quickly," Andrew whispered. "Run to the Trustees'
House and call Grady. Go that way," he said, pointing
directly east, "so they don't hear you. Tell Grady that

we are being robbed and he must come here immediately. *Go*."

Gennie scrambled like a frightened rabbit through the maze of trees and undergrowth. Going top speed, it would take her at least five minutes to reach the Trustees' Office, another couple to phone Grady, and then Grady still had to hop in his car and drive the eight miles to North Homage. It wouldn't take long for the thieves to load the wagon, even if they felt safe from discovery.

After fifty yards or so, Gennie gave up any attempt at silence. Her thoughts were racing faster than her feet. The thief in the Dorothy cloak—she had to be the ghost. It wasn't clear to Gennie exactly what it gained a thief to dress as a ghost, but there had to be a reason. Perhaps the reason had to do with Mina Dunmore and Brother Linus; perhaps they were killed because they'd discovered the identity of the ghost. Brambles scraped Gennie's legs, shredding her stockings and scraping the skin underneath. At that moment, she felt no pain. She would soon. It didn't matter. A few scratches were nothing if she could help stop this stealing, and maybe even unmask a ghost and a killer.

She reached the end of the woods and really took off, covering the distance to the Trustees' Office in less than a minute. She knew there was a small side door near the back of the building, on the west side, which would save her running around the front and up the steps in plain view. The door was unlocked, as she'd assumed. By now her legs were getting wobbly, but she propelled herself up the inside steps to the first floor, where the office and phone were located.

The night operator worked fast once she heard Gennie was trying to reach the sheriff for an emergency, and Grady, bless his heart, answered immediately.

"Gennie? What's wrong? Are you—"

"I'm fine, just listen. We've caught someone stealing from North Homage. There are two of them, and one is dressed like a sister. I suspect it's our ghost. You have to come right away, before they take off."

"Where are they?"

Gennie told him their location. "Andrew is watching them from just inside the woods around the holy hill. Please hurry, he's in danger."

"I'm leaving now. Gen, call Hank, he's on duty tonight, and tell him to call Bar. I want both of them to meet me at North Homage."

"Okay."

"And please, Gen, stay where you are. Don't go back and try to stop them yourself. Okay?"

Gennie only half heard him. She had pushed aside the sheer curtain and was watching out the office window, which gave her a view of the southwest corner of the village. She had seen movement in the moonlight, she was sure of it. She hung up the phone without remembering to say good-bye. Luckily she hadn't bothered to turn on the light in the office, so she probably couldn't be seen from outside. She tried to stay still, just in case.

Maybe she'd imagined it. The village seemed eerily deserted. Even the hostel looked as dark as it had all those years it had been empty. The people of the world must have decided it was too chilly and damp a night for ghost watching. Or perhaps they were finally losing interest. Then she saw it again, a swish of something dark that sped across the lawn, then disappeared be-

hind the South Family Dwelling House. This time she
thought she recognized what it was—a dark cloak flying out behind a running figure. The ghost.

Damn. She hadn't gotten to Grady in time. The thief
had returned to the village, perhaps to steal more before the night was over. If she could figure out where
the ghost was going, she could tell Grady when he arrived. She hurried to another window, which revealed
more of the southern and eastern sections of the village. Maybe she'd be able to spot the thief going into a
building. She stared into the night until her eyes watered. There it was again, a shadow against the white
Meetinghouse wall. The figure seemed to be heading
north, toward the path that ran down the center of the
village. She'd lose the trail if she didn't get out there
herself.

She let go of the thin curtain, but grabbed it before it
fell back across the window. Someone walked out of
the darkness beside the South Family Dwelling House
and headed toward the central path. A faceless vision
in flowing white. As it came closer, Gennie realized the
white was a nightgown, and she couldn't see a face because it was bent over. But she knew instantly who it
was—it was Mairin, stumbling through the grass. The
child reached the path and turned east. If she kept going, she would walk right into the arms of a killer.

TWENTY-TWO

ALONE IN THE DARK MEDICINAL HERB SHOP, ROSE TRIED to concentrate on the task at hand, but her mind drifted into worry. She wanted to be everywhere at once. Most especially, she wished she could be with Andrew and Gennie. She knew her presence wouldn't keep them from harm, but not being there left her to imagine all the worst possibilities. She prayed for their safety and for a peaceful end to this fearsome night.

For the fifth time, she circled inside the building, peering out each window into the moon-bathed night. She paid particular attention to the west windows, which gave her a view of the Herb House. Gennie had told the story Rose had concocted, and she promised she'd talked about Sister Sarina spending lots of time in the Herb House. Had it been too subtle, that hint? The Herb House had three distinct advantages—it was a building the ghost hadn't yet visited, according to Mairin; it was located at the northeast corner of the village, away from the buildings occupied at night; and Rose knew it very, very well. On the other hand, it was a large building, and Rose was only one person. She fervently hoped Andrew would arrive soon, with Grady and his officers.

She checked the windows a sixth time. A light snapped on in the Infirmary. Her stomach cramped for a moment, as doubt hit. What if her quarry hadn't gotten the hint about the Herb House—or had chosen to ignore it for some reason? Was the story too obviously a fabrication? If so, might Josie be in danger? Nay, it was more likely someone was ill, and Josie was just doing her job.

Rose returned to the west window, overlooking the experimental herb garden. This time she saw what she'd been waiting for—the faint, wavery sliver cast by a flashlight. The light appeared and disappeared through the uncurtained ground-floor windows of the Herb House. The wielder of the flashlight was searching a large room where the herb presses and other equipment were kept. The room had lots of corners and storage cupboards, so it should keep the searcher busy for some time. Rose was sure by now that the dancing in the windows only occurred when the so-called ghost saw people outside watching. The performance was intended to explain the presence of someone in the building—and to discourage folks from coming inside and confronting the intruder face-to-face.

The grounds around the Herb House were blessedly free of ghost watchers. Rose slipped out the back door of the Medicinal Herb Shop. She wore a dark blue work dress, hoping to meld into the night. She'd purposely left behind her cloak. The last thing she needed was to be mistaken for the ghost and chased around the village. Keeping as far north as possible, without trampling the herb fields, she wove around to the Herb House's small back door.

Rose eased open the door just enough for her to slip

through and into a small foyer used mainly during herb harvesting. The brothers would come in from the herb fields and change into clean shoes, leaving their muddy boots lined up along the wall. She could make out the line of boots in the darkness, cleaned up and ready for the next season. She removed her own shoes and arranged them in line, as if they'd been waiting all winter for someone to claim them. She'd move more quietly in stocking feet.

She couldn't stay here. Eventually the cloaked figure would work through the entire ground floor before going upstairs to the drying room. And the drying room was where Rose hoped to end the charade. She knew the room so well; she could easily navigate it in the dark, if she had to. If she could stay undetected until the intruder entered the drying room, she would close the door and wedge it shut, trapping the culprit inside. The windows were so high above ground that only a self-destructive fool would jump from one of them.

Unfortunately, the building had only one staircase, and it was in full view of anyone in the herb pressing room. She'd have to hide until the intruder moved toward the back of the building. Then she'd have a chance of slipping up the staircase unseen. Rose tiptoed up the few steps leading from the back landing to a short hallway. Two small rooms along the hallway were used for storing seasonal items, such as tools, extra tins, labels, hooks for hanging herbs to dry, and so forth. Rose took one step, stopped to listen, then took another step. The flooring was solid. She wasn't afraid of creaks so much as tripping in the dark. She passed the first room, had almost reached the second. A clatter sounded very near her.

Rose held her breath, hoping for a cry or even a curse to tell her where the intruder was—and whether she had guessed the identity correctly. All she heard was a scraping sound followed by a thud, as if an object had been dragged along the floor until it hit a wall. It sounded very, very close, perhaps just around the corner at the end of the hall. She needed to get inside the room just a few yards from where the intruder must now be. She was afraid she'd been too slow. The intruder had already worked through the pressing room and would enter the hallway at any moment.

It was now or never. She took three quick steps and reached the door of the second room. Just before dark, she had visited the Herb House to think out her plan. Luckily, she had thought to leave the door of the small storage room slightly ajar, so she wouldn't have to click the latch. She was able to squeeze inside without moving the door. Once inside, she stopped and listened. The scraping and clattering were fainter, but she knew the intruder was close. She had perhaps one or two minutes at most.

The room she'd entered looked smaller than it actually was. It backed up against an open storage area under the stairway. The Herb House was constructed for utility, but with neatness in mind. So only a portion of the area under the staircase had been left open for items that would be needed on a constant basis. The rest of the space had been enclosed in this room and turned into an odd-shaped closet. The closet door blended almost seamlessly into the pine wall; in the dark, even the narrow vertical handle looked like part of the wood grain.

Faint moonlight outlined obstacles in the room, so

Rose had no difficulty reaching the closet door without making a sound. Again, she'd earlier left the door open. She slipped inside. She shared the closet with spare and broken parts from the herb presses, machine oil, rags, and various repair tools, but she'd carved out an area large enough for her to stand in. She settled inside and reached for the door. In her earlier haste, she'd forgotten. There was no knob on the inside of the door. A rush of anger and fear paralyzed her. For precious seconds, she fought to recover, to think clearly again.

She pushed the closet door open enough to let some moonlight penetrate. She looked around her. All this junk; there had to be something . . . A narrow shelf next to her held several wooden boxes, each full of small objects. One of them held screws. As quietly as possible, she picked out a large screw with a sharp point. With her left hand, she reached around outside the door to hold it firm. With all the strength that years of daily physical labor had given her, she imbedded the screw tip in the soft pine and turned it with her bare hand. She felt the screw head scrape her fingers. She didn't mind the pain, but if she cut her hand, she would be a weaker opponent. She grabbed a nearby rag and used it to pad her fingers. The screw wound into the door with maddening slowness. When it felt firmly imbedded, she pulled it toward her, and the door followed, melding into the wall. It had been fitted so perfectly that its creator, Brother Hugo, had decided not to mar the door with any sort of latch, so Rose knew she would not be locked inside. She whisked a blessing heavenward to Brother Hugo, with the promise of many more to come.

The sound of scraping wood against wood told her

the intruder was now in the room with her. Her stomach did a flip-flop. Perhaps eating a full dinner had not been such a good idea. She forced herself to breathe as she listened to the sounds of methodical searching coming closer and closer. If she stayed still, she should be safe—as long as the intruder didn't turn on the light. That was the part she couldn't predict. If ghost watchers showed up while the intruder was in this room, the light would go on and the dancing would begin—and the intruder might notice the door in the wall. To make matters more frightening, locked away in her closet, Rose wouldn't know if the lights had been turned on until the door suddenly opened. She reached out her fingers and felt along a narrow shelf until she touched what felt like a wooden handle. She explored further and identified a hammer. For a moment, her fingers closed around the handle. She felt safer, stronger. She forced herself to let go. Holding the hammer as a weapon would be an enticement to violence.

The movements now sounded as if they were just outside her closet door. She heard a momentary silence that filled her with doubt. Had she been overconfident of Brother Hugo's skill? Had she underestimated the intruder? But the noise picked up again, softer this time. In another few minutes, Rose heard the door of the room creak as it opened more widely. Rose counted to one hundred, listening as she waited. The powerful smell of old machine oil was making her dizzy. She had to get out.

She pushed the closet door forward a fraction of an inch, then another. Finally, moonlight cracked through. No one leaped at the door and dragged her out. She could hear movement in the next room. She was safe.

But only for a while. Any hesitation and she might be the next victim.

Rose slid out and closed the closet door behind her, so the intruder wouldn't peek in the room again, notice the open door, and become suspicious. She wove through the small room with care—the searcher had left items out of place. She stepped down right on a sharp-edged herb tin lid tossed on a patch of floor hidden from the moon. It had pressed hard into her foot, slicing through her stocking. She bit her lip, stifled a cry. She steadied herself on a nearby chest of drawers and lifted her foot, careful not to clatter the tin. She stood balanced on one foot for several seconds, as waves of pain radiated through the ball of her foot. The worst subsided. She put some weight on her foot. Hurt, but usable.

Time was passing. Rose's biggest concern now was that the intruder would finish in the room next door and catch her in the hallway. Fear propelled her to the door. It had been left open. She peeked out. The hallway was clear. A few steps would take her into the herb pressing room and out of sight from the hall. She took a deep breath and walked as fast as she could. Tiptoeing on her injured foot was impossible.

Rows of windows allowed plenty of moonlight into the large herb pressing room. To avoid another mishap, Rose watched the floor as she hurried across the room to the wide staircase. With any luck, the intruder would now be searching the back foyer, far away from Rose. She took a risk. She lifted the skirt of her long work dress and took the steps at a half-run, flinching as the old wood and her hurt foot complained at the assault.

Rose reached the second-floor landing and glanced

back down the stairs. No one appeared below. Now for the final phase of her plan. She prayed it would work smoothly, that she herself would not be the trigger for further violence.

The drying room door stood wide open, inviting. Moonlight flooded the room itself, beckoning the curious to enter and explore. On the other side of the landing, across from the drying room entrance, a small room provided additional storage space. She'd cleared an area in the room so she could hide and wait. Next to the door, in shadow, a sturdy wooden chair stood against the wall, as if waiting for a tired Believer to take a break. Rose had placed it there.

She settled in the storage room, with the door closed. There was always the risk the intruder would resist the lure of the herb drying room and decide to search the storage room first. So Rose knelt in a corner behind a stack of boxes and baskets used during the herb harvest. After a long winter of rest, they still smelled faintly of the earth. They hid her like protective friends, and for a moment she felt safe.

The moment ended as Rose heard the distant creak of stairs. She had to strain to make it out. Long spaces between the sounds hinted at a leisurely pace. That seemed odd, but perhaps the intruder had tired. The squeaking grew louder, then stopped. A full minute passed in silence. The intruder must already be in the drying room. Try as she might, Rose couldn't hear any sounds from the room next to her; the thick walls muffled so much. It was time. She shifted her weight off her aching knees and prepared to stand.

She heard the soft click of a door latch. *Her* door latch. The door swished faintly as it opened. Noiselessly, Rose slid back to a kneeling stance and willed her muscles to be still. She had guessed wrong. The intruder had opted for the smaller room first. So much for her plan. This time, no handy hammer lay nearby. If she was discovered, she had few choices. She might be able to run. Or she might have to fight for her life.

The storage room had no windows. From her hiding place, Rose saw spots of light flick around, hitting the floor and the walls. *A flashlight.* The throbbing in her foot made her catch her breath. She willed the pain out of her mind. She had to be ready for anything.

The bouncing light stopped, and the door clicked shut. Rose didn't dare move, didn't dare allow herself to feel safe. She seriously considered staying where she was, then making a run for it while the intruder searched the drying room. They'd be no worse off than before. But this chance would never come again. Wilhelm's life depended on her choice.

With painful slowness, she stretched until she could see around her barrier of boxes and baskets. She was alone in the room. She pushed to her feet, shook the kinks out of her knees, and tried her weight on her sore foot. It was worse. Taking off her shoes had been a foolish idea. They wouldn't have made that much noise. Well, it was done, and she'd just have to accept the pain. She limped to the door, walking on the heel of her injured foot. With luck and heavenly help, she wouldn't need whole feet to accomplish her task.

She listened at her door and heard nothing. The intruder must be well into the drying room. That was good. She eased open her door. Still quiet. She opened the door enough to look out into the landing. It was empty. Dark spots on the normally clean floor marked where the intruder had tracked in mud. Rose felt a surge of resentment. She slid out the door. The wooden chair was right next to her. She lifted it and limped to the drying room entrance.

It was too early in the season for bunches of herbs to be hanging from every possible hook and rack, so much of the room was visible. Rose paused, put the chair down for a moment as she scanned the room from just outside the doorway. She didn't hear any sounds of searching, no furniture scraping or drawers sliding open and shut. What if the intruder had decided to stop searching and had already escaped? Well, then it wouldn't hurt to barricade the door anyway. She stretched out her arms toward the chair.

Like the strike of a poisonous snake, an arm shot out from just inside the doorway. A strong hand grabbed Rose's outstretched arm and yanked her into the drying room. She flew forward and sprawled on the floor. The door slammed shut behind her. As she tried to sit, she caught sight of her feet. Too late she realized what those dark spots on the landing had really been. The bottom of her left stocking was bloodstained. She must have left a trail of fresh blood all the way up the stairs and toward the closet.

She wasn't much use for the chase anymore. Besides, the intruder had turned her plan against her and trapped her inside the drying room. At least the room had its own phone. She could alert the village to be on the lookout for a very dangerous cloaked figure. She dragged herself to her feet and limped toward the phone. Before she could reach it, the sound of running feet reached her. Someone was flying up the stairs, someone who didn't care about being quiet. Her whole body wilted with relief. Grady had finally arrived.

As the door opened, she spun toward it. Her words of gratitude died before they reached the air. Someone in a long Shaker cloak, the hood pulled far forward, rushed through the door and closed it softly. One hand held a flashlight aimed at Rose's eyes.

"I'd hoped to be long gone," came a muffled voice from deep inside the hood of the cloak, "but there are far too many people outside. So you are going to help me."

Rose swerved to avoid the glare of the flashlight. She saw another hand appear from under the cloak. It held something long, thin, and sharp. Rose had seen it before, most recently in her own Ministry House work-room—it was a pair of tailor's shears.

Gennie stood on the top step, just outside the Trustees' Office, and frantically scanned the village. She'd been too late. Mairin, clad only in her night-gown, had disappeared. Gennie's worst fear was that the thieving so-called ghost had swooped up the little girl, probably to keep her quiet—at worst, to use her as a hostage. Standing around wouldn't do any good. Gennie thought about ringing the old fire bell next to the Meetinghouse to arouse the village. That might backfire, though. If the ghost felt threatened, Mairin would be in even worse danger.

Gennie ran down the Trustees' Office steps and into the road. She craned her neck to see if anything was coming from the west, like a nice, dusty, brown Buick, driven by Grady. She didn't see so much as a farm wagon full of ghost seekers. There was no point in trying to find Andrew; he had his hands full. She hopped back onto the grass north of the unpaved central road. She'd be less visible. She'd last seen both the cloaked figure and Mairin walking toward the path. Now she saw neither, so they must have crossed to the north side of the village. Her best bet was to see if Rose might still be in the Medicinal Herb Shop. Together they could comb the area. She ran the rest of the way to the shop and burst in the door.

"Rose? Are you here?" She didn't dare turn on the light. She didn't need to. The building was small and decidedly empty. She'd just have to think of some other way.

Gennie hurried back into the night. If the cloaked figure was holding Mairin somewhere, it was probably in one of three nearby buildings—the Laundry, the barn, or the Herb House. The Laundry was closest. As soon as she slipped inside, Gennie sensed the building was empty. She wasn't willing to trust her senses with Mairin's life at stake, so she methodically searched the first floor. She inspected the huge washing machines, only one of which was used anymore; they could easily hold a body. Both were empty. She peeked inside the gigantic basket attached to a pulley that lifted it, filled with clean, wet clothing, up to the second-floor ironing room. The basket could accommodate at least two people. It gave off a faint lavender fragrance but held nothing. Finally she did a quick and fruitless search of the upstairs ironing room, which had fewer places to hide.

Discouraged, Gennie checked the ironing room windows. The village had come alive. Several folks, dressed in clothes of the world, had gathered on the Meetinghouse lawn, and a wagon holding more visitors trotted down the central path toward them. *Now what?* Gennie checked the barn and the Herb House through the east and west windows. Nothing suspicious going on in the barn, as far as she could see. But the Herb House . . . She thought she had seen a sliver of faint light waving around the ground floor. It disappeared almost instantly. She waited nearly a minute, but it didn't reappear. Yet she was certain someone was there. It made sense. Rose had told her to be sure to mention the Herb House in her story about Sarina. She must have wanted the ghost to go there. Which meant Rose was probably in there, too. She might have no idea that Mairin was in any danger.

With a half-formed plan in her mind, Gennie left the Laundry and ran toward the strangers now clustered on the Meetinghouse lawn. She recognized one of the women as the intrepid Betty. The others must be her husband and their friends. She might have known a little damp and mud wouldn't keep these folks away from their favorite entertainment.

"Hey there, ain't seen you in a while," Betty called as Gennie approached. "Anything worth seein' around here?"

"Nothing at this end," Gennie said. "She must be on the other side of the village. I thought I saw something in the Carpenters' Shop. You go ahead, I'll be along when I catch my breath." The Carpenters' Shop was far enough away. It should keep them out from under foot for a while.

Betty waved her group toward the southwest, and they took off eagerly. Gennie waited until they'd begun to fade into the darkness, then she made straight for the Infirmary. The light she'd seen earlier must mean Sister Josie was up and about, probably seeing to a patient. There was a time to call in backup, as Grady always said, and this was it.

Sister Josie sat at her desk measuring powders together when Gennie burst in the front door. Josie stood at once and bustled toward her cloak, hanging on a wall peg. "Is someone ill at the hostel?" she asked. "Tell me quickly so I'll know what to bring. It isn't another murder, is it?"

"No, Josie, no one is ill. Yet, anyway. But I need your help, and I don't have time to explain. Grady and his officers might be in the village, maybe on the west side of the holy hill. Andrew, too. Or they might be on their way back to Languor. I want you to call both the Sheriff's Office and the brethren. Somehow we've got to find Grady and send him to the Herb House. Thanks. Gotta go." She knew Josie would try to keep her safe indoors, but she had no intention of missing the action.

"You might as well keep still. I can see now that I never gave you enough credit. However, I know you're hurt, and I suspect you're alone. The faster you help me, the sooner we part company." The voice was low and gruff. Rose sensed a lie when she heard one. Her death would be necessary. She now knew the ghost's identity. Her only hope was to stretch out the search until Andrew finished and came looking for her.

"What do you want from me?" she asked.

"You are familiar with this building. Where are the secret hiding places? I want those jewels."

"We Shakers have no need for secret hiding places."

"Nonsense. Everyone has secrets. Shakers are no

better than anyone else. You just want those jewels for yourself. Now, I can see this is the room where Sister Sarina would have worked, so this must be where she hid her fortune. If you don't help me, I'll simply kill you now and look for myself."

"The cupboards in the walls," Rose said, stalling for time. "She might have pulled out a loose board in one of them."

"Go try it. Go on." The flashlight waved Rose toward a cupboard. She limped over to it, opened the door and peered around inside. Anything to delay the process.

"Try the boards."

Rose clawed at the insides of the cupboard, but of course nothing loosened. Shaker buildings were solid and strong. "There's nothing," she said. "I'll have to try the others."

"Fast."

The room held two other cupboards and some built-in drawers. Rose examined them all, as slowly as possible. Not a single board had even the slightest crack.

"It's got to be here. I've looked everywhere." The voice was sounding desperate, angry. "You're no help. I might as well get rid of you now."

"You've been duped." Rose spoke quickly. Now her only hope was distraction.

"What do you mean?"

"There is no fortune. Those stories were just fantasy. There was no Sister Sarina, no tragic death."

"You're lying. You just want me to go away so you can find it." The voice was a shade less gruff.

"Nay, we have no wish to profit from anyone's

death. The stories are false. They were planted by someone who wanted to embarrass us. Someone you have lived in the same house with, eaten meals with for many days."

Keeping close enough to stop Rose from bolting, the cloaked figure crossed the room and glanced out the large south-facing window. "You know who I am, don't you?" This time, the voice no longer strained to sound foggy. It was clearer and tougher than Rose remembered it sounding during her evening meals at the Shaker Hostel, but it was the same.

"Is your real name Clarissa Carruthers, or is that just a stage name, like Daisy Prescott?"

The cloaked figure rested her flashlight on the worktable in front of the window. With her free hand, she reached up and pulled back her hood. Her face and head were covered with a knit mask, leaving only her blue-green eyes showing. "It really is Clarissa," she said. "I've had many others in the past few years, but I've always been partial to Clarissa." She peeled off her mask. Her hair had been pulled back in a tight bun; now fine tendrils, pulled free by the removal of her mask, framed her face.

Clarissa retrieved her flashlight but didn't bother to shine it in Rose's eyes. "I should have guessed those stories weren't true," she said. "Horace had something to do with them, didn't he? It was right in front of me; I should have known." There was no hint of anger in her voice, as if all she'd done was make a minor mistake in arithmetic, and she'd know better next time.

"How long have you known?" she asked.

"I suspected ever since I learned you were an actress—that you'd been engaged to a wealthy man and had disappeared from the stage shortly after your fiancé broke your engagement. I suspected Saul Halvardson, too, of course. You two were the only ones with the physical agility to carry off the hoax."

"Saul?" Clarissa laughed, one short bark. "He hasn't the brains to accomplish something like this. I caught on to him fast. I got suspicious when he kept plying us all with liquor, but he never seemed to drink much himself. I figured he wanted us to sleep soundly. He's a petty thief, no more."

"And you are a highly successful jewel thief," Rose said. In part, she was pandering to Clarissa's obvious pride, a ploy to keep her talking. She didn't admit that she hadn't been completely sure until she'd heard Clarissa's voice. Saul was no actor. He wouldn't even have tried to alter his voice. He was a copycat, using the appearance of the ghost to steal items from the Shaker buildings. He was the "pregnant" ghost. With all the curious folks around, he simply stole from buildings farthest away from wherever the ghost was appearing that night, then hid his booty under a cape. Where he'd found the cape didn't matter. He might easily have unearthed it in an attic during one of his nighttime adventures. He probably kept it in the woods somewhere and only used it when he was transporting stolen items. Rose suddenly remembered the tattered cloak she'd seen hanging in the South Family Dwelling House kitchen. Clarissa was wearing such a cloak right now. Hiding in plain sight—such bold cleverness was more Clarissa's style than Saul's.

Clarissa glanced out the south window again. A

small smile played around her lips. Rose took it as a warning that she was busy developing a new plan— one that Rose was not intended to survive.

"Wealth is very important to you, isn't it?" Rose asked.

Clarissa shrugged. "Wealth, of course, and respect. I'm no different from anyone else." Her eyes slid up and down Rose's body. "I suspect that, underneath that costume, you're just the same as me."

Rose refused the bait. "So the failure of your engagement must have hurt."

"It made me angry," Clarissa said. She lifted her chin. "The first house I ever burglarized belonged to his father, the one who ruined my engagement. It was easy, and so much more lucrative than acting. In fact, I used all my talents more fully than ever before. This is the perfect job for me."

"You met the real Daisy Prescott at that house, didn't you?"

"Of course," said Clarissa. "It was rather bright of you to find out about that. I thought using a real person would be much safer than making everything up, and Daisy is such a frump, she was practically invisible. I'd run into her shortly before deciding to come here; I knew she'd been called home suddenly to care for her ill mother. It was ideal."

Knowing she was taking a risk, Rose asked the question that burned in her heart. "Why did you have to kill Mina Dunmore and Brother Linus? Even if they'd discovered what you were doing, couldn't you simply have left? There are so many other opportunities in the world—other houses, other jewels. Why kill?" She couldn't ask the question without anguish coloring her voice.

"I had to," Clarissa said, with a casual shrug, as if it had been merely a practical decision. "Mina Dunmore was nothing more than a lying blackmailer. Getting away from her would have been far more difficult than it sounds. That woman lied so much you all thought she was just making up stories when she talked about her wealthy husband, going to balls, and so on. She was stretching the truth, but it wasn't all lies. Her husband's cousin was the one with money.

"You see, I've found it wonderfully easy and exciting to wangle invitations to balls in rich houses all over the country. These people think they are so much better than I am. I adore fooling them, mingling among them and then relieving them of their trinkets. I went to one party in Louisville at the cousin's house. It was early in my career, and I hadn't honed my skills. I had a close call. The theft was discovered while we were all still there, and the police were called. Luckily, I'd found a clever hiding place for the jewelry. I wasn't caught. However, I did use a different name than Daisy Prescott, and I had a lovely Southern drawl."

"So Mrs. Dunmore recognized you at the hostel and—"

"Put two and two together, yes. You'd hardly have thought it of her, but she wasn't actually stupid. Except in her dealings with me, of course. She'd tasted wealth before, and she wanted it again. Her idea was that I would do the work and give her half, in exchange for which she wouldn't tell the police my identity. So you can see why I had to kill her. Luckily, she was foolish enough to brag about tracking down her father—your elder—thinking it made her sound more dangerous, I suppose. She tapped her bosom as she told me. That's where I found her birth certificate."

"And Brother Linus?"

"Foolish man. He had appointed himself the village guardian. He was going to catch the ghost and get things back to normal, or so I assume. One night he actually had the nerve to come into the building I was searching and try to corner me. I wasn't worried, I'd always been too quick for him, so he hadn't seen my face. Unfortunately, he found me just as I'd finished taking care of the Dunmore woman. I grabbed some yarn and got away fast, but he chased me into the basement of that big empty building, where I surprised him. It was easy. I was hoping he'd get blamed for a longer time, but that irritating little girl found him."

"That little girl thinks you are her guardian angel."

Clarissa let out a belly laugh. Her eyes closed momentarily, and Rose leaped toward the closed door. She'd grabbed the handle when a slender but surprisingly strong arm encircled her waist and pulled her back into the room.

"This has been fun," Clarissa said. "It isn't often I get to talk about my work." She said no more, but Rose knew what came next. Clarissa spun her around and held the point of the tailor's shears against her stomach.

Rose heard what sounded like a faint shout—outside, she thought.

"The time should be right," Clarissa said. She flipped on the lights. "Come along." She grabbed Rose's arm and dragged her toward the south window.

Still holding tight, she leaned over the side of the
worktable and looked out at the grounds below.

"Perfect," she said. "Take off your clothes."

"Why you clever little thing, you." Betty's voice
came from somewhere in back of Gennie. "You
wanted the ghost all to yourself, didn't you? Well, we
found you out. Come on Arlin, over here," she called.
"Y'all come on this way." A group of nine or ten materialized from the darkness and sprinted toward the
Herb House.

"So," Betty said, "she's up there, is she? Was you
gonna go in there, try and see her up close?"

"Well, I—"

"That's right dangerous, my girl. You stay here. Arlin, make sure this girl don't go off on her own. Look!
There she is, up on the second floor."

Betty pointed toward the south-facing window of
the herb drying room. A bobbing light appeared, but
that was all. The newcomers stared upward. Gennie
spun around at a slight rustling in the grass behind her;
more folks were approaching, at least ten of them. At
this rate, she'd never manage to get into the Herb
House. As the new group approached, she realized they
were not of the world. They were Shaker sisters. She
recognized Sister Isabel leading the group, her small
figure plunging through the grass with fierce determination. Another group appeared just behind the sisters—the brethren had come, as well. Gennie looked in
vain for Andrew or Grady, but surely the rest of the village had arrived. They spread out across the south lawn
and seemed to be waiting for instructions.

A racket started up behind them, and Gennie saw a lovely sight—a big dark car destroying the grass as it bounced toward them. Grady was at the wheel, with Bar beside him. Scrunched in the backseat were two more figures, probably Hank and Brother Andrew.

"Stay back," Grady yelled. "Let us through." Grady and his officers pushed through to the front of the crowd just as the light flashed on in the drying room above them. All eyes watched the empty window. The Shakers, who believed their eldress was trapped inside with a killer, began to pray out loud. Catching their fear, the visitors from the world joined in.

"Now get up on the table," Clarissa ordered Rose. "Go ahead, do it."

Rose lifted herself onto the large worktable and waited. Movement was awkward in the long Shaker cloak. Beneath the cloak, she wore only her plain white cotton petticoat and underthings. Her hair hung loose inside the hood. Clarissa had slipped into Rose's work dress and covered her hair with the white indoor cap. She'd be able to get away easily. In the dark, no one would think twice about a Shaker sister walking across the village.

"Stand up," Clarissa ordered. "Good. Now face the window."

Rose looked down on the south lawn, where a large crowd had gathered. She couldn't see the faces clearly, but they all seemed to be staring up at her. Three figures stood in front, pointing their arms up toward her. Something glinted in the moonlight, something in the hand of one of the figures in front. Even without seeing it clearly, Rose knew what it was. A gun. Three guns pointed straight at her. And she was dressed exactly like Clarissa—the killer ghost that Andrew would have told them about by now.

"Dance," Clarissa said.

Rose didn't move. She felt the cold, sharp point of the shears poke into her ankle, just below the cloak.

"You see, it's like this," Clarissa said. Her voice was calm, reasonable, as if she were simply explaining a dilemma to a friend. Rose's skin chilled despite the heavy cloak. The woman had no conscience. She couldn't be ruffled. Any setback was merely a problem to be solved. "I've killed two people," she said. "I have nothing to lose by killing you, too." With her weapon against Rose's skin, Clarissa craned her neck to look out the window. "Good, everyone is in place. This will work perfectly. One of those nice policemen will shoot you, thinking he is saving an innocent Shaker. Then they'll come up here and find you. All those people will assume that you were this ghost all along. Won't that be lovely? It's the perfect solution. Now, dance."

"Why should I, if you are going to kill me anyway?"

This time the point pierced the skin of Rose's ankle. She tensed against the pain but didn't move.

"Because if you don't dance, I'll still kill you, make it look like a suicide, and then I'll make time to find out where that cute but interfering young friend of yours lives when she isn't at your hostel. Do you understand?"

Rose stepped forward, away from the point of the shears. She bowed toward the window. She bowed to the side.

"That's right," Clarissa said. "Good girl."

Rose began to twirl around, slowly at first, then faster. As she spun she caught sight of Clarissa watch-

ing her with a smug smile. Her injured foot screamed
at this new insult, but she steeled herself to ignore the
pain. It was about to get worse. She hadn't been shot
yet, and she was less convinced than Clarissa that
Grady and his men really would shoot at her, but she
knew there wasn't much time. If no one shot her,
Clarissa would simply stab her and make it look like
suicide. She spun faster.

She stopped spinning with a suddenness that clearly
startled Clarissa. Before she got jabbed with the shears
again, Rose stiffened her entire body and jumped up
and down, rattling the strong table. Clarissa held her
arm straight out and pointed the shears at Rose, ready
for an attack. Still jumping, Rose turned back to the
window. She barked like a dog. She didn't dare sweep
back her hood to show her long, thick curls. Instead,
she stretched her stiff arms straight out and waved
them up and down, as if she were doing a jumping
jack. The cloak swung wide open. She glanced down at
the crowd and saw something that gave her hope. Now
only two men held weapons aloft. The third was conferring with a tiny individual who had to be Gennie.

Rose's foot wasn't going to take much more. She
lowered her arms, pulled the cloak close again, and
jumped around a half circle, so that she faced Clarissa.

"Okay, that's enough, get down now." Clarissa said.
"If those silly policemen won't do their part, I'll have
to take care of you myself."

Rose barked louder and began to spring up and
down.

"I said get down." For the first time, Clarissa's voice
showed irritation.

Rose barked louder still.

Clarissa lunged for her. With all her strength, Rose leaped sideways, cleared the table, and smacked down on the floor. Shock waves pulsed up her legs. Her injured foot felt as if she'd landed on a razor. She crumpled into a ball on the floor and rolled under the worktable. She kept rolling, aware that Clarissa had dropped to her knees and was reaching for her under the table. She missed. Rose rolled out the other end and struggled to her feet. Clarissa was caught in an awkward position, half under the table. While she was righting herself, Rose ran for the door and flung it open. With a hasty but heartfelt prayer of gratitude, Rose jumped aside as Grady burst into the room, followed by officers Hank and Bar.

Rose hadn't the strength or the heart to watch as the officers handcuffed Clarissa. She limped downstairs to find Gennie standing at the open front door, her arms outstretched. Josie was right behind her. Each took an arm and kept her from crumpling in the grass.

"Come along now, Sister," Josie said. "That's quite enough for one night."

TWENTY-THREE

"ROSE, I KNOW YOU'RE REALLY TIRED," GENNIE SAID, "but we've got to find Mairin. I think that woman got hold of her and maybe hurt her. Can you think where she might be?"

Josie had run on ahead to the Infirmary to prepare a bed for Rose. Supported by Lottie and Frieda, strong young sisters, Rose had relaxed to a state of semiconsciousness, from which Gennie had dragged her back. "What are you talking about, Gennie? I was in the Herb House almost the whole time. When would Clarissa have had time to kidnap Mairin?"

"I watched Mairin walk right in the same direction as the ghost—I mean, Clarissa. They must have seen each other."

Rose moaned. "It never occurred to me . . . We've got to go back to the Herb House."

"Nay, Sister, you're in no condition," insisted Lottie. "We're almost to the Infirmary. When we get you inside, we'll call the brethren to go search for Mairin." With a whimper of impatience, Gennie held the Infirmary door open for the sisters.

Josie bustled into the waiting room. "I've got a bed all ready for you, Rose. Bring her along, Sisters."

"Wait," Rose commanded. "Gennie, tell Josie what you told me."

After Gennie's intense explanation, Josie shocked everyone by chortling. "My goodness, you two have had far too much excitement lately. You are expecting the worst."

"No, listen, Josie—"

"Come along now, follow me." Josie led the group toward the sickrooms that lined a long hallway.

"But Josie—"

"There," Josie whispered as she stopped at the doorway of a sickroom. "Have you ever seen anything so precious?"

Gennie and the sisters clustered in the doorway. Inside the room, an adult-sized cradle bed held a small bundle. Mairin slept curled on her side, her face warm and soft against the white pillow. One arm lay outside the covers, curved around a tiny ball of calico fur.

"Angel wasn't hungry for her supper, so Mairin was afraid she was sick," Josie said quietly. "Mairin stayed with her for hours, and when Angel still seemed listless, she came to me for help. It was just a hairball, but Mairin couldn't know that. When I'd gotten Angel feeling better, I put them both to bed. And now, Rose, you are going to bed, as well, if I have to carry you myself."

"Believe me, I'm more than ready," Rose said, and gratefully let go of her responsibilities for one night.

"There's still something I don't understand," Gennie said. She and Grady sat on a blanket under a sweet gum tree on the Center Family Dwelling House lawn.

The remains of a picnic lunch lay scattered around them.

"What?"

"The man so many folks heard in Mrs. Dunmore's room Sunday morning—I realize Daisy was an actress and could sound like a man, but why? Mrs. Dunmore wasn't killed in her room, was she?"

Grady shook his head. "Nope, poor Mrs. Dunmore was already dead by then. Daisy—Clarissa—had met her in the Sisters' Shop, killed her, and then killed Brother Linus. She wanted to muddy the waters, make it sound like Linus had been in the room with Mrs. Dunmore. So she imitated both their voices. She hoped it would distract everyone long enough for her to find the jewels and get away. Also, if people believed Linus was the sort to visit a woman at night in her room, it would add credence to the theory that he would black-mail Wilhelm, as well." Grady shook his head, and a stubborn lock of straight brown hair fell across his forehead. "Clarissa should have stuck to stealing from wealthy homes; she was good at that. She got greedy."

"She got too big for her britches," Gennie said.

The two grew silent, avoiding each other's gaze. With her index finger, Gennie lightly traced a pattern in the blanket.

"You didn't get your three peaceful weeks away from me," Grady said.

Gennie curled her legs underneath her and settled into a more comfortable position. The warmth of the day spoke of summer, and she felt her concerns melt in the sunlight. "Maybe I didn't need peace. Maybe I needed to do just what I did. I mean, I'm awfully sorry about Mrs. Dunmore and Brother Linus. Yet I know

now that I just can't sit still and plan dinner parties. I love you with all my heart, Grady, but I can't be the quiet, proper lady you want me to be."

"Is that what I want you to be?"

Gennie leaned toward him and looked up into his face. "Don't you?"

Grady kissed her on the forehead. "I learned something, too, this time around. You were enormously helpful to us, Gen, and you quite possibly saved Rose's life. After Andrew told me about Rose's suspicions, I was ready to shoot that dancer in the Herb House window. I thought Clarissa was holding Rose hostage, tied up somewhere, maybe hurt. If you hadn't noticed how real the dancing was and seen that she was only wearing a slip under that cloak, I might have shot Rose. And what you told me about Beatrice Berg was enough to get her husband's murder investigation reopened. You and Rose saved Wilhelm's life, too." He reached over the edge of the blanket and picked up a half-rotted sweet gum ball. He sent it sailing across the grass. "You showed me how dangerous my own stubbornness can be."

He leaned forward and kissed the tip of her nose. "So the answer to your question is no. I want you to be Gennie. My Gennie. I'd be proud and honored to have you as my wife."

This time Gennie, being Gennie, rose to her knees, took his face in her hands, and gave him her answer.

"How is Wilhelm faring since his release?" Rose asked. She sat in Agatha's retiring room, her bandaged foot elevated on a short-backed chair borrowed from the dining room. Dazzling sunlight shone through the window and warmed her.

"Josie says he is regaining his strength," Agatha said. "According to Grady, the only thing he ate during his imprisonment was the one slice of Mairin's birthday cake."

"That's interesting."

"Isn't it?"

"I don't suppose he has expressed any gratitude to everyone who helped free him?"

"Nay, but I believe he feels it in his heart." Agatha smoothed a thin, shaky hand over her blanket, as if comforted by its softness. "There is something I must tell you about Wilhelm," she said. "He told me this in the early days, but it never seemed necessary to reveal it to anyone else. I know it looks like he came to us as a Winter Shaker, but his reasons were quite different. He is still deeply grieved over how he lived his life before becoming a Believer. He was wild, driven by his passions. He deserted his family because the responsibility felt too burdensome. He admitted as much to me, with great shame."

"Yet it took him thirteen years to reach us," Rose said. She had prayed for release from her anger with Wilhelm, but so far she'd been left to stew in it.

"He did not immediately feel his shame. It took another experience. Grady discovered, did he not, that Wilhelm had served in the war? He had volunteered, thinking it was just the thing for him—action, violence, excitement. It was the reality of war that changed him. The horrors—seeing the terrible destruction of life, the impersonal cruelty. He watched friends die. One day he shot a German soldier. When he checked, he found the man still alive—and no more than a young lad. The boy held against his heart a photo of his wife and baby. He died in Wilhelm's arms. I believe Mother Ann took pity on Wilhelm that day and opened his heart. But an open heart is not always a peaceful one."

"I see," said Rose. "So that is why he sought us out and became a Believer."

"And it is why he often goes in a different direction than you and I. I used to remind myself of that several times a day when I served as eldress alongside Wilhelm."

"Did it help?"

"Sometimes." Agatha laughed softly.

"And Elsa? Do you have any stories that might help me understand her?"

"Nay, but I have an idea she sees Wilhelm more clearly than the rest of us do. The trance you described to me—I suspect Holy Mother Wisdom might have had a hand in it."

"I wondered about that myself," Rose said. "In a sense, Elsa's revelations were correct. All the guests had secrets that drew them to the Shaker Hostel—with the exception of Gennie, of course. There was indeed a terrible soulless evil to be stomped out. And Horace started it all. He did not kill anyone, but he wrote the stories that brought Clarissa here, hoping for riches. His stories served as the catalyst for murder."

"Have we recovered all the items stolen from the village?" Agatha asked.

"I think so," Rose said. "Grady said Saul made the most charming and thorough confession he'd ever heard, in hopes of leniency. He even confessed he'd gone into Mrs. Dunmore's room the morning she was found dead. He'd found the door unlocked and the room empty, so he took a quick look around for something worth stealing. That's how he knew about the port bottle Clarissa had planted in her room.

"He admitted he'd romanced a widow living near here on a run-down farm, and she agreed to bring her wagon to the village every night to pick up whatever Saul had been able to steal. When Grady went there, he found everything still piled in her barn, waiting for Saul to find buyers. I've no doubt he would have abandoned the poor woman as soon as her usefulness ended."

"Unlike Wilhelm," Agatha said, "he would have felt no shame."

Rose gazed out the window to a large sweet gum tree, where two people sat near each other on a blanket. "It looks like Gennie and Grady are resolving their differences," she said.

"Does that still sadden you?" Agatha asked.

"Nay. Gennie is a wonderful friend, but she belongs in the world. I wish her every happiness."

"Besides," Agatha said, "you have another charge who might just make a wonderful Shaker, when the time comes."

"Mairin. Yea, I believe you are right, though she certainly is a handful."

"A handful of promise, Rose," Agatha whispered, as she relaxed against the back of her rocker. "A handful of promise."

The Jersey Shore Mysteries by
Beth Sherman
Featuring Anne Hardaway

"Anne Hardaway is a delightful mix of humor,
pragmatism, and vulnerability."
Margaret Maron

THE DEVIL AND THE DEEP BLUE SEA
0-380-81605-9/$5.99 US/$7.99 Can
The late night satanic activities of bored teens in the God-fearing
New Jersey Shore community of Oceanside Heights seem more ditsy
than dangerous to ghostwriter-cum-sleuth Anne Hardaway—until
she stumbles upon the corpse of a young, would-be witch.

Also by Beth Sherman

DEATH'S A BEACH
0-380-73109-6/$5.99 US/$7.99 Can

DEATH AT HIGH TIDE
0-380-73108-8/$5.99 US/$7.99 Can

DEAD MAN'S FLOAT
0-380-73107-X/$6.50 US/$8.99 Can